The Body Beneath

Nick Louth is a bestselling thriller writer and an award-winning financial journalist. A 1979 graduate of the London School of Economics, he went on to become a Reuters' foreign correspondent in 1987. He was for many years a *Financial Times* columnist, and a regular contributor to many other financial titles in print and online. *The Body Beneath the Willows* is the ninth book in the DCI Gillard crime series, and his thirteenth thriller overall. Nick Louth is married and lives in Lincolnshire.

www.nicklouth.com

Also by Nick Louth

Bite
Heartbreaker
Mirror Mirror
Trapped

DCI Craig Gillard Crime Thrillers

The Body in the Marsh
The Body on the Shore
The Body in the Mist
The Body in the Snow
The Body Under the Bridge
The Body on the Island
The Bodies at Westgrave Hall
The Body on the Moor
The Body Beneath the Willows

NICK LOUTH

THE BODY BENEATH THE WILLOWS

First published in the United Kingdom in 2022 by

Canelo
Unit 9, 5th Floor
Cargo Works, 1-2 Hatfields
London, SE1 9PG
United Kingdom

Print ISBN 978 1 80032 841 9
Ebook ISBN 978 1 80032 172 4

Look for more great books at www.canelo.co

Printed and bound in Great Britain by Clays Ltd, Elcograf S.p.A.

1

For Louise, as always

Chapter One

January 2020

Angela Blanchard was surprised to see her husband's car backing up the drive towards the house at four o'clock in the afternoon, while it was still light. The big white Volvo, sporting the distinctive tangled blue and green arrows logo of his employer, Aqua Western Ltd, rolled right up to the garage door. She put the kettle on. Normally he wouldn't be home until five, except on a Friday. But today was Tuesday. Usually she would hear his cheerful whistling as he approached the door. The kicking off of the work boots in the porch, if he'd been on site, greeting the cat which rolled over on her back to have her tummy rubbed. And, at the end of every week, the banging out of the car mats against the wall, to get the mud off. It was a fixed routine.

But today he came straight in wearing his boots, dumped his briefcase on the hall table, ignored Felix, who was miaowing by the door, and clumped straight upstairs without saying hello. Most unlike him. She followed him, calling from the foot of the stairs.

'Are you all right, Ozzy?' she called. Lumps of mud flecked the stair carpet. Angela made allowances. She was an understanding woman. He must be stressed about something.

There were mumbled replies. He was fine, apparently. Clearly not true, but no doubt he'd tell her in his own time. As she waited, the rising roar of the electric kettle seemed to mark her husband's blood pressure. Ozzy was already bustling from his home office with a couple of big file folders and his laptop. She squeezed to one side on the stairs as he thundered down, arms loaded.

'Do you want a cuppa?' she called after him.

'Fine for the moment, thanks.' He disappeared out to the garage for a few minutes. Angela heard the sound of the car boot slamming, and then he hurried back inside.

'Ozzy, what's the matter? Do you have to go back to work?'

'There's a bit of a flap on. A project crisis.'

She assumed that meant yes. 'The Winchester to Havant phase two again?' She was proud to be able to hold up her side of abstruse water engineering conversations, learning the names and techniques, taking an interest. Accommodating the technicalities. One time she had gone to lunch with Jill, and given her a five-minute overview of the ongoing problems with the narrow-bore deep reach pump, whose failure to reach technical spec on overcast days had been holding up WinHav II, as it was known. Jill, who worked part-time with Angela at the local pharmacy, was impressed but baffled. Angela had her explanation. 'It's my job to help him get stuff of his chest.' She explained that it was one of the reasons for the success of their twenty-seven-year marriage. To listen and pretend to understand.

Ozzy, now back upstairs, asked: 'Do you know where my old Thames Water jacket is? I thought it was in the wardrobe in the spare bedroom.'

'That old blue one? That's in the under-bed storage in the spare room. I was thinking of chucking it out. It's not waterproof anymore, is it?'

'It's good enough.' He thundered back up the stairs, and she could hear the sounds of activity.

'Ozzy. Why do you need that old coat now?

There was a few seconds' silence. 'I said I'd lend it to a friend.'

Angela was quite baffled by that. What kind of friend would need an old coat?

'Ozzy?' There was no reply this time, so she returned to making the tea. There was more activity up and down the stairs, a couple of cardboard boxes carried out. Something else moved from the garage she couldn't quite see. A flash of orange. The old tent? That was all she could think of. The Volvo boot went again. She stood on tiptoe to peer out of the kitchen window. Ozzy was moving more stuff out of the garage. In one hand he had his guitar case, and in the other the old leather briefcase that he'd used in his first job when they got married, half their lives ago. He stowed them in the back of the Volvo, and slammed the boot down again.

Now she had moved from baffled to alarmed. If he had to go back to work what did he need to take the guitar for? In all the years she had known him, he had never had to rush back in to work. That was for the maintenance people, dealing with floods and so on, But he was a new-projects manager. Half of it was desk work. In piddle management, as he liked to say. New sewers, overflow pipes. Lots of concrete. In all his long years as a water engineer, his projects had been carefully planned, the schedules laid out over many months. There was none of this seat of the pants stuff that she was seeing now. She

3

poured boiling water from the kettle onto a teabag in the teapot, and gave it a quick stir before putting the lid back on. While it brewed, she headed out to the front door and opened it.

'Ozzy? What's going on?'

'A bit of an emergency,' he said, staring down at the phone in his hand. 'I've got to go now.' He gave her a perfunctory smile. He'd always had a lovely smile. Back in the day, when they'd met in Goa, India, she'd been quite taken by the lean, tanned man who had nice teeth, brown eyes and lovely long blond hair tied back in a ponytail. He still had the nice eyes and good teeth, but only some grey fuzz for hair.

'What about your tea? You've got time for a gulp or two surely?'

'No, sorry.'

'Why are you taking the guitar?'

He stared at her, dumbfounded.

'I saw you carrying it out from the garage.'

He stared around the driveway, as if there were answers to be found there. 'Tell you later. I'll be back by six.'

As the car slid onto the suburban road, it left an ominous silence behind in the house. In that emptiness grew pain. Through all their quarter of a century of life together, from the moment she and Ozzy had settled down, Angela had thought she could see where they were heading. A long, straight, predictable pipe, where each section fitted snugly onto the one before, heading to the horizon, their life together safely channelled within. All thanks to his good job, two holidays a year, and a decent pension at the end of it, now just four years away if he took the early retirement option. She'd thought she was happy.

Angela was an accommodating woman, and a little old-fashioned, but she wasn't a fool. He was gone. He'd said he would be back by six. But actions speak louder than words. The tent, the guitar, the paperwork. It appeared to her he was leaving for good.

–

He'd been gone less than five minutes when the land-line rang. She recognised the voice. Kelvin Arrowsmith, regional financial controller at Aqua, she thought. He didn't introduce himself, but simply asked to speak to Ozzy. She told him that he had just gone back into work. 'The Aqua site office, or regional HQ?' he asked.

'He didn't say. Is that Kelvin?' she asked.

'Yes.'

'Kelvin, honestly, he did seem in a bit of a flap.'

There was silence at the other end, then Kelvin said, 'I can't reach him on the mobile. When he calls in, ask him to ring me urgently. However late. Thank you, Angela.'

There was the briefest gap between the end of that sentence and Kelvin hanging up, not anywhere near enough for the many questions that Angela wanted to ask. But in that gap she distinctly heard the sound of Kelvin cursing under his breath.

Chapter Two

Ozzy Blanchard soon ran into heavy rain and winter darkness as he left Hemel Hempstead. The Hertfordshire town, just north-west of London, had been his home for two decades. No longer. The die was cast. He wasn't going back. His destination was familiar, but this time the journey was urgent. The next hour would be crucial. Weeks ago he'd sketched out a plan B for this moment. Plan B wasn't detailed, because he'd never expected to need it. Plan A should have worked.

He hadn't expected to be this scared. The first part of plan B was that he should take a different route from usual. Minor roads, country lanes. Break the routine. His prep hadn't been great. Everything should have been packed and ready. Was he not a professional project manager? But to make the plan in all its detail would have meant considering the worst-case scenario. Ideally he should have taken his own car, not the company one. But this one had more space and was fuelled up. Taking the Ford Focus would have slowed him up and left Angela stuck without wheels. Only one of many ways in which she was destined to be screwed over by his unscheduled departure. He felt guilty, but that was a luxury he couldn't afford. She'd be all right, eventually. It was his survival at stake here, not hers.

As he drove he cursed the name, again and again. Just one man had put him in this predicament. A greedy, smug bastard. And now his life was at risk.

It was gone five when Blanchard sat impatiently at a set of roadworks traffic lights, a long queue of rain-smeared tail lights visible through the sweeping wipers. A huge four-wheel-drive, its lights on full beam, sat right on his tail, gunning the engine impatiently. He could hear the thump of music, too. It brought his enemies to mind and made him nervous. He reset the satnav, and turned off right on a minor rural road. As the Volvo splashed through the puddles, Ozzy Blanchard tried to think. Every change of route would cost him time, but unless they had discovered everything he would still be safe. Or should be. They couldn't have discovered everything, could they? Not yet. Once he arrived at that familiar village, got her into the car and away, they would be safe. Their new life could begin.

He rang her on the hands-free, and after six rings it went to the message. He whispered, as if being overheard: 'It's me, pick up if you can.'

–

An hour later, Blanchard was edging the big Volvo down the cramped, puddled lane of Victorian cottages. Familiar, welcoming, the soft warm glow of lights from within, families sitting down to an evening meal, a night in front of the TV. Reassuring. He edged up outside the house, flecks of rain drifting through the beams of the head-lamps. The kitchen light was on, and one upstairs behind curtains. He rang her again, and again left a message. 'Come on. It's me. I'm here.'

7

Suddenly headlamps flicked on from a big dark vehicle parked further down the lane, and an engine roared. The door of the cottage opened, and a man he recognised leapt out, running down the garden path towards him.

It was a trap.

Blanchard jammed his vehicle into reverse, gunned the engine and leaning over his shoulder guided the Volvo backwards at high speed up the narrow lane. The big car, a BMW X5, followed him, almost nose to nose. The first thirty yards were fine, then he sideswiped a parked car's wing mirror. At the village green, he reversed straight onto the grass, intending to turn out on to the main road. The BMW blocked his forward route, so Blanchard continued to reverse, right over the steps of the war memorial, back down to the footpath, then turned sharp right, smashing down the memorial green rose bushes and into the lane which led down to the dual carriageway. He sped past the Anvil Arms at sixty, overtook a van on a blind corner, then headed for the slip road. The big BMW was right behind him. His heart was hammering, and he was taking risks he had never taken before. But he couldn't let them catch him.

As he approached the dual carriageway he could see arc lights in the distance. Once on the slip road he realised why. There were major roadworks, traffic was stationary, and he was being fed right into the queue. He was still doing over sixty and had one second to make a decision. He flicked the Volvo to the right, crossing the slip road hatch marks. He was headed the wrong way along the dual carriageway exit lane. That sharply curved slip road, designed to slow down exiting traffic, caused his tyres to squeal. He was gambling his life on a single calculation:

that this was such a minor turn-off there would be no vehicles coming the other way.

He was right. But everything changed the moment he was on the carriageway. A closing speed of 120 miles an hour to oncoming traffic. A large white van swerved out of the way into the fast lane, horn sounding. Blanchard too pressed his hand to the horn and kept as far to the right as possible, but this was the start of an overpass across the River Wey. There was no hard shoulder, just a one-yard strip to the crash barrier which guarded the drop to the water below. The next two vehicles gave him space as he crested the top of the overpass at sixty, but 300 yards away one articulated truck was overtaking another coming up the incline towards him, and there was literally nowhere to go. The railings ended in 150 yards to be replaced by an embankment and bushes, and he had to get to that spot before the two trucks closed off the gap. Blanchard accelerated, and saw the needle flick to eighty as he squeezed the Volvo to the right, one wheel on the grass and one on the edge of the tarmac. The vehicle seemed to leave the ground almost immediately afterwards, and Blanchard had one last glimpse in the mirror.

He wasn't being followed any longer.

Chapter Three

The Hampshire Constabulary Range Rover arrived within ten minutes. PC Colin Andrews emerged from the vehicle into the pouring rain, while colleagues from other patrol cars closed off the carriageway. He donned wellingtons and latex gloves and picked up a powerful torch. The beam followed the trail of damage, which included a broken stanchion on a large green road sign, into the undergrowth. No tyre marks on the carriageway, perhaps not surprising in the weather. Still, the exit route was straight, which indicated the vehicle had remained under control. No evidence of last-minute braking.

Very strange. Almost as if this was intentional.

He set off to follow the path of smashed stems and flattened nettles, heading up and over the embankment then down towards the river. He radioed in his findings, then followed the trail of destruction, steadying himself with a hand on some saplings as he began the muddy descent. There, fifty yards further down in the beam of his torch, was the Volvo, on its roof, in the shallows. The tail lights were still on. With only one hand to guide him, the other holding the light, the steep descent through the wrecked bushes and churned earth was treacherous. Finally, he stumbled through the broken branches of a weeping willow and plunged up to his knees in water. The car lay ten yards from the edge of the bank, held above the full depth by the felled boughs of trees. Wading across, his wellies now full of water, he shone his beam in through the crazed windscreen and between the inflated airbags. There was no one visible.

'Call out if you can,' he shouted, over the sibilant waters, hissing over the stones. There was no reply. The driver-side door was creased inwards, the window frosted and broken, shards of glass curled outwards. He squatted down in the shallows and shone the torch horizontally. There appeared to be no one in the car. At the limits of what he could do without wading waist-deep into the river, he was relieved to hear the sound of approaching sirens. Back up on the bridge he saw fire appliances, an ambulance and a recovery vehicle, and made his way back to brief them.

'Any casualties?' asked the burly fire chief who greeted him.

'Not that I can see,' Andrews replied. 'Wriggled out somehow through the driver-side window. Miraculous, really. Probably a drugged-up joyrider. Who else goes the wrong way up a dual carriageway?'

The next day

DI Helen Kaplan of Hampshire Constabulary rang the doorbell at 14 Wycherley Crescent, Hemel Hempstead. The woman who came to the door was a trim fifty-something with silvery hair. Kaplan introduced herself to Angela Blanchard.

'Any news on the search?' Angela asked, showing the detective into the lounge. A long-haired cat was lying splayed out in the middle of a white leatherette settee, leaving the women to sit on the other two components of the three-piece suite.

'Nothing so far. We think he got out of the car. We traced the signal on his work mobile phone moving for about five minutes afterwards until it ceased. I take it you've not had any phone calls?'

'No. I would have let you know if I had. Why wouldn't he ring me?'

'Well, the phone may not have been usable, even though it was giving out a signal,' Kaplan said. She kept from Mrs Blanchard the news that the phone had been used to call another mobile phone nearby, an unregistered one, in the minutes after the crash. Such news was likely to be an unwelcome addition to the shock of hearing her husband had been in an accident.

'He might have been injured,' Angela said.

'Yes, that's quite possible,' Kaplan said. 'Suffering from shock at least, disorientated. He may even have lost his memory.' The detective got out her notebook. 'Now, Mrs Blanchard, I understand you told the PC who first visited that your husband had been behaving strangely.'

'That's right. He was clearly in a flap, and in a hurry to get out again. It's so unlike him. His work isn't like that, with last-minute changes of plan. He's a project manager, and these projects are measured in months if not years.'

'So, do you think it's possible that he was just giving an excuse, and it wasn't about work?'

'Yes. He took personal things with him, like his guitar, and an old tent. I thought he might be leaving me.' Her eyes welled up. 'But then I got a phone call from his boss, who did seem to be pretty anxious to get in touch with him. So I then thought maybe it was about work.'

Kaplan made detailed notes. 'I'll be speaking to Aqua Western later on.' As she left, she thought this was unlike any other disappearance she had covered. Fleeing from an old life, yes. But urgently enough to head off into a new one the wrong way on a major road, and end up upside down in a river. And then gone, vanished.

Chapter Four

Six months later
Wednesday

Detective Chief Inspector Craig Gillard had visited most parts of Surrey in his decades in the police, but the tiny hamlet of Rissington Common was new to him. A body had been found there by workmen, close to the River Wey. Right in the south-west corner of the county, the map had shown a thorn-shaped valley sticking painfully into the top edge of Hampshire. On this showery morning he'd taken the A286 past Haslemere, and then the new dual carriageway from Camelsdale heading towards the A272. Once off this elevated link road he followed the signs and the road soon narrowed and deteriorated, over-shadowed on both sides by dense woodland. After a few hundred yards a mildewed sign announced his arrival at Rissington Common. A small triangular green divided the hamlet between a whitewashed pub on the left and a village shop on the right. The few dozen cottages he could see were all Victorian, and there were few of the signs of gentrification that the rest of the county had in spades. It was only four miles from Liphook and Haslemere, but it could have been a thousand.

Gillard eased his unmarked grey Vauxhall along Bourne Lane, past a large and untidy builders' yard, and a dozen more cottages. The road deteriorated further as he headed downhill towards the river, becoming a potholed track, crammed with untidily parked vehicles. There were fewer homes and cars in the final 200 yards. The last house on the right was a larger rectory type with a wild garden, and on the left was a tiny stone church with a squat tower and overgrown graveyard. Beyond it, the land opened up as marshy pasture, grazed by scraggy cattle, and dotted with alder, silver birch and stands of willow.

In the distance to the left, Gillard could see the upraised orange arm of a tracked digger, and the flash of blue lights, his destination. The Vauxhall bumped and ground along the heavily rutted track until a dead-end at some bollards, and swung left through an open metal gate, avoiding the two deep muddy trenches left by the crane's tracks. The detective gingerly steered the car across the meadow, following tyre marks, and then mounted a new crushed-stone track which led up through a dense stand of willows to an embankment at the river's edge.

The twenty-two-ton tracked JCB excavator, atop the embankment, dominated the scene. Below it, near the water's edge, were two water company four-wheel-drives, and a police patrol Range Rover. A group of a dozen face-masked individuals, three of them police, congregated around the water's edge, between the stumps of two trees, staring into a large water-filled hole.

Gillard got out of the car and went to the boot. He pulled on a Tyvek coverall and a pair of wellingtons, donned a pair of blue latex gloves and a face mask, and made his way down the embankment to join them. As he approached, three uniformed male officers turned to greet him. Of the rest, four were wearing water company hi-vis in lime green, and one who seemed to be in charge was a short, dapper man wearing a suit and a hard hat. The detective introduced himself.

'Kelvin Arrowsmith, regional financial controller for Aqua Western,' he responded, bumping elbows with Gillard.

'They've just found human remains,' blurted out one of the uniforms, a fresh-faced PC in his early twenties.

'So I was told. Down here?' Gillard asked, crouching down to look into the hole. He could see something grey and slimy in the cloudy water. The smell wasn't too bad, considering. Like old cheese rather than rotting flesh.

'Only part of it,' said one of the contractors, a shortish but solid guy with a gingery crewcut, who introduced himself as Aidan Tickett. 'Most of it is still in the bucket.' He gestured towards the excavator with a thumb over his shoulder. 'Some of it got crushed.'

Gillard and Aidan made their way over to the huge metal bucket of the excavator. Amongst huge clods of clay were more grey slimy lumps, and pieces of what could be bone. Torn fragments of black plastic were in there too, along with soggy residue which had the look of textiles. The cheesy stink was stronger here.

'It's a mess, isn't it?' the contractor said.

'It's often the way,' Gillard said. 'Who was operating the excavator, and who else was here when it was found?'

Aidan scratched his nose with a grubby finger. 'Female apprentice, her first week on the JS220. She was upset so we sent her home. Trev Collier, the engineer from Aqua, witnessed it, I came down a bit later.' Aidan pointed out Collier. He was one of the hard hats, a lean man in his fifties, with a deeply lined face that spoke of decades of outdoor work. Gillard took Collier aside and made notes as the engineer described how the JCB's bucket had dug into part of the riverbank and lifted soil and roots further back to make a higher embankment. 'That's when I saw body parts,' Collier said. 'I've been in this business twenty years and we've found all sorts of historical stuff, but I've never seen a dead body before. The woman working the JCB was freaked out when I told her. She thought it was her fault for not spotting it, but I told her that it could have happened to anybody.'

The detective peered downriver where the water-course widened into a broad meander that led into tangled woodland under the link road overpass. 'So what is the project you're working on?'

Collier sighed. 'We've been trying to stop sewer over-flow into the river with some bigger pipes and a protective embankment. It's a joint operation with the Environment Agency. It actually should have been done when the link road was put in,' he said, pointing half a mile downriver, past Bourne Lane where Gillard had driven in.

'You'll have to stop work until CSI has finished, and that could take a while,' Gillard said.

The sound of vehicles arriving made them both look up. Two CSI vans were making their way carefully across the marshy meadow, and pulled up next to Gillard's car. They were followed by a Hampshire Constabulary patrol car. Gillard smiled to himself. The county boundary ran right through Rissington Common, so he wasn't surprised that Hampshire was showing an interest in a Surrey case. A male uniform emerged followed by a fit-looking woman in her late forties wearing a grey trouser suit and mask, who immediately began speaking to the CSI team.

Oh no, Gillard thought, it's her. Just my luck.

–

Detective Chief Superintendent Stella Anderson made her way across the muddy meadow and up the embankment towards Gillard. Her hair was quite different from the long ponytail he had known. Now it was silvery blonde, shorter and shaped, with highlights. It suited her. She held out her arms for balance as she picked where to put her feet amongst the sloppy cowpats and rutted mud behind the striding uniformed officer. Unexpectedly needing wellingtons was always a danger for detectives. Particularly when you didn't bring your own vehicle but had hitched a ride in a patrol car. That showed some inexperience. Gillard couldn't help noticing that she'd already got muddy splashes at the bottom of her trousers, and on her highly polished black shoes. His mask hid an uncharitable smile.

'Craig, how are you?' she asked. 'It's been a long time.'

'I'm fine, ma'am,' he replied. 'I'd heard that you were in the Hampshire force.' Stella, then under her maiden name Taylor, had trained with him years ago in the Met Police, and was quickly promoted to sergeant when they were both in uniform. She was smart, perceptive and adventurous, having hiked the entire Andes from Colombia to Tierra del Fuego when she was twenty-three. They had worked together happily for three months and become friends until an unexpected Friday evening and night in a Basildon hotel after a training course, which in the morning felt more than a little awkward. She cut contact with him soon after and a few months later left the police. At the time he had no idea what he had done wrong, although in those days his behaviour with women had often been cavalier. It had taken him years, and the prodding of some of his remaining female friends, to realise that. He probably owed Stella an apology.

And here she was, back in the force, and senior to him.

'I was recruited three years ago. I normally specialise in fraud, given that I've been working in forensic accountancy in the intervening years.'

'Ah, that's why then.' He had wondered why she had been parachuted back in at such a senior level. There was a well-established level of resentment amongst detectives working their way up through the ranks at those who got brought in without having to pass the exams, or suffer the tedium of day-to-day work such as checking CCTV and the car licensing databases.

'So this is a little outside your bailiwick,' Gillard said, indicating the excavator behind him.

'Don't worry, Craig, I'm not planning to pinch the case from you. I'm just curious about what you've found.' Her smile was the same broad grin he had found attractive all those years ago. Her eyes were hazel, with just the traces of laughter lines.

'So am I.' Knowing her sharp mind, Gillard felt that this would be anything but idle curiosity. He led her around, first to the watery hole and then to the digger's bucket, while the CSI team were marking up posts from which to hang blue and white crime scene tape. 'I'll happily keep you in the loop for any developments, ma'am,' he said.

'Yes please,' she said crisply, glancing down at her spattered shoes. 'When there's a positive ID.'

'Not much call for wellies in fraud, is there?' Gillard said, following her gaze.

She smiled again. 'I'm not so sure. There's nothing muddier than dodgy accounts. So just blind copy me in on everything you find, okay?' She began to make her way back, watched by the various contractors.

'Is that your boss?' asked Aidan, leaning on his spade.

'Thankfully, no,' Gillard said. 'We're Surrey, she's Hampshire.'

'Territorial, like magpies, is it?' He looked amused.

'More like reverse territorial. Given the current resource problems we have, every force tries to dump work on its neighbour. Especially when it's arguable which side of the border the crime scene is.'

'I've seen her before,' he said. 'Poking about in the village a few months ago. Asking questions in the pub.'

'What kind of questions?'

'About the missing water guy, as I recall,' he said.

'Ozzy Blanchard?' Trevor Collier had mentioned to Gillard that his predecessor as regional surveyor had crashed a company car in the area six months ago and then disappeared.

'That's him. It was just before lockdown began, and it was so obvious she was a cop.'

'Do tell,' Gillard asked, intrigued.

Aidan's eyes lit up. 'Something watchful about her, like she couldn't relax. I was sitting at a table with my brother, and she was at the bar, and clearly didn't know anybody. I called Guy, the manager, over and asked what she was drinking and he told me soda water. So I asked him to get her in a vodka and soda on me.'

'Did he tell her what was in it?'

'I don't know, but he did say it was from me. I saw her stare at me in the mirror behind the bar, and take a careful sniff of the drink. Very wary, she was.'

'Professional, perhaps.'

'No doubt. She didn't drink it, except a little sip. Ordered another soda water, switched the glasses when she thought I didn't see, and drank that.'

'What else did you learn from her?' Gillard asked. It was a rare treat to be offered an insight into undercover policing from the other side. The other guy knew it, too, and was enjoying telling the tale.

'Guy told me that she had described herself as a sales-woman, but I never believed it,' Aidan said.

Gillard wondered quite why this construction worker would care so much.

'Anyway, it's all above my pay grade,' Aidan said. 'I just dig holes for a living, and keep my head down.'

Gillard nodded towards the digger. 'So, have you any idea whose body this may be? Ever lost a member of the crew?'

'Nope. Not one of ours.' He shoved his hands in his pockets and gave a little smile, as if there was a joke Gillard wasn't getting. He followed Aidan's gaze, towards an animated conversation between the two water company officials. They were maybe forty yards away, but it was clear that Arrowsmith, the smaller but more senior of the two, was berating Collier for something.

Not one of ours, Aidan had said. But maybe one of theirs. The missing Ozzy Blanchard, perhaps.

–

Gillard left the CSI crew and the uniforms to do their job. It was fairly clear from the poor condition of the body that this was not going to be an easy ID job. Dr David Delahaye, the Home Office forensic pathologist, would be down in an hour, but Gillard wasn't expecting too much. Purely based on the photos Craig had emailed him, Delahaye had warned that it was likely that he couldn't shed much light on cause of death, and suggested that it would be good to get not only a forensic archaeologist, but the county archaeologist too, who could give some clues as to whether this was a historical death.

The detective had already taken a quick look through missing persons for the local area. How big a task it was depended on how far into the past you wanted to go, and how large an area you wanted to use. There was the infamous unsolved case of Sally Whitchens, a ten-year-old girl missing since 2005 in Winchester, thirty-two miles west. Of those old enough to have chosen to disappear, there were probably thirty within a fifty-mile radius since 2000. Like most 'mispers', there often seemed a family reason: arguments, divorce, bereavement. Many of them were originally from other areas of the UK, three of them foreign nationals. There was nothing that really stood out.

Gillard walked back to his car and changed out of his wellingtons. He then drove back across the meadow and up into the village which, unlike the river valley, was in Hampshire. Parking outside the Anvil Arms, he looked longingly at the faded blackboard, which advertised real ales and home-cooked food. Clipped to the blackboard was a plasticised menu listing a mouth-watering array of dishes, under the heading: 'Hampshire Young Chef of the Year'. The pandemic lockdown was four months old, and due to end the coming weekend. Like many he was nostalgic for the pre-Covid world.

He gelled his hands, re-fixed his face mask and emerged from the car. The weather was genial, so he took a five-minute stroll through the village. One shop, formerly a post office. Forge Cottage nearby, a nod towards the blacksmith's it presumably used to be. The distant rumble of the link road reminded him how Riss-ington Common, probably always an obscure hamlet, was now totally off the beaten track. It wasn't on the way from anywhere to anywhere else. Even to get to Upper Rissington you now had to go back almost to the main road and drive under the flyover.

A short but broad young man in his twenties emerged from a cottage two doors down from the pub, and laboriously fixed a mask over his nose and mouth. He had the characteristic features of Down's syndrome, and was towing a skinny dog. On spotting Gillard, he approached.

'Hello. Did you hear about the dead body down by the willows?' he asked.

'I did, and I'm here to investigate.'

'Are you a policeman?'

'Yes, I'm a detective. My name is Craig Gillard.'

'I'm Stewie, and this is Sprocket,' he said, pointing at the dog, which had the long melancholy face of a whippet.

'Glad to meet you, Stewie. Hello, Sprocket,' Gillard said.

'My mum is Sheila. She has gone to the shops. What's your favourite game? Mine is Cluedo.'

'I used to be a Monopoly fan, years ago. So what do you know about this body?'

Stewie winced. 'It was all broken. Nasty. Was it a man or a lady?'

'We're not sure yet.'

'Was it murder? With the lead piping in the library?'

Gillard couldn't suppress a smile behind his mask at the Cluedo reference. 'We really don't know, Stewie. It may take a long time to find out.'

'I like Miss Scarlett. But the murderer is always the vicar.' He nodded. 'Mum is very good at the game.'

'The Rev Green, if I remember rightly.' Gillard remembered a few of the characters of the game, which he hadn't played for decades.

Stewie shook his head. 'The Rev Cleaver. He's a bad man.' He looked over Gillard's shoulder as if worried about being overheard.

'Did somebody tell you this?' Gillard asked.

'Don't tell tales,' Stewie said, shaking his head emphatically. 'Mum says don't tell tales. Goodbye.' He tugged the dog, which followed reluctantly as Stewie walked up the street. 'Come on, Sprocket.' The dog looked over its shoulder and gave Gillard a reproachful stare.

–

Gillard made his way down to the builders' yard, which according to the sign belonged to CJT Contracting (Hants) Ltd. There was also a shipping container labelled Buckingham Pallets Ltd, beside which hundreds of wooden pallets were stacked. Someone clearly had a sense of humour. Behind the padlocked gates and wire-mesh fence paced a couple of doberman guard dogs, their cropped ears giving them a devilish appearance. Gillard recalled reading in some police briefing paper that it was no longer legal to crop ears in this way. Behind them were a couple of old Portakabins, three or four caravans, a brand-new long wheelbase Transit, and a collection of older flatbed trucks. Further back in a weed-strewn paddock were a half-dozen elderly diggers and excavators. As he watched, a dark blue BMW X5 pulled out from a driveway adjacent to the yard, with a thickset silver-haired man at the wheel. He gave Gillard a hard stare as he drove off.

The detective memorised the number plate, and entered it in his notebook as he headed back to his car. Once inside, he took out his iPad and looked up the directors of the building firm from Companies House. The managing director was Mr C. J. Tickett, and there were several other Ticketts on the directors list, including Aidan, the man he'd talked to. Not just a hole digger, then. Something about the unusual surname triggered a vague memory. A Google search brought up the name of an aspiring middleweight boxer, Rory 'Typhoon' Tickett, who had done quite well for several years until being knocked unconscious by Ukrainian Denys Lasorenko in 2016. There were few mentions of him in the last four years. Gillard, no fan of boxing, didn't think this was what he had remembered. He delved further into the search results and found a few articles from the 1980s, about a Hampshire man being sentenced for murder. There it was: Christopher John Tickett, of Bourne Lane, Rissington Common.

The same address. Tickett had been thirty-one when he had been sentenced to seventeen years for killing a neighbour, Henry Willow, in 1982. Tickett would now be sixty-nine. That could well have been him in the car.

Interesting that a dead body should be found so close by.

Gillard closed up the device, and drove off to Haslemere. He had some research to do.

–

Haslemere was a well-to-do Surrey town, and Gillard knew there would be no difficulty finding what he was looking for. He parked the Vauxhall by a parade of shops outside a row of three estate agents. He asked the same questions in each, but it was only on the third that he got the comprehensive answer he was looking for.

'Rissington Common?' answered the middle-aged suit, barely able to restrain his surprise. 'And are you looking to buy or rent?'

'Buy,' Gillard said. He passed on some bogus details about his budget, before asking what there was in the area. 'We got some very nice places in Upper Rissington, still within your price bracket. That's a very up-and-coming area.' He tapped a ballpoint pen at his screen.

'But Rissington Common?'

'Do you have connections there, is that why you're interested?' The man asked Gillard to take a seat, and he did.

'No. It just looks nicely out of the way.'

The estate agent's woolly eyebrows shot almost to the top of his head 'It is certainly that, sir. And I have to admit you do get a lot for your money.' He stood and turned to a filing cabinet, reached right to the back, and brought out a handful of dog-eared property listings. 'We've got three or four cottages, with plenty of scope for modernisation, the sort of character projects you could really put your thumbprint on. How many bedrooms are you looking for?'

'At least a couple. But I have heard stories about bad sewers and so forth.'

The estate agent sat down and appraised Gillard. 'Indeed, and you will appreciate that's why you get so much for your money.'

'So what exactly is the story?'

'Well, all the land around there is on the floodplain, which used not to be a problem until the 2009 floods.

Unfortunately there was also a sewer bottleneck there, supposedly fixed a year ago. There had been quite a few instances of discharges into the river during heavy rainfall. I'm not aware that many of the houses themselves have been flooded with it, but getting buildings insurance for many of those properties is difficult. Planning permission isn't straightforward either because the land is designated as contaminated.'

'That's difficult for the inhabitants.'

The estate agent steepled his fingers. 'Absolutely. And that's why I would thoroughly recommend Upper Rissington. Got a lovely Victorian semi just come on the market, no chain, beautiful aspect, absolute bargain in my view.'

Gillard let the man pass across the property sheet, and after giving a bogus email address and mobile number returned to the car.

Chapter Five

By the time Gillard got back to the crime scene, Dr David Delahaye was already there. Gillard saw his Tesla parked at the bottom of the lane, and spotted the balding dome of the Home Office forensic consultant as he was talking to a couple of others within the blue tape at the crime scene. Delahaye looked up as Gillard made his way through the increasingly muddy meadow that led to the water's edge. He was standing with a tall wild-haired man in his sixties with a bushy beard and thick spectacles.

'May I introduce Dr Clive Hancock, Surrey county archaeologist,' Delahaye said.

Gillard touched elbows with them both. 'I remember you, Clive, from the Forest Bridge clay pit killings. I was only a DC then.'

Hancock scratched his head. 'That was a long time ago.'

'If I remember rightly, it was 1996,' Gillard said.

They continued chatting as Delahaye led them towards the bucket of the excavator, about chest high. 'So what we seem to have is head and upper body here, mostly anyway, and parts of the lower limbs still in the hole over there.' He pointed back towards the muddy pit by the river. 'Now there's been serious damage to the corpse, some of which was clearly caused by the current excavation. We're missing the entire lower mandible and many upper teeth, plus two fingers on the left hand.' He turned to Gillard and smiled. 'I must say it's absolutely delightful at my age to be able to get a close look at a body in situ without bending down.'

'I'll second that,' said Hancock.

'So is this a piece of history, or could we be looking at a modern crime?' Gillard asked.

'Or perhaps a historic crime,' Hancock said.

Delahaye began. 'First impressions are that we are seeing almost complete putrefaction. In these anaerobic conditions the flesh becomes adipocere, a kind of waxy soap-type substance. Not good news, because adipocere doesn't hold DNA. Generally, we'd be talking about an absolute minimum of three months in exactly the right conditions to get to this stage. The aroma of cheese is quite indicative. However, it's not all bad news. Modernity is indicated by the presence of an amalgam filling, and the fact he's dressed in jeans and scraps of a shirt. From the plastic tatters it is possible he may have been buried in a bin bag.'

Hancock took up the story. 'I agree with that. In any case, we are not talking about some ancient burial site, because the soil here along the water's edge has already been disturbed as recently as the 1990s because of work by both the Environment Agency and the water company.'

Delahaye nodded. 'I'd say there's fairly strong evidence that we're talking about someone who's been here less than fifty years.' He reached into the bucket and with a pencil pointed at several jagged splinters an inch or two long, plus some smaller pieces.

'Is that glass or ceramic?' Gillard asked.

'Plastic, from a ballpoint pen,' Delahaye said. 'They were nearby, rather than on the corpse, so we can't be sure they were his.'

Gillard nodded. 'It makes it difficult, given how much disturbance of his last resting place has occurred.' He inclined his head back towards the excavator. 'For forensic purposes I'm going to assume this is a crime, so I'll let CSI examine the entire area and bring out the body, or as much of it as we can find. It's a long shot, but I'd like to see if we can get any DNA from the biro fragments, if we can't get any from the body. In the meantime it would help if you would both stay around to spot anything CSI might miss.'

They agreed.

Gillard stepped away to answer messages left by his boss, Detective Chief Superintendent Brian 'Radar' Dobbs. The DCS, who'd got his nickname from his prominent ears, was a thirty-year veteran of policing and had spent his early years as a detective in Hong Kong. More recently he had an acquired reputation as a bit of a paper pusher and this, together with bouts of severe depression, meant he was rarely seen outside Surrey's police headquarters at Mount Browne in Guildford. However, since Gillard had been pulled from a high-profile case early in the year, Dobbs had been tasked by Chief Constable Alison Rigby with more closely supervising him. In practice this involved second-guessing almost every conclusion Gillard came to, making him nostalgic for the days when Dobbs was off sick and he had almost complete operational independence.

Terse message returned, Gillard made his way back to the car and left the experts to it. He sat there for a few minutes checking his messages. The Environment Agency and the water company Aqua Western Ltd had sent him the requested maps of dates and times of work commissioned in the immediate area. Glancing at them, it didn't immediately help establish how recently the soil at the riverbank had been disturbed. No doubt the archaeologist could make more sense of them.

A tap at the window made him look up. An unmasked distinguished-looking woman in her early seventies with neat silvery hair, was looking in at him. He buzzed down the window. 'Excuse me, are you with Aqua Western?' she asked.

'No. Surrey Police.' He hurriedly put his mask back on, but the woman showed no signs of stepping away.

'Oh, is that about the body?'

'Yes. I'm afraid I can't tell you very much—'

'It could be an Anglo-Saxon burial site, there are quite a lot of them around here. Of course it could also be that fellow who drove his car off the bridge back in the winter.'

'Are you referring to Ozzy Blanchard?'

'Yes, everyone thought he survived because there was no body found in the car. But it could be him, couldn't it? Seeing as he used to work for this lot.' She indicated the construction site with a thumb.

'You mean Aqua Western?'

'Yes. I crossed swords with the man on numerous occasions. Slippery fellow though he was, I preferred him to the new one, Collier, who is just plain obstructive.'

Gillard made a mental note to look into the relationship between the village community and the water company.

'My name is Sheila Ransome,' she said, offering a delicate hand through the window. Gillard leaned back and offered his elbow in exchange, which she squeezed in an overly-familiar fashion.

'I've just met Stewie,' Gillard said.

She beamed. 'He's everyone's friend.'

'Lovely man. I hear you're a bit of a demon at Cluedo.'

'He's obsessed with the game,' she said, with a smile. 'He'd play it all day every day if he could. He's thirty-one now, and I worry what will happen to him after I'm gone.'

'I'm sure that won't be for many years.'

She peered into the distance. 'And I've got plenty to keep me occupied in the meantime. I'm leading the legal campaign to bring Aqua Western to book over all the pollution here. It's made our lives a misery, and we can't sell our homes.'

'I'd heard something about that,' he said. 'Perhaps you be good enough to stand back a little, in the interests of social distancing.'

She moved back, but soon closed in again. 'I've spent years accumulating legal ammunition against them. I'm happy to share my evidence—'

'That would be a civil matter, I'm afraid. I know it must be frustrating, but the police really can't get involved.'

'No, that's not true, I have incontrovertible evidence that they have committed criminal offences. If you give me your email address I will send on some of the most relevant pieces—'

'I'm really sorry, madam. There is a dead body by the river, and my job is to investigate that. If Aqua Western has breached statutory rules in some way, there are other organisations such as the National Rivers Authority, the Environment Agency and the Health and Safety Executive—'

She looked angry now. 'You look at their website, and it's all environment, pictures of happy kids drinking glasses of water in sunlit meadows. Meanwhile, underneath it all they have allowed thousands of tons of human excrement on the quiet into the river, and onto our land. The private equity owners have taken hundreds of millions in dividends, siphoning away cash that was intended to be spent on repairs.'

'I appreciate your frustration, madam—' Gillard restarted the car, desperate to get away from this conversation.

'You're just like the rest of them,' she said. 'You don't want to get to the truth. I can tell you, there is an awful lot hidden by that company. If you ever want to find out about it, come to me.' She slapped the roof of the car heavily. Gillard said goodbye, put the Vauxhall in gear and slid the car away. In the mirror he could see her son, emerging from the cottage. They embraced, looked towards Gillard's receding car, then she led him back inside.

–

Gillard found the operator of the excavator at the Anvil Arms, which she ran with her partner Guy Naylor. Vicky Willow was a robust-looking woman in her mid-thirties, about five foot nine with a shock of dark wavy hair and a handsome face. She had a baby on her hip as she showed the detective into the deserted lounge, where one large table was devoted to a large scale model re-enactment of a medieval siege, with dozens of carefully painted metal figurines gathered round a plastic castle. After passing the child to her partner, who looked old enough to be her father, she sat opposite Gillard at the far end of an adjacent table. Above them, traditional horse brasses, horse collars, and various rural paraphernalia hung amongst the darkened beams. In a back room, a child could be heard running around. 'Sorry about the mess,' she said, indicating the wargame table. 'Half of them end up on the floor. I've vacuumed up more of Callum's soldiers than you can imagine.'

'So you run this place as well as operating a JCB?' Gillard said.

'Well, seeing as I'm still on furlough at the pub I took the opportunity to keep myself occupied. I've got a small stable across behind the Tickett place, and the pandemic has done for that as well. We had to keep ourselves going until pubs reopen on Saturday.' She glanced at her watch. 'Phew, there's so much still to do.'

'And I understand it was your first week on the excavator?'

'Yes. I was brought up on a farm, so can drive a tractor, a tele lifter, a truck up to the HGV limit, and am pretty good with trailers. I've worked a basic JCB, but the twenty-two tonner is a bit of a step up. It's always nice to have a new skill. Aidan showed me.'

'That's Aidan Tickett, the guy with the ginger crewcut?' Gillard recalled that the man Christopher Tickett had murdered in 1982 was a farmer called Willow. Vicky's father perhaps? It would be odd if the two families got along.

'Yeah. Aidan was a man short for rebuilding the embankment after the recent flooding. It wasn't tricky work, just digging out at the water's edge and heaping it up behind, but he was behind schedule. I had done about fifty metres of it that morning when we discovered the body.'

'And who actually made the discovery?'

'Aidan was there, with the Greenpiss surveyor.'

'What—?'

'Sorry, it's just our name for the water company.' She smiled. 'They saw the body in the hole I'd just dug.'

If she was upset before, she certainly seemed to have recovered now. That wasn't necessarily odd. A harried mother has little time for reflection.

'You'd been working on the embankment earlier in the week?'

'Yes. Monday was just practice, and the next three days I carried on under Aidan's supervision. I enjoyed it. Makes a change from changing nappies.'

Gillard was impressed with the woman's adaptability. 'I'll write this up as a basic statement and get you to sign it later.'

She nodded. 'Any idea who it is?' she said.

'Not yet. I'm sure you'll get to hear. Look, I heard there was an accident at the flyover earlier this year, involving a man who worked for the water company.'

'That's right. They found his car in the river, but never found his body. Do you think it could be him?'

'We're keeping an open mind.' Gillard wished he'd earned a pound for every time he'd trotted out the stock police phrase. On most occasions, of course, it was accurate.

The woman was staring out of the window. 'I feel terrible, as if I'd killed whoever it was. Stupid, isn't it?'

'It's entirely natural.' He started to pack up his notes. The door burst open and a boy of about seven ran in, dressed in a plastic Viking helmet and furry boots. He made warlike sounds as he clattered through the chairs, slaying imaginary foes.

'Callum, I've told you before. Calm down!' Vicky bellowed. The boy hurtled back out, slamming the door loudly enough to shake the woodwork. She turned back to Gillard. 'It's war, every day. He's big for his age, and so boisterous. Now he's furious because I won't let him see

Game of Thrones. It's not suitable for seven-year-olds. Too much bonking.'

'I've not seen it,' he said.

'I suppose your kids would be grown up?'

'Something I never got round to,' Gillard said. As he said it, he thought of Sam and her two miscarriages in the last couple of years. He felt a pang.

The woman seemed to read his mind, and gave him an indulgent smile. 'We can do you a lunch, if you like. We've got a freezer full of steak, fish, you name it, and we're not allowed to keep it more than three months. Some of it is still okay, but we're restocking on Friday. We had to pour the real ale away, but the lager is still fine. If you wanted one, I can do it on the house.'

'That's very kind,' Gillard said. 'But I have to pay. I can't be seen to accept favours. I couldn't help noticing your menu. Have you got the hunter's chicken?'

–

The hunter's chicken was awful, barely defrosted, cold in the centre and overcooked at the edges. The cabbage was overdone and the curly fries looked like deep-fried ginger pubes. It occurred to him that the body by the river may well have died of food poisoning. Gillard ate only a little of the meal, but made no mention of it when Guy came to collect the dishes.

'So when did Vicky get her young chef award?' Gillard asked.

'Nah, that was me. She can't cook for toffee.' He scooped up the dishes, and wandered back behind the bar shedding cutlery and leftovers onto the carpet as he went. Young chef? The man must be pushing sixty. While his bill was being prepared the detective went over and scrutinised the award certificate on the wall. Guy Naylor, 1983, it said. It must've been a fluke, or maybe he'd just stopped making an effort a decade or so ago. Gillard drained his half of lager shandy, and headed off to the gents. It was a smelly traditional pub toilet, sorely in need of renovation. The cold tap was jammed, there were no paper towels in the dispenser, the wall-mounted liquid soap dispenser was empty, and there was a sliver of greying soap glued to the top of the washbasin by its own fossilised lather. A sorry state of neglect, typical of the village. Time to get away, and back to the crime scene.

–

Gillard found Aqua Western engineer Trevor Collier down on the site well away from the crime scene, overseeing the digging of a trench that from the wooden markers would bisect the meadow parallel to the river. The water engineer agreed to step away from the gaggle of orange-clad contractors and the clank and roar of heavy machinery.

'I just want to get a bit of context about the discovery of the body,' Gillard said.

'Righto,' Collier said, pushing back his hard hat to reveal dark curly hair, flecked with grey. From the bulging front of his high-vis, it seemed he was fond of a pint. Over the next few minutes he entirely corroborated Vicky Willow's account of how the body was found. Still, Gillard had more questions.

'What work is it that you're doing here, and when did it start?'

'What you see right here is the flood management phase, second phase of the infrastructure plan for the area.

We're putting in water pipes and sewers to serve the new estates planned for the far side of Upper Rissington. We started on it three months ago, and just got up to there, where the body was found, last week.'

'And what about the first phase?'

'That was the main sewer modernisation, started nearly a year ago.' He sucked his teeth. 'It was designed to stop the storm drain surcharge problems they've been having round here.'

'Did Ozzy Blanchard work on that first phase?'

Collier stared at him. 'Yeah, he did. Then, as I say, he disappeared, and his company car was found down there in the river in January. It can't be him, though, can it?'

'Why not?'

'The archaeologist said the body is probably years old.'

'Did he indeed?' Gillard clenched his teeth.

'And it's upriver from the car, so he didn't get washed up here.'

Gillard made a couple of notes and looked back at Collier. 'Some in the community say there's been a lot of pollution over the years.'

Collier sucked his teeth at what was clearly an often-expressed opinion. 'Yeah, we've been having our ears bent about it from all sides. The trouble is it's not so easy to solve. The original pre-war sewer for all the villages to the north-east of here runs parallel to the storm drains. Normally they run side-by-side, not interfering with each other at all, until they join just prior to the water treatment works five miles that way.' He pointed west past Gillard, downriver past the flyover. 'The storm drains are designed to vent rainwater into the river in extreme circumstances. But when you get heavy rain, rainwater gets into the sewer, and it too will vent into the storm drains at certain locations when the water level gets high enough, and certainly when the streets get flooded. And Rissington Common, and the land around, is the lowest point.'

'So when there is exceptional rain, basically you get shit in the river?'

'And all the other stuff people flush down the toilet.'

'Don't you have gratings to hold that stuff back?'

'We do, but they get blocked very quickly. It only needs a few nappies for example to inhibit the flow. At a certain pressure, the gratings are designed to lift as an escape valve, which allows everything out.'

'Why?'

'Because otherwise we'd flood out the water treatment works and that would take weeks to put right. So we are allowed to vent a certain amount of raw sewage in exceptional circumstances, but the Environment Agency gets upset if there's too much and we can get fined millions, which has happened.'

Gillard stroked his chin. 'Do you ever get dead bodies flushed out of the system?'

He laughed. 'Of rats, certainly. In London they probably get all sorts, but out here I've never heard of human bodies in the system.'

'Where the body was found, had that area flooded often?'

'Ah, you need to speak to the Environment Agency about that. That's outside my remit.'

Gillard suppressed an inward laugh at the bureaucratic reflex. 'One final thing – I noticed you and your colleague having a bit of an argument about something. May I ask what?'

Collier took his hat off and scratched his head. 'There appears to have been a bit of a screw-up. Between you and me, it's only become clear while working on phase two that what was done in the first phase didn't match what was on the spec.'

'In what way?'

'I'm surprised the police are interested in this,' Collier said.

'Indulge me.'

'Look, I'm not supposed to admit anything, or even discuss it, because we could get fined by the water regulator. But what was done in phase one was botched. Those higher up than me will have to decide what to do about it. And I was getting bollocked as if it was my fault. I didn't have anything to do with phase one.'

'But Ozzy Blanchard did?'

'Yeah. He was the main on-site engineer.'

Chapter Six

Gillard let Collier go and retreated to his car, still feeling slightly bilious after the meal. It certainly wasn't helped by the nature of the conversation he'd just had. He took out his iPad and looked up the news stories about the accident in January. It told him little he hadn't already heard, except for the alarming fact that Blanchard's vehicle had been driven against traffic on the dual carriageway for more than quarter of a mile before leaving the road. He then looked up Blanchard's employer. Aqua Western Ltd was part of a group of four UK-based water suppliers, each with a point of the compass as part of its name, and a fifth company, Aqua Clear Ltd, which seemed to concentrate on cleaning up industrial sites and former rubbish tips. They were all owned by Aqua Holdings Plc, but the ultimate owner was a New York registered private equity company called Clearwater Partners LLC. There were pages of aspirational verbiage about how clean, green and socially responsible each of the companies were, so Gillard instead switched to news stories about the parent company, and the two young billionaires who ran it.

The most prominent of them was Titan Willard III, known as Ty. A former professional football player, a handsome six foot five, Ty Willard came from a patrician New England family. His partner was Eric Lishman, supposedly the financial genius, who had met Willard at

Harvard. They were both thirty-eight, firm friends, and had made their first billion before there were thirty.

Clearwater Partners had acquired the company that later became Aqua Holdings a dozen years ago, paying £3.5 billion. Within six months they had outsourced much of the maintenance operation, sold off thousands of acres of land for development, and with the proceeds paid themselves a £500 million dividend, via a Bermuda-based holding company on which no tax was due. Gillard found a *Financial Times* analysis piece which said that the two billionaires had brought their money-making strategy to the UK, but warned there were bound to be claims of asset stripping, and the danger of leaving potential liabilities for repairs uncovered by the now-depleted capital reserves and huge debt accumulated.

This all seemed to Gillard to dovetail neatly with the accusations made by Sheila Ransome, the woman who had spoken to him through the car window. It clearly was a battle of David against Goliath. Quite how the elusive Ozzy Blanchard fitted into all this wasn't clear. However, no one of sound judgement drives at high speed into oncoming traffic on a busy dual carriageway unless drunk, drugged or very, very scared. If it was either of the first two, his body would almost certainly have been found at the scene. But it wasn't. So a man capable of that dangerous manoeuvre was fit enough to exit the vehicle and then escape. He must have been terrified. Perhaps the finding of this body would prove whether that fear was justified.

–

Gillard was just finishing saving all the documents he'd found when the head of CSI rang him. Yaz Quoroshi was quite excited about a discovery they had made as they were shifting the corpse carefully into a body bag. 'Craig, we're making good progress towards an ID.'

'That's quick,' Gillard said. 'I'd feared that we would struggle to get much information without some time-consuming and expensive tests.'

'Well, first off the victim is male. The archaeologist and I agreed about that. The skeletal remains are indicative, even though the hip girdle is fractured in numerous places, as is the jaw. We've got a few upper molars still in place, one of which has an amalgam filling. There is also a wedding ring, plain gold band, no inscription. But we made an even more exciting discovery, which should accelerate the inquiry considerably.'

'Good.'

'I was really pessimistic at first when I saw the kind of soil conditions the body was in, but we've now established that the upper half of the corpse was in was a modern shirt, artificial fibres. The jeans were in better condition, and in the back pocket we've found a comb, trapped within which there are quite a few hairs with follicles still attached. They are in far better condition than the few hairs that we found on the scalp. It looks easily good enough for a DNA analysis.'

'That's brilliant news. Any further thoughts on how long he's been there?'

'All we can say is an absolute minimum of three months to get adipocere, right up to a handful of years. We can certainly already rule him out as a historic body, simply based on the modernity of much of what we found upon him. The fillings, the comb and the bits of ballpoint. There's enough tattered plastic around the body to make it likely he was buried in a couple of refuse bags.'

'It's all beginning to look coherent then,' Gillard said.

'Yes, we finished on the upper torso in the excavator bucket, but there's quite a bit more fingertip-search work to do in the hole by the water's edge. A few of us will be busy on that up to our waists until the late evening I imagine, and when we've finished we'll get the excavator to dig out the last bits just in case we've missed anything. One more thing. The archaeologist has been pestering me to allow his volunteers to sift parts of the site while the digging is halted. The riverbank has seen some Anglo-Saxon finds in the past, and he thinks it might be a good opportunity.'

'Only once you've finished at the crime scene, and assuming the water company has given permission'

'Aqua Western is okay with it. And we'll be done by midday tomorrow.'

'All right then. Who knows, they might finding something we missed.'

Gillard thanked Quoroshi and finished the call. The CSI chief, originally an Iraqi refugee, had proved an invaluable asset to Surrey Police over the last decade. He'd worked his way up in the forensic service which Surrey and Sussex shared, and proved his worth not only for his knowledge but also his managerial skill. Crime scene investigation is a dirty and often repellent business, and unlike some senior officials, Yaz liked to stay at the sharp end. If there was a long overnight investigation, shivering in a forensic tent in the pouring rain, you could bet your bottom dollar that Yaz would be there right through. Consequently, his staff were ferociously loyal, and would do literally anything for him.

The detective looked out of the car window. Rain was beginning to fall. He didn't envy the job they would have to do that night.

Gillard checked his watch. He'd have to hurry back to Mount Browne by six to brief Radar Dobbs. And it was already just past five. He would probably make it, given the rush hour was far less of a hold-up in these days of lockdown. As he put away the iPad and tidied up his notes, he noticed a silver Nissan Qashqai making its way down the lane towards the crime scene. At first he thought it was probably someone from the water company, but they normally worked straight office hours. As the Nissan squeezed past Gillard's Vauxhall the driver stared at him. He was a big, bald, bullet-headed man in his mid-fifties with rectangular sunglasses, wearing a suit but with his tie loose around his thick neck. There was something about him that looked familiar. As the car continued to the dead end of Bourne Lane, Gillard made a note of the registration number, and drove off back to Guildford.

Who was he? He had a good memory for faces, but couldn't quite place the man.

—

'So are we dealing with a murder or not?' Dobbs asked, sitting back in his chair with his hands cupped behind his head.

'We're awaiting full forensics,' Gillard said, describing the modern aspects of the body and the prospect of a DNA sample from the comb. 'But a few things stand out. One is that it is a recent death, probably less than five years. The fact that he was partially dressed, without jacket, shoes or socks, and probably wrapped in bin bags, is indicative that someone else was involved. He clearly didn't bury himself, and even though his body was found within an embankment, it doesn't look like he could have been swept down the river and deposited there from somewhere else.'

'Is this something we can pass off to Hampshire?'

This was exactly the kind of comment that Gillard had expected from his boss. Bureaucratic jostling for position, attempting to pass the parcel on time-consuming and resource-heavy investigations to another equally overworked constabulary.

'He was found in Surrey, sir, just.'

'But Rissington Common is in Hampshire,' Dobbs persisted. His short iron-grey hair and pencil-thin moustache made him look like a door-to-door insurance salesman from the 1960s. Light from the window behind him made his enormous ears look baby pink.

'We've already committed resources, including our county archaeologist and Home Office forensic consultant,' Gillard said levelly. 'With respect, I think this case is ours.'

Dobbs turned a pen over and over between his fingers, like some mini-majorette. 'I had a call this afternoon from Hampshire Constabulary, DCS Anderson. She wants to be kept informed of every development.'

Of course. Stella was bound to go over his head. That was just her style. 'I've already told her that I would copy her in. It would certainly be useful to have Hampshire's input on some of the locals.'

After another few minutes of instruction and suggestions, Dobbs let him go. Gillard blew a sigh as he walked down the corridor. He had preferred the days when Dobbs was off sick, and he had reported directly to Alison Rigby. The chief constable was smart, decisive and generally supportive of her officers. With Dobbs, Gillard felt that he was being watched until he made a mistake. Stella Anderson's involvement would simply be another opportunity to second-guess his work. Still, this connection could work both ways. He didn't routinely have access to the Hampshire crime database, and it would be useful to speak to her.

He picked up the phone and rang her. The call went to voicemail, so he dropped in the name of Ozzy Blanchard. 'I need to know everything you've got on him, ma'am.'

–

Gillard headed home early, knowing that DI Mulholland was on evening duty. Claire was a very safe pair of hands, one of Gillard's closest colleagues and his best friend in the force. He knew that she could handle anything that emerged from the Rissington Man case.

Before lockdown began, Gillard had tried to match up with Sam's work schedule once a week so they could both go to the swimming pool at the same time. Now, with gyms and swimming pools closed, they missed that shared exercise, but had switched to a new one. He had for years been a regular cyclist, but since the lockdown in March they had ridden together, Sam using the new lightweight racer that Gillard had bought her for Christmas. Tonight was a perfect opportunity to make use of the light summer evenings to notch up some longer distances. She was very nearly as fit as he was, though she still lacked confidence in jousting for space on the busy Home Counties roads. They stopped halfway round their route in a layby to drink from their water bottles, but by the time they got back home in the failing light, they both needed more.

'I'm so thirsty,' she said, wiping her mouth with the back of her hand, while Gillard opened the garage. He smiled. She looked as good as she had ever done, her trim Lycra-clad figure still showing traces of tan from the holiday they had enjoyed just after Christmas. Upstairs, they jumped into the shower cubicle together. Sam washed her hair, and with fleeting touches, he helped her rinse suds from the long dark tresses.

'That feels nice,' she said, leaning backwards into him, her hot sudsy head against his shoulder, her firm buttocks against his groin. After a few minutes, the words ceased, and they exchanged hot wet kisses. Slick, slippery movements and wordless murmurs took over, and became a gentle rhythmic symphony under the steaming nozzle. It was gentle, unhurried and delightful. When it was over, Sam's eyes popped open, a huge grin on her face. 'Oh Craig, I got there.'

'Fantastic. I didn't want to ask.'

'It was a little one, but they all count.'

He held her close, and kissed the top of her head. There had been numerous attempts at lovemaking since Sam's kidnapping ordeal a year ago. Faltering to begin with, each in its own way had been a stepping stone to rebuild the trust and intimacy that her PTSD had shattered. Today was the first time since then that she had been able to surrender to the pleasure. He knew it would get better from here.

For the rest of that evening Sam was in a bubbly mood, affectionate and relaxed. Abandoning plans to cook, they ordered a Chinese takeaway, and instead of drinking wine, shared a pot of loose leaf jasmine tea. For once the crime gods were kind to them and Gillard's mobile stayed silent all evening. As they slipped into the cool sheets, they both knew they were going to make love again. After a few minutes under the covers, she pulled his head up from between her thighs. 'God, I'm ready. I think today's the day. Let's build a new future.'

–

While Gillard was busy at home, someone else was busy at the crime scene. PC Sarah Noakes was sitting in her patrol car at the bottom of the lane in Rissington Common next to the gate which led to the meadow. She could see the embankment and the silhouettes of the motionless machinery against a Prussian blue sky. The CSI team had finished for the night, but she was to keep an eye on the crime scene until they came back at seven the next morning. She had with her a takeaway coffee, now cooling, and a magazine of sudoku puzzles. She was just finishing a fiendishly complex one when she saw movement in her peripheral vision. Looking up, there was a figure moving in the meadow amongst the willows that marked the water's edge. Male, large, hooded, stealthy. Carrying something heavy. The silhouette passed behind a thicket and disappeared. She picked up her radio and called it in, then repositioned the car so she could shine the headlamps towards him. With the lights on full beam she stepped out, and called across towards the water. 'This is a crime scene. You are not allowed here. Come away immediately.'

There was no reply. Muttering to herself, she went to the boot, changed into her wellingtons and picked up a torch. She locked the car, ducked under the crime tape and went through the gate. The torchlight showed no signs of the person she had seen. She splashed across the muddy field, and climbed up the embankment to where the excavator sat, like some giant metal bird, halfway through scooping a meal from the water. She called out again, but got no reply. Slightly unnerved, she called in her position on the radio. The operator in the control room was a friend of hers, and advised caution.

'Don't worry, I'm not going to take any risks,' Sarah said.

Then she caught him in her beam. A man crouching down at the very pit from which the body had been removed, just twenty yards away. 'Oi!' she called out. 'This is the police. Stay exactly where you are.'

The man had his own torch, which he shone in her eyes. Briefly dazzled, she then saw he was running away along the riverbank. The object he was carrying was now clearly a metal detector. From her position on the embankment, six or seven feet higher, it seemed easier to run on the hardened earth than to make her way down the weed-strewn slope to the riverside path. She was running in parallel to him and gaining, although she was aware that the river curved away to the right while the embankment carried on straight.

Whatever it was she tripped over, she didn't see, but it was enough to send her tumbling down the slope. By the time she got her feet, and retrieved the torch, the man had made good his escape.

Thursday

Gillard was notified about the intruder by the Mount Browne control room as he was driving into work the next morning. He rang Yaz Quoroshi at CSI on the hands-free, and asked if they had finished at the crime scene.

'I keep getting the same question from Hancock. Just a couple of hours now,' Quoroshi said. 'We've dug another ton of soil immediately around the body, looking for the missing fingers and teeth. Then we removed the topsoil to a depth of twenty centimetres in a five-metre radius from the discovery of the body, but didn't find anything except bits of the plastic bag. Hancock's archaeology volunteers have arrived ready to go through it. He's badgering me to use ground-penetrating radar to search for a murder weapon.'

Gillard laughed. 'He's trying it on. We already have enough dental proof that this is a modern body,' he said. 'No doubt the archaeologist is getting very excited about the prospects of the police paying for a sophisticated dig, but if the county council won't pay for it, it's not going to happen.'

'That's almost word for word what Radar Dobbs told me.'

'Well on this occasion I agree with him. Oh, hang on, I've got Dr Delahaye on the other line,' he said. 'We might have the answer already.' Gillard said a hurried goodbye and switched call. The dry and cultured voice of the forensic pathologist came onto the line.

'There have been some new developments, rather surprising ones in my view,' he said.

'Let's hope we are closer to some answers.'

'When I saw how much adipocere there was in the body, I was pretty certain that I wasn't going to be able to tell you very much about the cause of death, but actually I may have been wrong. The conversion of soft tissues to this soapy texture is the major problem, because the internal structure that any pathologist would rely on has broken down. I've got him out on the slab right now, in about six different pieces. There's clearly been considerable damage to the body, broken bones, damaged neck vertebrae, a couple of missing fingers and so forth, much of it obviously caused by the excavator. I had assumed that trying to tease out whether any of the trauma predated the machinery damage would be quite difficult, and that most of the information would be derived from the wealth of associated material, clothing, pens and so on.'

'You're keeping me in suspense, David.'

'I am, and for the good reason that you're still going to need a forensic archaeologist to tie up the loose ends. There was an interesting puncture wound in the neck, which might possibly account for the damage to the vertebrae. It didn't on the face of it seem to me likely to have been caused by the excavator. I X-rayed the head and neck, and discovered a sliver of what appears to be heavily corroded metal, partially embedded between two neck vertebrae. This would have severed the spinal cord, probably cut the right common carotid artery and was certainly embedded with some force. If it turns out to have preceded the damage caused by the excavator, it could well turn out to be the cause of death.'

'What exactly do you mean by a sliver of metal?'

'It's essentially a thumb-sized fragment, but much less thick. My suspicion is that it originally could have been very sharp. I've copied the X-ray to Dr Clive Hancock and to you as well.'

'Sorry, I can't open it because I'm driving. Are you saying it was a knife, and that he was stabbed?'

'I'm saying nothing of the sort, Craig, at least not for the moment. We don't know what this thing is yet. Nevertheless, the puncture wound has *prima facie* similarities with the use of a knife, even down to a slight element of gape rendered in the adipocere on the point of entry. If so, a fragment of the weapon has remained behind in the wound. In the context of a modern stabbing that would be most unusual. I have conducted over four hundred autopsies involving a stabbing in my career, and I cannot recall a single case where a blade fragment remained behind in the wound.'

'But you say this thing was corroded; would the adipocere have done that?'

'It's too early to tell. It does appear to be metallic because of the bright image on X-ray, and the uneven shape may be indicative of corrosion. One remote possibility of course, is that during the excavation, a piece of debris got pushed into the neck to cause the observed injury. If the corpse had been in better condition I might be able to ascertain whether the injury was pre or post-mortem, but I'd rather not try to remove the item at this stage, because it might break up.'

'What are the possibilities?'

'As I see it, there are only three ways it could have got there. One, as we mentioned, is a stabbing, though it was clearly a very unusual weapon. Two, it's a piece of debris that got forced into the neck during the excavation, or three, it's a piece of debris that got forced in some other way.'

'How are we going to narrow those down?'

'I'm hoping that Dr Hancock will have some ideas. He's on his way now, and seems rather excited.'

'May I come and join you?'

'Of course.'

Gillard thanked the forensic pathologist and hung up.

Gillard was delayed by phone calls once he arrived at Mount Browne, and only got to the mortuary at eleven. He made his way to the examination room, where Dr Hancock, wearing a white coat, beard net and hairnet and latex gloves was deep in conversation with Delahaye, similarly dressed. Between them, on the slab lay half a dozen grey pieces of humanity, like a first disastrous clay mould made by an apprentice from Madame Tussauds. The two men looked up at the detective's approach.

'Ah, Craig, I think we've got something fantastic here,' Hancock said, leading Gillard to a lightbox, where an X-ray was on display. 'This is Dr Delahaye's first image, using a conventional medical setting on the machine.'

Gillard could see the bright fragment, alien amongst the softer greys of the body. It was clearly embedded between two vertebrae, and seemed to have displaced the line of the spine. 'That is a pretty graphic injury,' he said.

'Most certainly,' Delahaye said.

Hancock took over. 'By adjusting the exposure to an archaeological setting, we have been able to look inside the object found in the corpse's neck.' He placed a second X-ray on the lightbox, side-by-side with the first. 'Here we are able to delineate a little bit more of the object, which I'm now convinced is mainly iron, and even to see inside it, beyond the corrosion.'

'So can you tell how old it is from how much it's rusted?' Gillard said.

'In laboratory conditions, yes,' Hancock said. 'The trouble with iron is that unlike most metals, its rate of corrosion isn't purely geared to elapsed time. It depends on the level of moisture, oxygen and salt it is exposed to. So in the field we can never be precise.'

Delahaye exchanged a knowing glance with Gillard, then resumed gazing indulgently at the archaeologist, whose enthusiastic hand movements emphasised his excitement.

'What this shows,' Hancock said, 'is extensive corrosion, but not right through to the core of the object. On the surface there are traces of copper, or possibly bronze. You can't see it easily on this one but we did a close-up.' The archaeologist switched the X-ray image to a far more detailed one.

Gillard squinted at a series of darker shapes in a line which punctuated the mainly white bulk of the image. 'It looks like writing.'

'Very good,' said Hancock. 'That's exactly what it is.'

'Does it say "Made in Sheffield"?' Gillard asked, thinking of what might be written on a knife. He turned his head sideways but couldn't make out what the letters said.

'Oh no, I think not. This is not a modern object.'

'But we appear to have a modern victim?'

'Yes, slightly tricky, to put it mildly,' Dr Delahaye said, folding his arms.

Hancock laughed to himself. 'That's what makes it so fascinating.'

'How old are we talking? More than a hundred years?' Gillard asked.

'Oh, yes. Much more than that. Indeed, much more than a thousand,' Hancock said. 'I think this is a fragment of an Anglo-Saxon dagger, and very rare indeed.'

Chapter Seven

Gillard's jaw hung open. 'How did a modern man end up being stabbed in the neck by a thousand year old weapon?'

'Maybe he worked in a museum,' Delahaye said.

Hancock chuckled. 'I think the crucial thing here from an archaeological perspective is to identify the dagger, and then we can tell if it is from a known collection. If it is an unknown item, then that is very exciting.'

'How long will it take you to decipher the writing?' Gillard asked.

'Well, it could be several weeks, but hopefully less.'

Delahaye turned away to take a phone call. As he was listening, he turned to Gillard with his hand up. 'So you have identified DNA from the body? Okay, from the comb. Good. Thank you.' After he had hung up, he pointed at the corpse and said. 'Our victim is not on the national DNA database.'

'What other tests are they doing?' Gillard asked.

'I sent off a fragment of the shirt for analysis, and fingernails for toxicity tests as I can't check out the liver or any other organs. As you heard, the lab tried to extract DNA from the hairs on the head, but the roots have deteriorated. The comb was in a plastic sleeve inside a rear pocket of the jeans, which seemingly made for a better environment for DNA preservation. Having just heard what Dr Hancock has to say, I think we should send off some samples of bone and hair to Glasgow for carbon-14 dating. Somehow we've got to reconcile the ages of what we have in front of us.'

Hancock rubbed his hands in anticipation. 'That's exactly what I would have suggested. This could be a major discovery.'

'That's all very interesting, but my priorities are a bit more down-to-earth,' Gillard said. 'I need to know as soon as possible if a crime has been committed, it's as simple as that.' He was a little alarmed that Hancock seemed to be inserting himself deeper into the investigation, and steering it away from the primary objective.

'I take your point,' Hancock said. 'However, given the minimum length of time it takes to form adipocere, I think your murderer, if he exists, has made a clean getaway.'

Gillard nodded. 'It clearly seems to be a crime, but this being the pandemic, police resources are quite stretched. Clive, I don't know if you'd heard, but a metal detectorist was spotted on the site late last night. We're doubling up on the overnight officers for tonight, but that will be the last. It will be down to the county council to arrange security if you're planning to pursue anything on the archaeological side.'

Hancock sucked his teeth. 'That won't be easy. I might instead be able to persuade the water company to fence it off for the three days we've been given. After all they've got equipment there, and there are health and safety concerns too. Lots of uncovered pits. Kids running all over the place too.'

Delahaye nodded. 'When I was there, some children were throwing stones. One hit Arrowsmith, from the water company, fortunately on his hard hat. He wasn't hurt.'

'Did anyone see who threw it? Take any pictures?'

'No, but the water company isn't popular in the village,' Hancock said.

'Arrowsmith was furious,' Delahaye said. 'He ran after them shouting "I'm the one trying to put it right, you idiot".'

'There's a huge backlog of work, the rivers are awash in sewage, and they seem to be using cowboy contractors,' Hancock said. 'I'm just glad that Aqua Western is responsible for the water in only a small part of the county.'

–

On his way back into the car park Gillard's mobile rang, a private withheld number. 'Hello Craig, it's Stella Anderson.'

'Hello, ma'am,' he replied.

'I'm quite impressed. It didn't take you long to figure out that Ozzy Blanchard might be of interest.'

'Locals mentioned him, but he hadn't come up on the missing persons search.'

'He is listed at his home address in Hemel Hempstead. So if you'd been looking for a missing person in the vicinity of Rissington Common, he wouldn't have come up.'

'What have you got on him?'

'Nothing concrete, despite the industry he worked in.' She permitted herself a small chuckle. 'I've forwarded you the crime report, and a statement by his wife, who has not heard from him.'

'Thank you. Have you got a DNA sample for him? We'd like to compare it to samples from a comb we found on the body.'

'No. It didn't seem necessary at the time, because we were simply following up on an accident. I'm sure Mrs Blanchard wouldn't object to someone coming to collect a toothbrush or something. Look, Craig, I would draw your attention to one element of the investigation. Blanchard's work mobile was in use on the night of the accident, at that location, a few minutes afterwards. He was clearly alive then, even if he isn't now.'

Gillard was looking forward to more details, but didn't get them. Anderson gave a hurried goodbye and cut the call, blaming a meeting about to start. What she'd said hadn't explained why someone of her seniority was involved in something like this. It had to be much more than a missing persons case. She was a fraud expert, so was it that? Examining his phone, the records she had sent him indicated nothing more serious than dangerous driving had been levelled at Blanchard. Aidan Tickett had described seeing Anderson in the pub months ago, but Gillard hadn't had an opportunity to ask her about it. What was she hiding?

–

Gillard drove back to his office to a backlog of other work. DCS Dobbs had sent him a huge folder of training courses that he was supposed to have taken, but had never had the time. In his nit-picking way, the detective chief superintendent had underlined each of them where the word 'mandatory' appeared. There were certainly several forensic courses he would like to have taken if he had the time, but the mandatory ones included racially sensitive stop-and-search techniques, and preparing rape cases for the CPS. He hadn't conducted a stop and search since he was in uniform, while rape evidence was these days handled by a specialist unit. Each course was a day or more long, and Dobbs needed a response today on when he could book himself in.

Gillard tossed them aside for later. As he did so, DC Carrie Macintosh walked stiffly over to the desk. A bright and quick-witted Glaswegian, formerly a junior doctor, she was known universally as Rainy.

'Is our wee body a murder victim then, sir?'

Gillard smiled. 'Probably.' He described the latest forensic findings. 'If the victim turns out to have been there for half a century or more, then we can turn it all over to the archaeologists. If he hasn't, he might well have been murdered. But even if you had a rusty Anglo-Saxon dagger over your mantelpiece, there would be better and more effective weapons to use. There are other accidental possibilities that Delahaye listed, but they do seem quite unlikely.'

'Och, best check if any antique weapons have been nicked recently.' She looked down at her notebook. 'I did the registration trace you asked for on the Nissan Qashqai. The owner is RAS Services Ltd of an address in Croydon. I looked the firm up Companies House and it simply says business services, but a little more digging turned up that it's a private detective agency. The owners are Raymond and Anne Slater. They share an address in Croydon, just round the corner from where the firm is based. Do you want me to dig for more?'

'Yes please.' The name Slater was definitely familiar, from many years ago. 'What else are you working on at the moment?'

'A break-in at a pharmacy. The usual type. Addicts for sure.'

'All right, I may need you full-time on this case if it develops into anything. We're expecting some forensic results in the next couple of days, so don't get too deep into anything else.'

'It will be good to have something with a wee bit of spice to it,' she said, as she headed back to her desk. Gillard couldn't help noticing that she was limping.

'Have you hurt your leg?' he asked. Rainy wasn't tall and had admitted to struggling with her weight on and off for years. He suspected she may have been on one of her occasional fitness kicks.

'Dinnae worry, it's nothing,' she said, sitting down heavily at her desk. It was clear she was in some pain. Gillard didn't want to make a fuss about it, but thought he would keep an eye on her. The rest of his team wasn't exactly fighting fit. DS Vikram Singh had Covid, and had already been off for three weeks, DC Michelle Tsu was self-isolating after a family member had tested positive, and DC Shireen Corey Williams from the economic crime unit was stuck in Greece with an elderly relative who had fallen ill months ago. That left DI Claire Mulholland and the old reliable DC Carl Hoskins.

Mulholland was out of the office, and Hoskins was at his desk, eating some kind of deep-fried food. Shaven headed, clinically obese and something of a dinosaur in terms of sexual politics, Hoskins represented the traditional past of British policing. But you had to hand it to him, he was hardly ever sick, did long hours week in, week out, and uncomplainingly tackled tedious tasks like looking through CCTV. Gillard often thought of Hoskins as being like the bass player in his little band. His steadiness helped hold it all together. Even now, he was on the phone while looking through the ANPR database.

Line after line of traffic camera number plate matches were flicking up on his screen.

Curious, Gillard heaved himself out of his desk and wandered over. Hoskins hurriedly wound up the phone call, and clicked off the database.

'What are you working on, Carl?'

'Bit of this bit of that,' he said, swivelling on his seat. The detective constable had finished his meal, but had showered bits of breadcrumbed fat on the floor around his chair and on his lap. There was grease on the screen, on the keyboard, and all round the detective's mouth.

'Look, Carl. I don't mind a sandwich at the desk; we all work hard and have to work through lunch. But once we get to hot-desking at the new HQ, there's no way you'll be able to eat chicken nuggets at the keyboard.'

'It wasn't nuggets, sir. A battered saveloy and a Scotch egg.'

Gillard shuddered inwardly. 'It doesn't matter. No one would want to sit at the desk after you.'

Hoskins face creased in satisfaction. This was clearly part of the plan to mark out personal territory when the force vacated the historic Mount Browne site and moved into its planned new headquarters in Leatherhead. That wouldn't happen until 2024, and just like the water project he'd seen, might well be subject to delays and cost over-runs.

'The cleaners have complained, you know,' Gillard said. 'They're on a pittance, and they say your part of the room takes as long as the rest of the floor.'

The detective constable apologised, and began to use the paper bag his lunch had come in to wipe the screen. The bag was already translucent with grease, and it only made things worse.

'Clean it properly before you go home,' Gillard said.

His mobile went, and he turned away to take the call. The caller identified herself as Sheila Ransome. He recalled she had earlier buttonholed him in the car about the supposed crimes of the water company.

'How did you get this number?' he asked her.

'I borrowed the business card you gave to the archaeologist.'

'Did you indeed?' Gillard made a mental note to have a word with Clive Hancock about making free and easy with contact details as well as facts about the case. Mrs Ransome was undoubtedly a capable and determined campaigner, which was even more reason that she should not know how to get hold of him. Still, it was too late now. 'How can I help?'

'I just want to report what I saw last week, which may have some bearing on your case.'

'Go on then,' he said, with a due sense of dread.

'I saw this man skulking around the village at night. A stranger, large with a bald head. I'd heard that someone was trespassing around the crime scene. I wondered if it might be the same man.'

Gillard returned to his desk and grabbed a notepad and pen as the woman continued her tale.

'It was about nine p.m. last Thursday. I was at the church, locking up after evensong. And I saw this man in a suit walk past, climb over the gate into the meadow and on towards the river.'

'What did he look like?'

'Medium height, solid build, fiftyish and bald.'

'Was he carrying anything?' Gillard was thinking of the reports of the detectorist, and of the man in the Nissan.

'No.'

He thanked the woman, and asked her to use the main number to report any further details, before hanging up.

–

Desperate to get out of the office and stay away from Radar Dobbs, Gillard returned to Rissington Common. He was getting frustrated at the slow pace of the forensic tests, but until he knew who the dead man was, most other investigative leads risked being dead ends. Still, some dead ends are more pleasant than others, and Bourne Lane, Rissington Common fell into that category.

Gillard parked in the lane. He made his way across the meadow and over the embankment to see that Hancock hadn't wasted any time since CSI had packed up and left. There was what looked like a full-scale archaeological dig marked out with a chequerboard grid of string and posts, dividing the site into yard-wide squares, including the spot where the body had been found. A dozen volunteers crouched or sat, carefully socially distanced, while sifting through samples of soil. Aqua Western had put up a perimeter fence around the field, and it was certainly more difficult to get in, although anybody who was determined to do so could wade in the shallows of the river. Clive Hancock was at the centre of the dig, his wild hair pluming in the wind. He had a sheet of plastic on which various small items had been placed. He looked up as Gillard approached.

'Found anything?' Gillard asked.

'A few coins, not much else so far. However there is this, just found a few minutes ago.' He picked up a marble-sized muddy pebble and showed it to the detective.

'What is it?'

'I think it's an amber bead. I won't know for sure until we've cleaned it, but it may be from a necklace or something similar. Anglo-Saxon, quite probably, given where we've found it.'

'I've found another one, Clive.' The call came from a girl on the far edge of the dig. The archaeologist carefully stood up and made his way across to where she was squatting. Gillard followed. The teenager, slim and tousle-haired in T-shirt, jeans and engineer's boots, was pointing to a raised lump in a patch that she had cleared carefully with a decorator's brush. Hancock knelt down and looked at it as closely as he could, a magnifying glass between him and the ground. 'Just a hand-width away from the last one,' he observed.

The girl, about sixteen, looked up at Gillard, beaming. 'I hope we find the rest of the dagger. That would be so cool.' She had an elfin face and short brown hair.

'What dagger?' Gillard glanced balefully at the archaeologist.

'The one with a broken bit in the neck of the dead man,' the girl said. 'Are you from Greenpiss?'

'No, I am nothing to do with Aqua Western.' He rested a hand on Hancock's shoulder. 'I'd like a word, Clive, in private.' The archaeologist stood, and with Gillard leading they threaded their way away out of the dig towards one of the large willow trees which leaned over the river.

'Clive, did I not make it clear to you that this was to be treated with the utmost confidence?'

The archaeologist squinted and scratched his head. 'Well, I didn't mean to say anything. But they all knew I'd been to the mortuary to see the body, and naturally they wanted to know all about it.'

'You shouldn't have told them anything. This makes it very difficult for the investigation. It was extremely unprofessional of you.'

Hancock wouldn't make eye contact. 'I think that's a bit unfair. I can hardly not tell them why they are here for this dig. They're volunteers, and they need to be motivated to get out here in the mud and the muck.'

Gillard had come across academics like Hancock before. All enthusiasm and no discretion. 'All I can say Clive, is that now it seems it was a recent murder, you've given all and sundry every reason to go scavenging here.'

'Craig, I can vouch for my volunteers. I've known all of them several years. Some of them, like young Rowena, are already very knowledgeable. They understand the importance of not disturbing a site of such historic significance.'

'Maybe. But there are motives. If an Anglo-Saxon sword was discovered, how much would it be worth?'

'Phew.' Hancock squinted into the distance as if he had never considered such a question. 'Well, it's irrelevant really, because anything found here would belong to the Willow family, who own the land. Unless it was found with coins and deemed treasure trove, of course. If you found it you couldn't keep it.'

'There are always thieves, Clive,' Gillard said. Like most cops, he was aware of his own cynicism, quick to discern the basest motives in humanity. Hancock, immersed in a scientific community which revered the Anglo-Saxon world, seemed to have the opposite problem.

'Yes, but you wouldn't get the full value unless it could be professionally restored, and its provenance confirmed. An Anglo-Saxon artefact is not like a stolen car. You couldn't sell it on a layby to a passer-by.'

'I'm absolutely certain you could. I mean, what would that Sutton Hoo helmet be worth?' Gillard had done a little bit of his own googling on the subject of Anglo-Saxon finds.

'It's priceless, obviously.'

'I mean we're talking millions aren't we? So even if the thief only got ten per cent of its value to a private collector, that's quite an incentive. I can categorically assure you that there are not only bent collectors but bent valuers, bent auctioneers and bent restorers. Almost everyone has their price. And if it is the murder weapon, we as the police need to find it, before a criminal gang gets its hands on it. Are you with me now?'

'I'm really sorry, Craig. But the cat's rather out of the bag now, isn't it?'

'Yes, I'm afraid it is. Sheila Ransome rang me on my direct mobile today, saying you had given her my business card.'

Hancock scratched his beard. 'She is rather relentless, so I gave her that to shut her up.'

'Please, Clive, exercise total discretion from now on.'

–

After Hancock had returned to the dig, Gillard sat on the protruding root of a willow and stared out at the river. It should have been a place of beauty, and probably was once. But it was rather spoiled by the drone of traffic from the overpass half a mile to his right, and the huge amount of rubbish washed up into the bushes on the steep bank on the far side. That waste, greying tatters of plastic bags, and numerous bottles, cans and face masks, undoubtedly washed through during the recent floods, would stay there for God knew how long until some organisation, probably staffed by volunteers, cleaned it. The water looked reasonably clear, but according to the spam which he'd now started getting from Sheila Ransome on his work email, there was a higher than average amount of agricultural run-off as well as untreated human waste in the water. No one was taking responsibility for it.

He pulled out his iPad to see if any of the tests had come back, when there was a flash of blue along the river. He looked up to see a tiny kingfisher, little more than the length of his finger, dart down to the water, grab something and fly off. He spent a couple of minutes peering into the overhanging bushes on the opposite bank, until he finally spotted the giveaway silhouette on a low branch. A beak almost as long as the bird itself. Another quick sparkling movement, and off it flew, moving down the river. It lifted his mood immensely.

Finally turning to his emails, Gillard saw a sheaf of lab test results had come in. The body that had been found on the riverbank just a few tens of yards away was confirmed as modern. Carbon dating on the bones showed that they were post-1950, while the adipocere seemed to show that the corpse had been buried for several months at least. That pretty much confirmed what Gillard had suspected, and was consistent with the amalgam filling found in the upper jaw, and associative elements of textiles which had been found on or with the body. Analysis of the limited dentition showed evidence of an adult male, old enough to have had wisdom teeth. Full skeletal analysis would take longer, but confirmed an individual in good bodily health at the time of death and who would have stood roughly five foot nine. The University of Glasgow, which co-ordinated the testing, still had more analysis to do, some of which might take months. Separately, he was waiting for a familial analysis of the DNA from the comb. The sample already analysed didn't match anyone on the national database, but there was a good chance that a partial match to somebody else on the system would turn up.

Gillard's original hope that the corpse would be of merely archaeological interest had been dashed. This would now be a resource-intensive case, just at a time when Surrey Police was short-staffed. He emailed Rainy Macintosh and Carl Hoskins, and asked them to attend an inaugural incident room meeting at six p.m. Subject: the murder of Rissington Man by person or persons unknown.

Chapter Eight

When Gillard made his way back to his car he saw the young archaeology volunteer walking down the lane towards him eating something from a ball of white paper. A face mask was slung around her neck.

'It's Rowena, isn't it?' Gillard asked.

'Yeah. Got my lunch from the Anvil. Do you want a chip?' She offered the package to him. The distinctive tang of vinegar was enticing.

'Thank you, no.'

'So I understand you're a copper.'

'I'm Detective Chief Inspector Craig Gillard, from Surrey Police.'

'Who's the dead bloke then?' She indicated with her head towards the river, and resumed eating her lunch.

'You tell me.'

She waggled her head sideways as if considering the question. 'I don't know. But I tell you what I do know.' She pointed at him with a chip. 'There's a prophecy about a killing here. It's quite famous. Hasn't Clive told you about it?'

'What prophecy?'

'It's in the church. Come on, I'll show you.'

Maybe there was something the Anvil's kitchen was good at. Gillard suffered the torment of watching hot chips and tangy vinegar being consumed for the next few minutes as they walked down towards the overgrown churchyard. Having finished her chips, Rowena screwed up the paper and dropped it into a litter bin in the church-yard, and wiped her fingers down the side of her jeans. She then made her way up to the portico of the church. She pulled open an iron gate which led to a short gloomy passageway and an ancient wooden door. From beneath a rusted umbrella stand she retrieved a cast-iron key the length of her hand. She braced her hand against the church door, fitted the key and, jiggling it carefully, turned it. There was a satisfying clunk of the lock opening.

'It's quite a technique,' she said. 'There haven't been any thefts for a while, but we have to be careful. Lead got nicked off the roof five years ago, which I'm sure you know all about.'

'I don't, actually,' Gillard said.

'Well, I don't want to spread rumours. But there was a big falling-out about it. There was a fight at the Anvil. In fact there always used to be fights at the Anvil. It's all a lot quieter now.' She pushed open the door, which creaked ominously, and Gillard ducked under the low lintel to enter the gloom of the nave. 'Some in the village said the stolen lead was bound to have ended up at the Tickett yard. Being travellers, they get blamed for everything. The fly tipping, the burglaries, stuff like that.'

'They look like they have been a settled family for decades.'

'Yes. They've been here since before the war, but that's not as long as some of the other local families, like us Willows. We go all the way back to the time of King John.'

Gillard realised he might be talking to the grand-daughter of murder victim Henry Willow, and presum-ably the niece of Vicky. He kept his conjecture to himself.

71

Rowena flicked a switch which illuminated the tiny church. 'There's a history of St Crispin's which goes back to the early seventh century, when St Augustine came through on his way to Winchester.' She pointed to an interpretation panel on the wall which gave the history of the place.

St Augustine of Canterbury is believed to have founded St Crispin's church in 602 AD, making it the third oldest parish church in England. Much of the original construction was of local flint and spolia, repurposed Roman bricks thought to have been scavenged from the original crossing of the River Wey, and associated military buildings. St Augustine was on his way to Winchester to meet the Frankish princes who at that time controlled this part of Britain. It is said that he baptised 700 people in the river. The Venerable Bede wrote that the church here was an outpost amongst a 'particularly difficult group of pagans' who inhabited the dense willow forest along the edge of the river. Although Bede implies that in Roman times there was already a temple on the site, modern scholarship has called this into question, suggesting that it may simply be a seventh century structure built of Roman materials. St Augustine was said to have chosen the dedication because of the local weaving and tannery, of which Crispin was the patron saint. There is a notable engraved historical stone in the foundations, of Cornish or possibly Scandinavian granite. This can be found on the obverse side of the apse, facing south near the Galilee porch.

Shortly before 1842, a hoard of gold coins which may date from the late seventh century was found in the churchyard, one of which is the Godwin medalet, which bears an image of a diademed figure with a legend referring to Godwin, Earl of Wessex (d. 1053).

'This is what I wanted to show you,' Rowena said. From a wooden box she picked out a laminated card and then led Gillard out, back through the wooden door and into the graveyard. He followed her around the overgrown edges of the church where stacks of moss-covered headstones, their engravings now illegible, leaned against the walls. Behind the church apse, she crouched down behind a bush, and pointed to a worn, pillow-sized rock which formed part of the foundations. The stone was dark, quite unlike the honey-coloured masonry which was built upon it, and there were light-coloured scratches in it. With her finger she traced along the line of the marks. 'This is the prophecy, written in Anglo-Saxon runes, and actually dated in the late sixth century, a little earlier than Augustine's visit.'

ᛁᚾ×ᚨᚷᛖᛋ×ᚻᛖᚾᚳᛖ×ᚹᚻᛖᚾ×ᛖᛝᛚᚨᚾᛞ×ᚠᛚᛖᛖᛋ×ᚦᛖ×ᚠᚱᚨᚾᚳᛁᛋᚻ×ᚨᚱᛉ×ᚻᛖᚱᛖ×
ᚨᚾ×ᛁᚾᚾᚨᚳᛖᚾᛏ×ᚹᛁᛖᛚᛞᛁᛝ×ᚨ×ᛚᚨᛋᛏ×ᛋᚳᚱᚨᛉᛋᚨᚳᛋ×ᚹᛁᛚᛚ×ᚠᛖᛚᛚ×ᚨ×ᚠᛁᚳᛁᛝ×ᚳᚱᚨᚹᚾ×

'What does it say?' Gillard asked.

She looked at the laminated card. 'Roughly translated, it says: "In ages hence when England flees the Frankish arm, an innocent wielding a lost scramsax will here fell a Viking lord".'

'Have they figured out what it means?'

'Well, as is common in archaeology, there are various interpretations.' She laughed. 'The Frankish arm could mean the Norman invasion, which was five centuries in the future. But the Normans were themselves descended from Norsemen and Vikings, not Franks. Of course there were many Viking raids in this area over the following centuries, and indeed some of them settled.'

'Fascinating,' Gillard said. 'But I don't get the relevance.'

'To me the word that stands out is scramsax. That is a term for a dagger, not commonly used in England at the time but referenced originally by Geoffrey of Tours in the sixth century.'

'You're pretty young to be so knowledgeable.'

She shrugged. 'I'm sixteen. I've been an archaeology geek since I was five, when I found my first Anglo-Saxon coin. When all my friends were playing with dolls I was at the library ploughing through history books.'

'I'm sure it's all very interesting, but it's not going to help us identify the dead body.'

'I'm not so sure. The chunk of blade lodged in the neck of your dead guy is exactly the right size to be from a dagger.'

Gillard chuckled. 'Which from the prophecy would indicate that the victim was actually a foreign monarch of some kind.'

Rowena laughed with him. 'Well, it's one possibility anyway.'

Gillard heard footsteps. He turned and stood to face a large bearded man with shoulder-length dark hair. 'Hi there Rowena, how are you?' asked the man, who was wearing an open-necked mauve shirt, leather trousers and cowboy boots. A face mask dangled around his neck.

'Hello Matt,' she replied. 'I was showing Detective Chief Inspector Gillard here some of the features of our wonderful church.'

'Matt Cleaver,' the man said, offering Gillard an elbow. 'How's it going?'

'The investigation? Slowly, I suppose.' Cleaver had dazzling blue eyes and a piratical countenance, further enhanced by the profusion of black hair visible above the top opened button of his shirt. 'I understand you're the vicar here?'

'Well, I've got half a dozen under-used rural churches in which I conduct services on a rota. Congregations aren't what they were, as I'm sure you know.' He turned to Rowena, whose eyes hadn't left his face since his appearance. 'I was on my way for some murderous fun with Sheila, Callum, and Stewie, do you want to join in?'

'Definitely. I spent all morning squatting down at the dig, so it'll be good to sit on a chair.'

Cleaver turned to Gillard. 'Our regular garden game of Cluedo, with full social distancing,' he said with a conspiratorial smile. 'Pastoral duties can be fun.'

'If you find out who did it be sure to let me know,' Gillard said.

–

Gillard got back to Mount Browne at half past five. As he was pulling into the car park, he got a call from Hertfordshire Police to say that an officer had visited Angela Blanchard in Hemel Hempstead to seek a DNA sample. It hadn't been straightforward. Ozzy Blanchard had taken his toothbrush and most personal items when he had left back in January. Mrs Blanchard was apparently an efficient housewife and now burned with the indignation of the abandoned woman. She had washed, packed away or disposed of many of his clothes to a charity shop. She wanted him out of her life.

Gillard was annoyed that no one at Hampshire Police had at least alerted her to the possibility that personal items should be retained in case a DNA check was needed. The visiting officer had taken samples from Blanchard's favourite chair and some footwear. There seemed a reasonable chance of a result. The only other route to an elimination sample, tracking down the wrecked car, seemed even more of a long shot.

Armed with this limited information, Gillard gathered together his team for what turned out to be one of the emptiest incident room meetings of his career. Detective constables Carl Hoskins and Rainy Macintosh sat at opposite ends of one of the larger conference rooms, staring at a whiteboard and laptop projector. They had coffee and a few biscuits, but little inspiration.

'Why are we even looking at this?' Hoskins asked, as he watched Gillard writing down various details of the Anglo-Saxon murder weapon alongside the more modern finds of pens, wedding ring and comb.

'Quite simply because the coroner insists upon it,' Gillard said. 'We've got a modern body, with DNA, and we need to find out who he is. The wound to the neck is, according to Delahaye, unlikely to have been caused by the excavator or any other movement of the body, so we have a presumption of homicide. We've got familial DNA analysis, as well as mitochondrial being undertaken from the hair follicles found in the comb, and we're looking to see if we can match them to any of the degraded hair on the head, and anything we get from Blanchard's home. All that may take a couple of weeks.'

Rainy leafed through the folder in front of her in which were bound statements of each of the witnesses to the discovery of the body. 'Aye, we've plenty of witnesses to the discovery of the body. Water engineers, workmen, and the lassie with the digger. It all looks consistent. Is it just a question of waiting for the forensics, sir?'

'No, I've never believed in waiting,' Gillard said. 'There's more we can do in the meantime. There's a lot of friction between the water company and the locals over pollution, and some question over whether the original work on the site had been done correctly.'

Hoskins groaned. 'I hate that kind of stuff.'

'We're sifting for motives, Carl, not policing a civil engineering project.'

'What do you mean?'

'The point is that if Ozzy Blanchard was driving that car, then he was terrified of something. You do not head the wrong way up a dual carriageway at rush hour unless you're even more scared of whoever is behind you than of a fatal collision.'

'But who was behind him?' Rainy asked. 'We dinnae have that information.'

'The witness statements to the accident mention only Blanchard's Volvo – for obvious reasons, each and every driver would have been focused on it. But that doesn't mean to say that he wasn't being chased, or at least wasn't convinced he was. From the statements given by his wife, it was clear he meant to be away for a considerable time.'

'Well, he certainly managed that,' Hoskins said.

'What we need to find out is what he was scared of,' Gillard continued. 'The fact that his boss called him at home within an hour of his leaving seems to indicate that there were some work issues. Now they may not turn out to be the crucial ones, but I think they should be investigated.'

'I can't imagine a water engineer getting into that kind of trouble,' Hoskins said.

'Up shite creek without a paddle? This is the wee laddie who installs the creeks. Seems to describe him perfectly,' Rainy observed.

Hoskins shook his head. 'I don't get it. He doesn't control money, does he? It's not like he's a bank manager with access to the safe. He's not a jeweller, or even the manager of a car dealership with access to expensive vehicles. I don't have a financial angle on this.'

'Maybe it was love,' Rainy said. 'Not fleeing from anything, but towards something.'

'Then how do you explain the mad dash against the traffic?' Gillard asked.

'Easy. He runs off to join his fancy woman, and finds she's either got cold feet, or another boyfriend. Maybe a big, brutal, jealous guy.'

Gillard hadn't considered this, but conceded it was possible. 'So he was either running from the jealous boyfriend...'

'...or the wee lassie had dumped him, and he was driving into traffic to end it all.'

'Clearly a failure even at that,' Hoskins said. 'Seeing as he didn't die in the crash.'

Straight after the meeting Gillard returned to his desk to find DI Claire Mulholland waiting for him. 'Did you know about Rainy?' she said, looking around to check that the Glaswegian officer wasn't in earshot.

'I noticed she was limping.'

'Her ex-partner assaulted her, apparently. He'd come down from Glasgow last weekend. Her son witnessed it, and ran away for a day.'

'She was off on Monday and Tuesday. That must be why.' Gillard steepled his fingers over his mouth. 'Does she want to press charges?'

'No. I only know about it because the boy texted one of my own kids. You recall Ewan stayed at my house for a while last Christmas?'

'Yes. I knew something was up, but this is worse than I thought. Her ex is a doctor, isn't he?'

'That's right,' Claire said. 'A paediatric consultant, would you believe. Has a mighty temper, apparently. He came down to see the boy for a weekend, and it all went pear-shaped. I took Rainy for a coffee and spoke to her about the texts. She broke down and told me all about it.'

As her line manager, Gillard knew he would have to tread delicately. 'She's a great member of the team, and I want to do anything I can to ensure she gets the best support. I'd hate to lose her to sick leave, especially now when we're so short-staffed. What would you suggest, Claire?'

'She's really embarrassed, obviously. I wouldn't say anything to her directly if I was you, but I can pass on your messages of support. If you could just be aware of this if she requests time off.'

'Of course, thank you.'

Gillard trusted Claire's judgement. Staff issues were one of the most awkward and intractable elements of his job, and he felt much less confident dealing with them than he did with the pure detective work. It was one of the main reasons that he hadn't yet applied for the vacant post of detective chief superintendent. At that level, people problems crowded out most of the detective workload. He didn't want to end up a desk jockey like Radar Dobbs.

It was late that evening when Clive Hancock rang Gillard at home. The county archaeologist was bubbling with excitement. 'We managed to get much more detail about the metal fragment lodged in the man's neck. I've managed to decipher some of the lettering, which confirms that it is a dagger blade, made by one of the most well-known swordsmiths of the late Anglo-Saxon period.'

'Very good,' Gillard said, peering at the clock, which showed it was nearly eleven o'clock. 'I suspect that is much more of archaeological interest than investigative.'

'Not necessarily. This is not a known item. That means it was not stolen from some museum or collection. It's a new find.'

'So what you're saying is that someone has kept this weapon concealed?'

'We don't know when it was found, that's the trouble. Given that the victim is a modern man, we can assume that the crime took place in recent years, but the big question for me is whether this man was killed over a new archaeological find, or whether the dagger had been found many years or indeed centuries ago and kept concealed.'

'Well, given that we have seen evidence of detectorists locally, the idea of a fight over ownership of a newly discovered relic is quite enticing,' Gillard said. 'However, it would seem to me pointless if, having just discovered how valuable and rare this weapon was, someone was to then damage it by using on another person.'

'That's certainly true. Anyway, when I get back to the lab at Guildford, I'll send you a selection of X-ray images.'

'I'll look forward to it,' Gillard said, then ended the call.

Chapter Nine

Friday morning saw Gillard take a different tack. He'd been considering getting a magistrate to issue a financial order so he could look into Ozzy Blanchard's bank account activity, but discovered after ringing Hampshire Constabulary that they already had one, still open after four months. The officer at the Winchester HQ wouldn't say any more, but asked Gillard to call the SIO for further details. So, reluctantly, Gillard once again rang Stella Anderson to ask her to share what she knew. She had been largely ignoring his calls and emails, but as the phone rang out and he prepared to leave another message, she picked up.

'What can I help you with, Craig?'

'It's about Ozzy Blanchard, ma'am. I'm looking for evidence he might still be alive, seeing as we haven't yet got an ID on the body. The usual thing: have his credit cards, bank account and so on been used?'

'No. As of yesterday morning, the only payments from his account were the usual standing orders and direct debits, and withdrawals by his wife from their joint account.'

'So he could well be dead,' Gillard said.

'That's a reasonable opinion,' Anderson responded. 'However, my feeling is that our Ozzy is a lot brighter than he gets credit for.'

Gillard sighed. That could mean a number of things. 'Ma'am, I really do need to know what the nature of your inquiry is. Are you examining a fraud at Aqua Western? If you shared information with me, it would save a lot of time.'

'Craig, I wish I could. There is something a lot bigger going on here, and I don't yet have the authority to bring you aboard. However, matters are moving apace and I predict that in a couple of days you will no longer have to worry about Ozzy Blanchard in your inquiry.'

'You mean that you think he's still alive?'

'I'm not saying that.'

Gillard stared at the ceiling in frustration. He knew that he would have to go to his own boss to get Anderson to release more information. But Radar Dobbs was clearly no match for Stella Anderson, even though they had the same rank. 'Then what are you saying, ma'am?'

'I'm sorry, Craig. I shouldn't have said anything.' She hung up.

Gillard slammed the phone down so hard that both Rainy Macintosh and Claire Mulholland looked up. He stopped swearing and waved his apologies across the open-plan office. As he did so his mobile pinged with a text from the lab alerting him to the results from the Hemel Hempstead DNA check.

He swiped straight through to his emails, and speed-read the results.

There was a match. DNA extracted from hairs on the comb found on the body matched three different samples from footwear and clothing belonging to Ozzy Blanchard at his home.

'Yes!' he shouted, and punched the air. The same two faces looked up from across the office. 'We've got a positive ID on the body,' he called across to them. 'It is Blanchard.'

The two female officers came over, leaving Hoskins deep in some phone call.

'So what's next?' Claire asked.

'I've got to speak to Delahaye and the archaeologist to get their input. But it seems DCS Anderson was wrong. She predicted that we'd be eliminating Ozzy Blanchard from our enquiries. But now a lot of it begins to make sense: a man leaves home in a hurry, grabbing some vital possessions, disappears off towards the very area where he was working on a project, sufficiently terrified to drive at high speed into oncoming traffic, crashes the car, escapes on foot and disappears close to the village of Rissington Common.'

'And now the poor wee laddie's turned up dead a few hundred yards away,' Rainy said.

'Maybe the people that were chasing him finally caught up with him,' Claire said.

Gillard nodded. 'Stella Anderson told me that Blanchard made one call on his work phone to an unregistered mobile a few minutes after escaping from crash. That seems to me a very important call.'

'Aye, if your first call after surviving a road accident isn't to your wife, that tells us he had some major worries,' Rainy said.

–

Dr Delahaye was busy most of the afternoon in London, but his secretary set up a video-conference call with Gillard and Rainy Macintosh in Guildford, and Clive Hancock from the church in Rissington Common. They spent the first few minutes figuring out the mutes, background reflections and sound quality and the next making sure everyone had seen the emails that Gillard had circulated.

'That's a very encouraging result,' Delahaye said, having looked through the evidence. 'However, I really would prefer to see a match with the few surviving hairs on the victim's own head. That would make the connection much more robust.'

'Unfortunately, the lab couldnae recover any DNA from those,' Rainy said.

'Well, we have made a find of our own,' Hancock interjected. 'A section of the left-hand lower jaw, it seems, with five teeth, just a few feet away from where the upper torso and head were found.'

'Are you sure it's modern?' Gillard asked.

'Yes. There are two fillings in the molars, one lead amalgam at the rear and one near the front in white composite.'

'Well we should certainly be able to date those to within a decade,' Delahaye said.

'There's something else even more exciting,' Hancock said excitedly. 'About the murder weapon—'

Startled, Gillard asked him to explain. 'With the help of Guildford University I've been able to decipher the lettering on the section of blade within our murder victim's neck.'

Hancock then shared an image on the screen.

✠ BIOR ELM E ÞOR

'Those are the letters we were able to decipher,' Hancock said. 'It's Anglo-Saxon, and typical of a mid-ninth-century artefact. Filling in the missing letters, we think we have this.'

✠ BIORTHELM ME ÞORTE

Gillard could understand why for an archaeologist this was terribly exciting. But he needed to find out what relevance it had for the crime. 'What does that mean, Clive?'

'It is the signature of the swordsmith. Literally it means "Biorthelm made me". Biorthelm was the pre-eminent smith of the period, and ownership of one of his weapons conferred huge status. Perhaps the most significant part of this discovery, as I mentioned, is that this is an unknown weapon. Not from any collection that I'm aware of. Biorthelm tended to make full-length swords, and as far as I'm aware only one other dagger made by him has ever been found. This is a reconstruction of how it would have looked undamaged.' His screen now displayed a fifteen-inch-long weapon with a narrow blade reaching a wickedly sharp point, a hand guard separating the blade from the hilt above it.

Delahaye chuckled. 'That is quite fascinating, Clive. So it shows my little joke about the victim having been stabbed by someone who worked in a museum is false.'

Hancock beamed. 'Yes indeed. In fact I find it very hard to envisage what circumstances could have given rise to this murder. It's almost as if some thousand-year-old warrior has emerged from the mists of time and struck a blow of vengeance against those who disturbed his rest.'

'Who just happened to be a middle-ranking water engineer from Hemel Hempstead,' Gillard said.

Hancock couldn't have missed the sarcasm, and could be seen vigorously scratching his head in frustration. It made him look a bit mad.

'What I'm saying, Clive, is that the more we know, the less likely it seems that this piece of blade can have been the cause of death,' Gillard said. 'We have to look at the broader context of this killing. Whoever it was that wanted to kill Ozzy Blanchard had managed to scare him well in advance. They were clearly organised, capable of acting out a premeditated plan. Who then in their right mind would choose a rusty Anglo-Saxon weapon, even if they had it to hand, to dispatch him when a kitchen knife or a baseball bat would have done a more reliable job?'

Hancock shook his head in frustration. 'But David here confirmed that the damage caused to the spine would have been fatal—'

Delahaye interrupted. 'Yes, I did, but that doesn't mean to say that our victim hadn't already been killed by another method. On the balance of probability it seems more likely that the excavator caused this unusual wound.

'But both possibilities seem to be extremely small,' Hancock protested. 'I mean, what is the chance of criminals burying a body so close to an undiscovered Anglo-Saxon dagger that when the bucket of the excavator dragged him out of the earth, the two were pushed together with enough force to drive the blade into his neck?'

The forensic pathologist was nodding. 'It's beyond my remit as an expert witness.'

'Okay then,' Gillard said. 'Give me a third possibility.'

There was a long silence. 'Suicide?' Hancock said eventually.

'After which he wrapped himself in a bin bag and then dug himself a grave?' Gillard said.

'He was a very scared man, apparently,' Hancock said.

Delahaye spoke. 'He might well have been, but I can't think of a more agonising and less reliable way to end your own life than stabbing yourself in the neck with what inevitably would have been a fragile and corroded weapon.'

'And who was it buried him?' Gillard added.

After a few more inconclusive exchanges, Gillard thanked the two participants and after a reminder about confidentiality, ended the call and filed the recording, under the title *Hancock's Half Hour.* The electronic case file was already bulging with fascinating details, expert insights, and plenty of witness statements. But despite establishing the identity of the body, the main questions remained unanswered. Who had killed Ozzy Blanchard? How had they done it, if not using an Anglo-Saxon weapon? And the most fascinating question of all: why?

-

Gillard sifted through Hampshire Constabulary's inquiry record on the night of Ozzy's accident. Mostly it had been done by the book. They had traced not only his phone, but also the unregistered mobile phone number that he had rung both before and immediately after the accident. They had triangulated the recipient phone to Bourne Lane in Rissington Common at the time of those calls. Some well-meaning plod had rung the recipient's mobile and left a message the following morning, when the inquiry was thought to be no more than clearing up after a road traffic accident. Of course in hindsight that wasn't so smart. It had simply tipped off whoever it was that the police were chasing down Blanchard's communications. It was thus no surprise to Gillard that the unregistered mobile had ceased activity after that. Once DCS Stella Anderson was involved, the inquiry had broadened: the financial order to look at his bank accounts, examination of the metadata of his personal and work mobile going back months. The summary documents he saw referred to text messages and emails extracted from the service providers, but the details of those were not for some reason available on the local system, and he couldn't find them on the police national computer either.

The next thing to look at was the car. Hampshire uniforms had recovered quite a bit of Blanchard's luggage from the wrecked Volvo, including a work laptop. There were no details of whether it had survived being submerged in the river. However, the document trail did show the vehicle had been taken initially to a garage on the edge of Haslemere because of lack of storage space at the nearest police station. Within six weeks it had been shuttled off to a breakers' yard on the edge of Winchester. Someone from Stella Anderson's team had gone to find it in March, when her inquiry began, but couldn't locate it in the enormous and chaotic yard. No doubt Aqua Western's insurers had released the company car as scrap. It didn't look to Gillard that she had pursued this angle very hard, but for a murder investigation being able to examine the car would have been very useful. He would like to have seen any satnav records which showed where the vehicle had been in the preceding weeks, but again he did not have access.

He sighed. This was like banging his head against a brick wall. Somewhere along the line the misper inquiry into Blanchard had become something more, judging by the involvement of someone as senior as Stella Anderson. He'd got individual records from Hampshire, but he was clearly being stonewalled on the extent of the inquiry. He emailed Radar Dobbs, and copied in Chief Constable Alison Rigby, asking them to exert pressure on Hampshire to release all relevant records. Given that this was a Friday, it would inevitably take until next week to get to the top of the chief constable's bulging in-tray. In the meantime, he would use the weekend to start at the other end. There were two people in particular who lived in Bourne Lane, who had serious criminal records, and may have had a motive for killing Ozzy Blanchard.

One was Christopher Tickett, and the other was the Reverend Matt Cleaver.

Chapter Ten

The prison record of Christopher John Tickett stated the bald facts. Found guilty of the murder of Henry Harold Willow in November 1982 and sentenced to seventeen years, of which he served twelve. Generally good behaviour inside, much of it served in Parkhurst on the Isle of Wight. Since release, a few speeding tickets, a caution following an altercation in a pub, and interviews about fly-tipping and the theft of lead from the roof of a church.

To fill in the blanks it was quicker and easier to search the archives of the local papers, some of which were online, than to make formal requests for the release of paper documents by Hampshire Constabulary dating back to its investigations in 1982. The newspapers showed that Henry Willow, a local farmer, was reported missing in March 1981. After an extensive police search, his body was found in June, buried in a pre-existing grave in the medieval section of the cemetery at St Crispin's church in Rissington Common. Several of the newspapers reported that the body was considered to be in very poor condition, making identification almost impossible. This was of course in the days before DNA testing, but the victim was eventually identified through dental records. A forensic source quoted anonymously by one of the papers made mention of 'unusual soil conditions' in the area which contributed to a rapid transformation of bodily tissue to a 'waxy substance similar in texture to soap'. That was exactly the same process which has been observed in the body that had been found by the excavator. Henry Willow's corpse had turned into adipocere.

It was time to interview Mr Tickett.

–

It was with some trepidation that Gillard approached the yard of CJT Contracting (Hants) Ltd. Even as the detective approached, the two boisterous dobermans bounded into view, snarling and barking. The chain on the gates was unlocked, but a hefty bolt secured them. A sign on the gate asked visitors to ring a mobile phone number and wait to be shown in. Gillard did so, and left a message. It was a couple of minutes before there was any sign of activity, a masculine bellow from somewhere back in the yard, which had the dogs lying down, looking back towards their master. 'It's safe to come in now,' the voice said.

Far from convinced, Gillard reached through the fence, slid the bolt and pushed open the chain link gate. As calmly as he could, he walked between the two guard dogs, which eyed him balefully. A low warning growl emanated from one of the creatures, which clearly had the detective on notice. Fifty yards into the site, Gillard caught sight of an imposing silver-haired man standing on the steps of a large static caravan, hands on hips. It was the same man he'd seen in the BMW two days ago. To get to him, Gillard walked between piles of discarded tractor and truck tyres, stacks of wooden pallets, rusting oil drums and heaps of reclaimed timbers.

'I didn't think it would be too long for you lot to come sniffing round,' the man said, beckoning Gillard inside.

The caravan had a characteristic bottled gas odour mixed with stale cooking. The detective took off his shoes and left them with the other boots at the door, and followed the man onto the deep pile green carpet. The walls were lined with black and white photos of a boxer, various certificates, and a glass case with newspaper coverage of the triumphs of Rory 'Typhoon' Tickett.

'My name is Detective Chief Inspector—'

'Got that from the message,' he interrupted. 'I'm Chris Tickett, but I'm sure you know that.' He had the intimidating stance of a nightclub doorman, with pale grey eyes, a florid face and just the hint of an Irish accent. Tickett indicated that Gillard should set himself down on an enormous settee, facing an even larger TV screen which blocked out the light from the biggest window. 'You want a cuppa? I'm just making one.'

'No thanks.' Gillard sat down and waited while Tickett busied himself in the kitchen. Only when the big man had returned with a mug and sat opposite him on a big recliner chair did the detective begin his spiel.

'Mr Tickett, as you will have heard, a body was found close to the river a few days ago, on a site that was being worked on by your family firm.'

'I know that, obviously.'

'And the foreman was your son, Aidan.'

Tickett nodded. 'And?'

'I just wondered if you had any ideas who this person might be?'

'The uniformed coppers already asked me.'

'I know, but I just thought—'

'You just thought that, seeing that I was a convicted murderer, you'd come round here and poke your nose in.'

'I'm just doing my job, Mr Tickett. There's not much detail on your statement.'

'That's because I've got nothing to tell you. You know, every time anything happens in the area, a missing person, a stolen car, a pub fight, whatever it is, Hampshire Constabulary are here.'

'I'm from Surrey Police.'

'Same difference. My crime, nearly forty years ago, was a crime of passion. Me and Henry were in dispute over Jeannette.'

'His wife. Who later took her own life.'

'Yes, poor Jeannette.' Tickett's eyes lost focus for a moment. 'But because I'm from traveller stock, the assumption is that I'm some kind of habitual criminal. It's just prejudice. We Ticketts get on right enough now with the Willows, and everyone else in the village.'

Gillard could see there might be some truth in that. 'I think from my point of view you can see it would be remiss of me not to come and talk to you.'

He shrugged. 'Well, now you've met me and had a chat, you can go.'

There was the roar of an engine, and a large black car rumbled past the window and came to a halt in the yard. Gillard, who had been preparing to leave, decided to hang around for a moment or two. Tickett stood up, looking slightly nervous. There were some heavy approaching footsteps, shouts to the dogs to shut up, and the caravan door flew open to be filled by a tall and muscular young man with a shaven head, carrying a cardboard box in his arms. The lad had started speaking before he'd even looked around.

'Pa, the bastards have disappeared—'

'Hold your horses, Rory,' Tickett said. 'This fella here is from Surrey Police.' He gestured a thumb at Gillard, who introduced himself.

The young man scowled, and shouldered his way into a back room. In there he must have dropped the box, for the clatter it made, and then he emerged back into the lounge, seeming to fill it with a disruptive energy. He was wearing a dark blue T-shirt embroidered with the Tickett company initials, a pair of brick red canvas shorts and yellow construction boots. There was no sign of dirt or builders' dust on him.

'Rory's been looking for some missing equipment,' Tickett explained, smiling for the first time since Gillard arrived. The detective knew he was lying. He really wasn't very good at it.

'You're Typhoon Tickett, aren't you?' Gillard said, as a conversational gambit.

'What's it to you?' he replied, looking him up and down.

'So who is it you couldn't find?' Gillard said.

The two Ticketts started speaking over each other. Rory mentioned Aidan, while his father talked about generators.

'If you had something stolen, please let us know,' Gillard said. The two men exchanged dark glances; clearly they had plenty to say to each other once Gillard had left.

'Are either of you aware of anyone going missing in the village in recent years?'

The Ticketts again looked at each other before the older man said, 'No.'

'Does the name Ozzy Blanchard mean anything to you?'

'Is that who the body is, then?' Tickett senior asked.

'It may be, but we're keeping an open mind,' Gillard said.

'I heard of the man, that's all. My sons met him through contracting work at the water company.'

The two men clearly had something to hide, but another ten minutes of questioning elicited little useful information except some background. Christopher Tickett said he and the Willow family had long ago mended their differences. The farm was now run by Michael Willow, Henry's eldest son, while the two daughters, Vicky and Crystal, and her own daughter Rowena, were well known in the village. 'If you're looking for evidence of a family feud between us, you won't find it,' he volunteered.

Gillard thanked them and made to leave. Tickett senior bellowed at the dogs, allowing the detective to make his way, calmly and with no sudden movements, past the watchful animals. Once back on the road, he memorised the number plate of the black Audi RS Q8 that the younger Tickett had arrived in, and walked back to his own car. Straining his ears, Gillard could just about hear an argument in the caravan, made easier for him when the squeal and boom of the opening door let the row out. He watched Rory Tickett stride angrily to his car, open the door as if intending to pull it from its hinges, and start the engine. The detective managed to reach the unmarked Vauxhall and get inside before the black Audi shot past. He did a quick three-point turn, and followed at a discreet distance.

Rory seemed to be in a tearing hurry, turning left at the village green and racing for the link road. He paid no heed to the forty limit on the 180-degree northbound on-ramp, and even as Gillard was doing fifty, he could see the Audi accelerating away from him, leaning over to the right, tyres squealing. Once up on the dual carriageway, the detective kept the Audi in view, leaving two or three vehicles between them. Rory took the Haslemere turning, and led Gillard down country lanes. Keeping up with him would have given the game away so he slowed, losing sight of the vehicle, but able to hear it through the open window. Gillard eventually passed a driveway where electric gates were just closing. The wrought iron barriers were set between high newly-constructed brick walls, and coasting past he glimpsed a sizeable new-build home, and a flash of black vehicle.

An interesting family and, on crude policing criteria, definitely of interest: Christopher with a conviction for murder, Aidan present or nearby when the body was found, and Rory 'Typhoon' Tickett, a man who for a few years at least had made a living with his fists. The big house and the brand-new black Audi didn't appear to be out of kilter with a briefly successful boxer. Still, plenty of inspiration for further research.

-

The head office of Aqua Western was in Windsor, on the top floor of a small modern office block in a residential area. Gillard parked in the visitors' section of a small car park which served the three businesses there. At reception, he was shown into a waiting area, and the secretary came down to take him up to Kelvin Arrowsmith's large, airy corner office. Arrowsmith was on the phone, leaning back in his chair, feet on the desk, but waved Gillard in. The detective was supplied with tea from a pot and a selection of biscuits while he waited for the apparently jovial manager to finish off his conversation.

'So what can I do for you, detective chief inspector?' Arrowsmith asked, coming to join Gillard on the low chairs by the coffee table. He had the broad conceited face of a tomcat, in command of his territory.

'I want to ask you about Ozzy Blanchard.'

'Is the body definitely him?'

'We've strong evidence that it is.'

Arrowsmith shook his head. 'This must be truly awful for Angela. The poor woman is trying as best she can to put her life together after he left, and now this.'

'How long did you work with Ozzy?'

'Well, he was one of six regional surveyors that reported directly to me, although I have fifty-two other direct reports in other roles. So although I knew him reasonably well, I can't say I had much insight into his life outside work.'

'What about his work?'

'Ozzy had some good soft skills. You know we had all this trouble at Rissington Common? That dreadful woman, Sheila Ransome, even managed to find my home phone number somehow. She's absolutely relentless, the typical one-issue campaigner.'

'You've got to sympathise,' Gillard said. 'Your company was paid to manage the sewers and manifestly failed. The whole village is blighted by that.'

'The official company position is to dispute that. But anyway, Ozzy went to their meetings, and for a long time he seemed to have it under control. Then about a year ago it all flared up again. I mean, you know what happened to me? I went down there, and this vicar who looks like a pirate cornered me, bellowing about all sorts of things.'

'That would be the Rev Matthew Cleaver.'

'That's right. Quite a scary individual, if you ask me. When I got back to my car, someone had ripped the wing mirrors off. So I didn't envy Ozzy dealing with them.'

'Was he truthful, trustworthy and competent?'

'In all my experience, he was, yes. He was methodical, hard-working and *generally* had a good eye for detail.' The caveat was there, and Gillard picked up on it.

'So what went wrong in phase one of the project at Rissington Common?'

Arrowsmith rubbed his chin. 'A lot of it is quite technical, I'm sure it's not of much interest to you.'

'Indulge me.'

'I'd love to, but if you are really interested, I think you're going to have to go above my head to corporate. You probably think me terribly bureaucratic, but if this project fails to meet its regulatory benchmarks, the company will be fined a great deal of money. So I have to wait for a final assessment by outside auditors as to what extent it is deficient. It's out of my hands. As I said to your colleague Stella Anderson, I can certainly copy you in when the final report is ready.'

'When might that be?'

He looked out of the window and blew a sigh. 'Judging by past experiences I would say two or three years.' He seemed very pleased with his answer. 'I think you can see my predicament. If I was to give you a partial assessment, and this was quoted out of context it could prejudice—'

'Let's cut to the chase. These things are often simple. Could Ozzy have been creaming off money by constructing the new pipes on the cheap?'

Arrowsmith smiled. 'Well, of course that is certainly something we are looking into. It's not unknown in the industry. However, Aqua Western has exacting requirements as regards to the audit trail. It's not as easy as it used to be to take a firm like ours to the cleaners. And can I say that, once again, you are treading a path already well-trodden by Detective Chief Superintendent Anderson.'

'It's funny how everybody keeps telling me that.' *Except her.* Gillard realised he was spending a lot of time reinventing the wheel. If there was a fraud, he really needed to persuade Anderson to share all the evidence.

Gillard peered out of the window, and spotted a familiar silver Nissan Qashqai parking at the other end of the car park from his Vauxhall. It was too far to read the number plate, but Gillard recognised the big bullet-headed man who emerged from the car.

'Just excuse me for a minute,' Gillard said to Arrowsmith. Exiting the office, he ran down the two flights of emergency stairs which brought him out next to the ground floor lift. From there he could hear the receptionist and, just as he hoped, she announced the name of the visitor, who was clearly familiar to her.

'Hello, Mr Slater. Mr Arrowsmith has someone with him just now, but I'm sure he won't be too long.'

Gillard lifted his face mask into the correct position and made his way along the corridor into the reception area. He caught a look of surprise on Slater's face to see him there. 'Ray Slater, well well,' Gillard said.

'How are you doing, Craig?' he asked, standing and touching elbows with him.

'Very well, thank you. I knew your face first time I spotted you, but couldn't place it. Met Police dog handler, twenty-odd years ago if I recall correctly.'

'That was a long time ago,' Slater said.

'When did you leave the force?'

'Seven or eight years ago.'

'And you're in business with your wife, I understand?' Gillard said.

'My wife?'

'RAS Business Services, of which she is a director, right? Ray and Anne Slater. Private detective agency.'

'I have to earn a humble crust,' he said, spreading his arms.

'I would have appreciated you introducing yourself as being on the case when it crosses with mine, Ray. I need to know who else is sniffing around Rissington Common. Your presence has been noted by the locals. Now I see who's employing you, it all makes a little more sense.'

The receptionist was staring at them, and two phones at her desk were softly ringing, unanswered.

'I'm not obliged to tell you my business, which is client-confidential,' Slater said.

'That's all right, I think I can figure it out. Aqua Western was trying to find Ozzy Blanchard, as were we.'

'So the body is his? Judging by your use of the past tense.'

'We'll confirm it when we're absolutely sure. I assume he must've been on the make, and the company doesn't want to let the cat out of the bag.'

'I really can't comment,' Slater said weakly, his eyes sliding across to the receptionist, who was clearly entranced by this confrontation.

–

Friday night traffic was nowhere near as bad as it had been in pre-pandemic times, and Gillard got back to Mount Browne just before five. With so many officers opting to work from home, the CID floor was sparsely occupied. DC Rainy Macintosh, who had been asked to look in more detail at the Tickett family, was sitting disconsolately at a screen absentmindedly rubbing her knee. Still painful, Gillard thought. 'What have you got for me?'

'Och, a fair bit. Typhoon Tickett has been driving all over the place in that Audi,' she said. 'The family construction firm has three sites across Hampshire and Surrey, and most of the ANPR hits seem to reflect that kind of travel on a typical builders' early-start, early-finish schedule. But he's also made lots of journeys further afield, almost always in the evening. Aye, and he has a tidy wee house in Haslemere.' She flashed up some estate agent details and pictures, which showed the same five-bedroom detached home Gillard had driven past. The listing partic-ulars mentioned three acres of paddocks. 'It looks like the laddie paid £1.5 million for it, and that was a few years ago.'

'Yes, I glimpsed it when I was following him. That would have coincided with his European title contests,' Gillard said. 'That's unlikely to be incriminating in itself. What about Aidan?'

'He's got a tidy place in Upper Rissington, only two miles away from Daddy. Three bedrooms, and there's planning permission for a fourth and an indoor swimming pool, would you believe.'

'Interesting. He must have come into some money, just like his younger brother.'

'I've been trying to tie in some dates on this,' Rainy said. 'The planning application for the pool went in two years ago, April 2018. That same month, Rory Tickett registered the purchase of an Aston Martin DB11. That costs a minimum of £150,000.'

'Hmm. That might be a bit late for his boxing successes. He'd already had his jaw broken by Denys Lasorenko two years before that, which finished his career.'

'Aye, well here is the funny one. I've looked up the Tickett family on Companies House. Apart from the family construction business, they have another limited company.'

'Buckingham Pallets Ltd,' Gillard interjected. 'I saw the logo on the side of a shipping container.'

'That's the one. No results or financials reported since inception,' she said. 'Which was March 2018. They're pretty much up-to-date on the main construction firm.'

'Rainy, this is really good work. I suppose it's just possible that Typhoon was spreading his boxing purse around. But I would lean towards the family coming into some money back in 2018.'

'Well, that's me until Monday,' Rainy said, logging off. 'I take it you're working the weekend, sir?'

'Yes, there was a certain inevitability about it. Look, would you come into my office for a minute? Unless you have to hurry away.'

'Och, what have I done?'

'Nothing but good, believe me.'

She eased herself to her feet, and tried to smile away the pain it clearly caused her. She followed Gillard into his glass-sided office and he got her to close the door. He was aware that every time he closed his door, every detective in the open-plan office looked up to see who was in trouble or sharing secrets. This afternoon, there was only Carl Hoskins and Rob Townsend, but both glanced up as the door clicked shut.

He offered Rainy a seat and said, 'Inevitably, I heard what happened last weekend. I want to offer you whatever support that we can—'

'Sir, I really don't want a fuss about it, I'm embarrassed.'

From what Claire had relayed, Rainy had been at her flat when the row erupted. She was punched twice by Ross, her ex, and twisted her leg when falling. He had refused to help and walked out.

'I understand that, but you are an increasingly important member of my team. Yes, increasingly. Your work has been excellent, and I don't want anything to get in the way of your continued progress.'

'It's my boy,' she said. 'If I press charges, it will all go public. He's having trouble enough in that school in Reading because of his accent anyway. I really don't want to put him through anything else.'

'I don't want to interfere, but are there any court limitations on his visiting rights?'

'He's entitled to every other weekend, but because of the distance from Glasgow, and the hours he works, it's only been once every three months. The boy needs his father at least that much. Another thing, there's a family wedding in September up in Glasgow, and he'll be there too. I've got to keep things calm until then, at least.'

'Look, Rainy. We can get this done and stop it ever happening again. I've got contacts in Police Scotland who can take up the case. Or they could take him aside for an off-the-record warning.'

'Thank you, but no.'

Gillard sighed. He wished he had a pound for every domestic abuse case he had seen over his career in which the woman had refused to press charges for very similar reasons to this. 'All right, Rainy. It's your call. I would suggest you only meet him in public places where there would be witnesses, if you have to spend any more time with him.' He looked at her and wondered what else he could say that might lift her over the weekend. 'One other thing. I know you've only been a DC for a couple of years, but I think you'd be ready for the sergeant's exams. If you want to go for it, I'd support you.'

Her face lit up. 'Och, that's rare nice of you. That means a lot to me.'

He smiled and got up to open the door for her. He was pleased to see that her grin was still there for the rest of the office to see as she made her way out, somehow just a little taller.

Chapter Eleven

A bright sunny morning greeted Gillard as he left the car in the Mount Browne car park and brought in two sizeable coffees, one for him and the other for Rob Townsend, the only other member of his team not working from home that day. As research intelligence officer, Townsend took care of most of the technical and computing oversight needed by Gillard's CID team, often working with civilian specialists. He had been asked to follow up the burner phone which Ozzy Blanchard had briefly rung on the night of his accident in January. Gillard went over to see how he was getting on.

'It's like you'd expect,' Townsend said, pointing at documents on his screen. 'After Hampshire Constabulary left a message on the phone, no further calls were made on it. In fact it was only switched on twice for brief periods since then. I imagine whoever has it is just checking for messages.'

'What about the locations?' Gillard asked.

'Both times somewhere in Bourne Lane, Rissington Common.' Triangulation was fairly approximate in rural locations with widely spaced cell towers. In city centres it was often possible to get the position of a phone down to thirty yards or less.

'Was there much early history to the phone?' Gillard asked.

'First appears in November last year. Dozens of calls to Ozzy's work mobile, but unfortunately there is no triangulation available anymore because they only retain six months' cell tower data.'

'And Stella Anderson never asked for this, did she?'

'No. According to my contact, Hampshire didn't ask for anything earlier than a week before the accident. As it is, we've only got the metadata. It would really help if Hampshire sent us the contents of Ozzy's phone. Texts, email, stuff like that, to save us the trouble of getting another warrant.'

'I've asked Anderson, but I'm being stonewalled.'

'Okay, the earliest location data we have for the burner phone is at the start of January, a week before Ozzy disappeared. Not too many calls, but all from the same location. Not in Rissington Common, but on the southern edge of Haslemere.'

'Give me the location, and I'll see what's there,' Gillard said.

—

An hour later Gillard parked his unmarked Vauxhall on the B2131 Camelsdale Road, on the southern edge of Haslemere. From the location he had copied into his iPad, this was roughly the triangulation of the two contacts between Ozzy Blanchard's work phone and the burner phone. The road was lined with pleasant turn-of-the-century semi-detached cottages, and the odd bungalow. The calls to Blanchard could have been made from any of three dozen different homes. Google Maps flagged up a few businesses dotted amongst the houses. A PC repair outfit, an accountancy firm specialising in small businesses, and New-Age Therapeutics.

Some quick searches on the web added little more information, except one crucial name. New-Age Therapeutics, a business run by someone called Crystal Willow. Her name had cropped up before; Crystal was the older sister of Vicky, and the mother of Rowena. The website had a picture of her: an attractive, frizzy-haired fortyish woman of substantial build, wearing lots of jewellery and shrouded in a floaty dress. Very much New Age. The business address was just three doors down from where Gillard had parked.

The detective emerged from the car, and headed for the house. It was a 1960s semi, with an unkempt hedge shielding it from the road and a short drive on which an aged Fiat was parked. Approaching the front door, he saw a sun-bleached sign which indicated New-Age Therapeutics operated from the rear of the property. Gillard made his way around the back, where a UPVC glass door led to a large brightly lit sun lounge with a massage table, on which were stacked several neatly folded towels, several freestanding oriental wooden screens, and various hangings and knick-knacks. Glossy magazines were spread about on coffee tables, and there was a stand of what looked like skin creams and oil. There was no evidence of occupation. He rang the doorbell, which produced gentle tones of what might have been Tibetan bells. He tried the door. Locked. After a minute, he returned to the front, and rang the main doorbell. No reply. He checked up on the rusting Fiat via the Driver Vehicle Licensing Agency portal, and found it was officially off-road, the DVLA having received the statutory notice. Returning to his car, Gillard noticed a woman further up the road on the other side, a fit-looking woman in T-shirt and shorts, working in her front garden. He did a double take.

It was Stella Anderson.

If the Hampshire officer was a near neighbour of Crystal Willow, this gave a completely new angle to her interest in the case. In fact, with just over 100 yards between the homes it was even possible that it was she who owned the burner phone. Gillard's car was only four doors away from Stella Anderson's home, on the other side of the road. His first instinct was to drive away and think about the implications of what he had seen. But as he sat inside the vehicle, he could see in his wing mirror the woman's approach, garden fork in hand. He decided to get out and face her.

'Hello ma'am, didn't realise you lived in this neck of the woods.'

'I don't, Craig. It's my mother's home, and she's getting a little too infirm to do the garden. So I help her out on the heavy stuff. The more pertinent question is, what are you doing here?'

Gillard decided to pursue a policy of complete candour, hoping to elicit similar transparency on her side. 'Tracing some of the phone contacts between Ozzy Blanchard and the burner phone in the run-up to his disappearance. I was hoping to speak to the proprietor of New-Age Therapeutics.'

Anderson nodded. 'Crystal Willow disappeared at about the same time as Ozzy Blanchard.' Seeing Gillard's curious expression, she continued, 'My mother has severe arthritis, and was a regular client. She was quite upset, in fact, that Crystal hasn't contacted any of her customers for several months.'

'You know where she is?'

Anderson laughed; an infectious giggle which reminded Gillard again of how attractive he had found her all those years ago. 'That's the $64,000 question isn't it? I do have a bit of inside information I'm willing to share with you. Crystal had a boyfriend called Ozzy, because she used to discuss him with my mother during her massage and therapy sessions. No mention of course that Ozzy was already married. For several months now, I've been working on the assumption that wherever Crystal turns up, you'll find Ozzy. She has a motor caravan, missing from her driveway, so there are a lot of possibilities. The ANPR traces were not conclusive. Somewhere in the West Country was the best we could come up with.'

'And that's why you don't think he's dead?'

She stuck the fork into the tarmac between them and leaned on it. 'You see, Craig, Crystal hasn't been reported missing by any members of her family. Even her daughter Rowena seems unconcerned. If they were worried about her, you would see very different behaviour. It seems quite likely that she has been in contact with them, somehow. So they've gone to ground – the question is why.'

'I would have thought they would be a bit more worried after the discovery of the body.'

'Ah, the body, yes.' Her smile was one of concealed knowledge, and her hazel eyes roamed over his face. 'You know, Craig, when we met all those years ago, you behaved like a complete shit to me. We had a good friendship and, I thought, more. Until that night. The Craig Gillard seduction machine just kicked in, and in the morning you seemed almost embarrassed to know me. As if you couldn't get out fast enough.'

Feeling enormously uncomfortable, he said: 'I can only unreservedly apologise for my younger self. There were reasons—'

'I discovered that a bit later,' she said. 'After the Elizabeth Knight case. I'd already left the force, but I had friends within it. Still do, of course. I made a few enquiries.'

'I was very hung up on her,' he conceded.

'So I heard. And in the meantime, while you waited hopelessly to get her back, the rest of us were just easy meat, isn't that right? Stop-gaps and bedpost notches.' She pivoted the fork in her hands, grinding out pieces of tarmac from the footpath between them. She wasn't letting him off the hook. 'I was very upset, you know.'

'Thank you for making that clear... Stella.' He baulked at referring to her seniority in such a personal conversation.

'So you're married now?' she asked.

'Yes. Five years. Sam reformed me, or maybe I just grew up.'

Another brief smile. 'Yes, but too late for me. Much too late.'

'Is that why you left the force?' He had no idea that she had been serious about him. He'd just thought it a bit of fun. It showed the huge mismatch in their intentions on that fateful night in Basildon.

She shrugged. 'One of the reasons. Of course you did me a favour at one level. I'm a cynic now, particularly about men. It's amazing how useful that has turned out to be, particularly once I divorced and returned to the force. I meet male cops every day who are emotional teenagers, and the absolute worst are those close to retirement.'

He fought the urge to apologise yet again. He needed answers to more questions about the case, but couldn't bear any more of this digging into his soul. He was itching to get away.

'Unlike you, Craig, most of them are incapable of reform, and some of the worst are at senior level. My friend Alison Rigby has been retiring the dinosaurs in Surrey, but in Hampshire they still rule the earth.'

If Stella Anderson was a good friend of his chief constable, that would give her huge influence. Gillard had heard Radar Dobbs and others muttering about the encroaching 'sisterhood' at senior levels in British policing, and here was some evidence of it. Still, after decades in which senior police officers had scratched each other's backs in male-only Masonic meetings, it was only right that the pendulum had finally swung the other way.

'I'm glad you changed, Craig,' she said, pushing a garden-gloved finger into his chest. 'At least someone gets the benefit. Sam. Is that her name?'

'Yes.' Gillard looked down at his watch and said. 'I'd best be going now. I'm supposed to be at Rissington Sluice.'

'Running away again?'

'It's work.'

'Yes, that's what you said last time.' She turned and walked away without looking back.

–

Overshadowed by dark thoughts, Gillard drove slowly back to Rissington Common. Having read up on the recent history of the place, it seemed a good moment to visit the site of the 1991 suicide of Jeanette Willow, the widow of Henry and the sometime lover of Christopher Tickett. Her contested affections were the motive for murder back in 1982.

A mile upriver from the village, Rissington Sluice was reached on a narrow private road owned by Aqua Western. Parking next to a Victorian lock-keeper's cottage, Gillard was met as arranged by a water company employee who took him through a gate in a palisade of galvanised railings, and down to the Wey. At this point the river showed more evidence of an industrial heritage than a rural one, with numerous abandoned Victorian sheds overshadowed by the gloomy foliage of large sycamores on either side. The sluice itself resembled a canal lock leading into a tunnel under the riverbank. The young man gave him a brief overview of the sluice's function. While most of the river-flow slid over a broad shallow weir, the Victorian brick construction was designed as a storm-surge run-off, controlled by a pressure gate. In normal times water simply spilled over the swing gate, but during floods, the pressure of water pushed the suspended metal shutter against a sprung hinge and torrents of water would spill underneath until the pressure dropped. This was evidently where most of the effluent vented into the river. The sluice had been the location of a number of deaths over the years until it was fenced off in the 1950s. These were mainly of children drawn into its deep catchment. That didn't of course stop those who were playing in the water nearby. Although there were cast-iron rungs cemented into the wall at both ends and lifebuoy rings mounted on either side, the man said it was treacherous during heavy rain.

It was here during a thunderstorm on St Swithin's Day, 1991, that Jeanette Willow threw herself into the sluice, and was found dead the next day. Gillard had found online an article from the local newspaper on the twentieth anniversary of her death which quoted her daughter Crystal: 'My mum never got over being the inspiration for murder. She had an open heart, and loved her family dearly even as she loved another. She never got over the fact that her chance misjudgement years before inspired a feud, tearing apart two families in the village. She couldn't live with that, but we the survivors will have to.'

Gillard was puzzled. If Vicky Willow was working with Aidan Tickett for his father's construction firm, there was some evidence that the two families had mended their fences. Maybe Christopher Tickett was right about that. It seemed the real feud wasn't between the families; it was between the villagers and the water company.

–

DC Rainy Macintosh had collected a file of year-old press stories from online sources which detailed the ongoing fight between the residents of Rissington Common and Aqua Western Ltd. There were accounts of picketing of the company's regional office in Windsor, and at least one major demonstration outside Aqua Holdings Plc's headquarters in London's Victoria. Gillard clicked on a Channel 4 News video. There, standing on a crate addressing a modest crowd with a loudhailer, was the Rev Matthew Cleaver. He certainly knew how to whip up angry feelings. The newspapers focused on him too. In one photo after another he was the centre of attention: standing impassively in front of a police cordon, with an upraised fist, shouting some slogan. And finally a whole series of pictures of him being bundled away by at least seven policemen. There was something almost magnetic about his presence, which the press could not get enough of. One piece of video footage at the demo a year ago centred on Cleaver quoting scripture. 'Ezekiel chapter 34, verse 18: Is it not enough for you to feed on the good pasture, that you must tread down with your feet the rest of your pasture; and to drink of clear water, that you must muddy the rest of the water with your feet?'

Gillard reflected that the Bible could be co-opted to any cause, such was the diversity of its sayings. The only other person arrested was Sheila Ransome, who'd super-glued herself to the glass front doors of the corporate HQ. She had been pursuing this fight for years, but Cleaver was a new and powerful recruit to the cause; one with a serious criminal record in his youth. An interview with the Rissington Common vicar seemed long overdue.

–

It was six p.m. on the Saturday when Gillard reversed his Vauxhall up the drive. It was the only day of the week when he generally managed to get home at a reasonable time. He'd only just put the key in the lock when Sam opened the door from the inside, and greeted him with a hug. 'I've done something a bit special for this evening,' she said, and it was true there was a delicious aroma coming from the kitchen. Tonight was one of their key anniversaries, of the night he proposed to her. She was wearing a pinny, but underneath that a short black lacy dress, and heels. As she clicked back into the kitchen, he saw an open bottle of white wine in a silvery ice bucket. 'I've already started on it, cook's prerogative,' she said, handing him a chilled glass and filling it up.

Gillard loosened his tie and exhaled. Getting out of work was one problem, of course, for a busy detective, but getting the work out of his head was sometimes even more intractable. He relayed to her a summary of the day's investigation.

'The BBC said the body's been identified.'

'We're not quite there, but it does seem to be our missing water engineer.'

'So what about this Anglo–Saxon dagger?' she asked, as she sipped her own wine.

'I've no idea how that fits in,' he said. 'It's pretty hard to be sure that it was the murder weapon. When the body is in so many pieces, and in such condition, there are any number of other causes of death that might be missed. But it's certainly weird.'

Sam moved Gillard aside, and made her way out of the kitchen with a handful of serving spoons. She then went into the hall and crossed into the garage by the internal door. He followed her, and was amazed to see that she had transformed the garage into a restaurant. She had managed to hang some old curtains to mask the shelves of paint tins and tools, she'd installed a small folding table with a red checked tablecloth, and had suspended from the ceiling a network of soft white Christmas lights. A full–length mirror stood by the garage door, and in front of it on a coffee table were a couple of dozen large candles, their light reflected throughout the room.

'This is gorgeous,' he said, embracing her. 'What a clever idea.'

'I'd originally planned to book a restaurant tonight, seeing as it's the first day out of lockdown. But everywhere was booked solid. So I brought the restaurant in to us.'

'It's wonderful.' Gillard went upstairs, showered and changed. The meal Sam served was fitting to the surroundings. A ceviche of monkfish with lime and ginger, cucumber and spring onions, followed by fillets of sea bream with fresh local asparagus, followed by strawberries. Sam disclosed that she had cycled off to the pick-your-own farm eight miles away to get the berries. 'I think I ate as many in the fields as I picked,' she said.

They had just finished the meal, at half past nine, when the doorbell went.

Sharing a puzzled look with Sam, Gillard got up and went to answer it.

There, standing on the doorstep, was his Aunt Trish.

——

Chapter Twelve

Gillard's jaw dropped. 'The hospital didn't let us know you were coming out.'

Six months ago he had heard that his aunt had come round after more than a year in a coma. He and Sam had resumed their visits to hospital until they were barred under the terms of lockdown, and Trish had remained semi-conscious before her condition deteriorated again. The head injuries that had been inflicted on her by the assailant a year ago were still far from healed, and she was on very heavy doses of steroids to stop renewed swelling. Then in April she'd resumed consciousness properly, had promptly caught Covid-19, and was put into a medically-induced coma because the violent coughing was threatening to cause further inflammation inside her skull. The last Gillard had heard, a week ago, was that she was conscious again, but still needed another month in hospital.

'I discharged myself. I was fed up with the place,' she said, handing Gillard the handle of her wheeled suitcase. She was wearing an unseasonably heavy overcoat, and a beret. To Gillard's eyes she looked exactly the same. She must be almost eighty, still stick thin and upright with the same shrewd expression. 'Where are my cats?'

'With some neighbours, they're retired and were better able to look after them. Napoleon is still going strong, as are Billericay and Grizelda. I'm sorry to say that Lucretia ran away, and we don't know what happened to her.'

Trish was already through the doorway, staring at Sam.

'Hello, Trish,' Sam said weakly. 'How are you?'

'Hard to kill, I suppose. Everything aches, you know. No baby for me yet, then?' Trish looked at Sam's slim figure, then scanned the hall as if looking for signs of prams or toys.

'As you know, Sam had two miscarriages, and since her ordeal, well…' Gillard said.

'Gone off sex, I suppose. It gets worse as you get older, dear,' she said, resting a hand briefly on Sam's shoulder. 'I'll be staying for a few days at least, until I get my place sorted out.'

'I'm not sure we'll be able to look after you, because we're both working,' Gillard said.

'I can look after myself,' Trish replied. She made her way into the downstairs loo and closed the door. Gillard and Sam stood and stared at each other, mouthing phrases of incredulity. Once she re-emerged, Trish asked: 'Are you expecting me to carry my case up on my own?'

'No, I'll do it,' Gillard said. He trudged up the stairs with the luggage as if going to his own execution. He made his way into the second bedroom, and laid the suitcase down on the bed. Trish followed him and scowled at the place. 'Is there an en suite toilet? Only I have to go regularly at short notice.'

'No, you have to share the main one at the top of the stairs with us.'

He left her to her own devices and descended the stairs. Trish had exerted a baleful influence on his life ever since he was a child. Since the hit-and-run case a few years ago and the failed prosecution against her, she had been an inherited burden, having sold up from Devon and moved into a bungalow opposite him. But for all their relief at her coming out of a coma, her turning up like this unannounced was a nightmare.

'She can't stay for long,' Sam hissed.

'Three days. I'll get to work on her bungalow and make sure it's fit for her to move back in.'

'In what spare time exactly? You told me you were on shift tomorrow.'

'I'll start now,' he said grimly.

'Let me give you a hand,' Sam said. 'I don't want to be left with her on her own.'

'The hospital needs to be notified,' Gillard said. 'She might have medication she needs, all sorts of things.'

They were both silenced by the sound of a soft tread descending the stairs. Trish was smiling at them, having once again embedded herself in their lives. Gillard shivered at the prospect.

—

The Wagon and Horses wasn't far from West Croydon railway station. It was coming up to eight p.m. and Carl Hoskins was sitting at the newly-constructed outside bar, nursing an almost-finished pint, staring disconsolately at the football highlights which showed Arsenal a goal down. Although he was wearing a rugby shirt, tracksuit bottoms and trainers, sport for Carl Hoskins was strictly a spectator activity. His weight had gradually climbed over the years, but now it was undeniably a problem. The doctor who had handed him a diabetes diagnosis last week said as much. He had to watch what he ate and drank. The trouble was, it wasn't just a tweak here and there he needed to make, it was a wholesale revolution. Like many things that are too big to face, Hoskins had so far just turned his back on the whole subject.

He drained his glass and ordered another pint. He felt nervous about the meeting. Ray was almost half an hour late. Hoskins hadn't seen his brother-in-law for a couple of years before the call he'd got in March. After leaving the Royal Marines where he'd seen service in the Falklands conflict, Ray Slater became a cop, in the Met. Played up his experience to the family and friends; Carl had heard about it. But the truth was that Ray had been a dog handler for most of his working life, and retired through stress after a bad experience at a demo in central London. So all in all, not a meteoric career. But he had parlayed it into a tidy little private detective business. Starting with divorce, the bread-and-butter. Now he clearly had something bigger. It hadn't seemed too much to be asked by a member of the family, for an ANPR check as a favour. But that was just the beginning. Hoskins had spent a few hours trying to get information, as surreptitiously as possible, out of the Hampshire Constabulary local crime database. In the old days, any serving officer could turn up in person with a good excuse and get given a fistful of documents on any crime. Stuff that wasn't big enough to go up to the police national computer. These days, they would email you a link which would be good for twenty-four hours. What you searched for would be recorded on the system, so he'd tried to go for only the things he really needed.

But Ray just kept on asking. It had got quite embarrassing.

Hoskins was a third of the way down pint number two when Ray finally walked in. Still an imposingly big guy.

Dark grey suit, red tie open at the neck. A florid face underneath the shaven bullet-shaped head, and the usual rectangular glasses.

'How you doing Carl?' he said, slapping Hoskins on the shoulders.

'Fine, thanks Ray. You're looking well.'

'I'm keeping busy. So what'll it be?' he asked, pointing at the glass. Hoskins' reflex to accept any offer of a drink was ingrained. Ray ordered loudly to the barmaid who was standing checking her phone. Three pints was too much under drink-drive rules and Hoskins knew it. Still, this was the first night of reopening, it was only a twenty-minute journey home, and he knew it in his sleep.

Slater pulled up a stool and squeezed himself in next to Hoskins. They shared a few minutes' small talk about Arsenal, before the private detective said: 'The next phase is easier, Carl. Much easier, my son.'

'What do you mean "next phase"? I thought we were done?'

Slater laughed and looked around the bar. 'Trouble is, there are so many moving pieces to this. I've got to keep my clients ahead of the game. Not just of your gaffer, but the redoubtable Stella Anderson.'

'I can't go into the Hampshire database again, Ray, sorry. My excuse is wearing a bit thin, and bloody Gillard will catch me out. It's bound to get back to him. You've heard what he's like.'

'Well, this is your lucky day. Because what I need to know will be on the PNC. It's about the Ticketts.'

Hoskins shook his head. 'No, Ray. Every inquiry on the police national computer is logged. Look, I can't do no more.'

Slater squeezed out a huge sigh, and rotated his own glass between his hands. 'I thought you might say that, and I respect your position. You're family after all.'

'Was, until me divorce.' Brenda had divorced him years ago. He'd not seen her since 2015.

'You're still family to me,' Slater said, fishing in his jacket pocket and sliding out a fat envelope which he slid onto Hoskins lap. 'Call it an early Christmas present.'

'Nah, can't do it, mate. Sorry.' Hoskins slid the envelope back across to Slater's lap. For the next two minutes it was passed backwards and forwards with a variety of verbal labels. Slater finally said: 'It's not a payment, it's just to cover your legitimate expenses, all right?'

'You're making me bent, and I am not *fucking* bent,' Hoskins hissed. 'I did you a few favours. Let's leave it at that, okay?'

'All right, Carl, play it your way.' Slater sighed, and returned the envelope to his jacket pocket.

They switched back to talking football to take the heat out, and after ten minutes Slater slapped Hoskins' back, said goodbye, and walked out. He hadn't even finished his pint. Hoskins drained his own, and as the solitary barmaid came to collect the glasses they exchanged a glance. She was an attractive woman, young enough to be his daughter, and she had clear grey eyes. As he looked at her, he realised he was in that scene in the impressionist picture he'd seen at the Courtauld Gallery years ago, a print of which was rolled up in his garage, still awaiting framing. The girl at the folly bar or something like that. The look she was giving him was one of thinly veiled contempt, tinged with sadness. She had obviously overheard what they been discussing. This wasn't his local, but for some reason her opinion mattered to him. He gave her a small smile and tried to think of something to say, something to explain why he suddenly felt like a crook for helping a mate.

But before he had come up with anything, she'd turned away to use the remote and switch the TV to the news headlines. The second item was a report identifying the body found near the River Wey as being that of missing water engineer Oswald Blanchard. It cited 'sources close to the investigation' but said the police had declined to confirm it.

Hoskins knew that Gillard was being ultra-cautious about the identity of the body, and wondered who had leaked the report. Still, he wasn't at work now. With the barmaid now serving in the other bar, Hoskins leaned over the bar for the TV remote, and switched back to the football.

Sunday

Except for weddings and funerals, Gillard hadn't attended a church service for decades, not since staying with his aunts in Devon as a boy. This was the first Sunday that socially distanced religious worship could resume following a change in the rules. He arrived early at St Crispin's to be greeted by Sheila Ransome and a couple of other elderly ladies, masked up and spraying hand gel liberally on those arriving. 'I hope you haven't come to arrest our lovely vicar,' said one of them, her eyes twinkling.

'No,' he said in response, and smiled under his mask. Although directed towards the front of the tiny church, he sat at the back in a rather quaint box pew with its own door and latch. Over the next few minutes the congregation grew and grew. There was the usual collection of elderly, mainly female, worshippers, mostly carefully spaced, but a surprisingly large number of young women, who crowded together in the first two rows and chattered excitedly through their masks. Finally, at ten o'clock, the medieval door behind them closed with an echoing crack, and an unmasked Reverend Cleaver strode down the aisle towards the pulpit carrying a single guttering candle. Once he had mounted the wooden dais, he turned to the congregation and in a powerful voice proclaimed, 'Jesus said: I am the resurrection and the life. He that believeth in me, though he were dead, yet shall he live.'

He held up the candle, and the small flame seemed to fill the nave. If he had looked piratical before, now he looked almost Christ-like. He then proceeded to declaim a great long passage of scripture, ending with a prayer. Even as an agnostic, Gillard felt the power of the man, his hold on the congregation. After a hymn, whispered rather than sung, he began a sermon on his own conversion to Christ.

'In my life I have done many bad things, I think those of you who know me well have heard some of the stories. I was in drug gangs in Manchester, and I was imprisoned for many years, which gave me a chance to consider my sins. I realised I had the choice of a path of goodness or of evil. I had free will, and I have exercised it. It is a choice we all have and can transform our lives.'

Once the service had finished, Gillard became aware of Ray Slater standing at the back of the congregation. Like him, Slater was in a suit and didn't quite seem to fit in with the others there. They briefly made eye contact above their masks, but while Gillard had more questions to ask Slater, it was more urgent to speak to the priest. It soon became clear that getting the Rev Matthew Cleaver on his own would not be easy. A press of women had gathered around him with no regard for social distancing. Amongst them he recognised Rowena Willow. Gillard waited patiently as the vicar gradually extricated himself from several conversations to get to the detective.

'Welcome to St Crispin's,' Cleaver said, his bright blue eyes flashing and his mask now in place. 'Come and have a cup of tea and a slice of cake with me. Victoria sponge.'

'Only if we can do so safely. I'm here on a work-related matter.'

Cleaver chuckled. 'Of course you are! Let's go to my home, where there is a bit of privacy.'

In the churchyard, Gillard noticed Slater in conversation with Rowena Willow. Her body language was defensive, and she seemed eager to get away from the private detective.

The priest led Gillard out of the church grounds, followed by the gaze of a few of the ladies. They crossed the lane and went up a garden path to Dove Cottage, a small terraced house with peeling paint and unwashed windows. Cleaver let them in, offered the detective some hand sanitiser, then showed him through to a cosy but untidy dining room, heaped with clothes, books and papers. It looked like a cross between a library and a teenager's bedroom.

'Take a seat, detective chief inspector, I shall be in shortly,' Cleaver called as he ascended the stairs. When he returned, he'd changed into jeans, a loose black shirt and a slightly worn corduroy waistcoat. A mask dangled around his neck. 'I suppose this is about the body found by the riverbank?'

'That's right. I'm really trying to get a picture of what has been going on in Rissington Common over the last year or two.'

'So is this now being treated as a crime?'

'We're keeping an open mind, but you will undoubtedly have heard that the body we found is modern, not historic.'

'Yes, Rowena told me all about it. So you think Ozzy Blanchard may have been killed by someone in the village?'

'Well, that would be a bit of a leap at this stage. We're not officially confirming the identity until all tests are completed.'

'I met him, if that's what you're here to ask. I was appointed just over a year ago so only overlapped a few months with him, but he did attend a couple of village meetings last autumn. He seemed like a nice guy, quite easy-going. Wasn't his car the one that crashed nearby back in January?'

'Yes, it was. I was wondering if you had witnessed any tension between members of the community, or between families, that kind of thing.'

Cleaver nodded. 'Well, I'm quite new, but some things are obvious. This is a neglected backwater, as I think you can see. I was surprised when the bishop asked me to try to revive a collection of rural churches, given my background. I thought they would give me some urban wasteland in Liverpool or Leeds,' he chuckled.

'Because you spent time in prison?'

'Yes. And that undoubtedly is part of why you are speaking to me. I do get the police mindset.' He held up his hands, and for the first time Gillard noticed a faint tracery of tattoos across his knuckles. 'Now don't get me wrong, my resentments and insecurities have long ago been burned away by the power of the Lord. I understand that you have to come to talk to me, not just as a preacher but as a man with a criminal record. I have nothing to hide, and if you want to search this house you are free to do so.'

'That won't be necessary at this stage,' Gillard said. 'I just wondered if you had witnessed or heard about anything that might give us a clue.'

'I can't say that I have.'

Cleaver excused himself to go to the kitchen to make a cup of tea. Gillard perused bookshelves heavy with well-thumbed paperback literature, from Dickens to Marx, Schopenhauer to Saul Bellow. An electric guitar case was propped up by the lamp standard, and there were a couple of framed black and white photographs of Cleaver himself, naked to the waist, playing at some crowded gig. One of them had caught the beads of perspiration on his brow and well-muscled shoulders, along with one edge of an enormous bird of prey tattoo on his back. He looked every inch a rock star.

The priest returned with a tray laden with two china cups, a teapot and two slices of cake. 'The cake is courtesy of the ladies of the Women's Institute,' he said.

'Is this house officially church property?'

'No. It's rented. Things have changed a bit from the days when every parish vicar had their own rectory, you know. The Church of England is not immune to financial difficulty.'

'When did you first move in?'

'Almost exactly a year ago. Why do you ask?'

'Just curious.' Gillard was wondering how long the body had been buried by the willows.

Cleaver looked at his watch, and said, 'Now, to your question. There was a long-standing enmity between the Tickett family and the Willows, now largely healed, but I'm sure not telling you anything you don't already know.'

'I know about the murder of Henry Willow in 1982, and the jail term that Christopher Tickett served.'

Cleaver nodded as he chewed the cake thoughtfully. 'You have got to feel for the Ticketts. Everything that goes wrong in the village is frequently blamed on them. Fly-tipping, vandalism, petty theft. They're with the other lot, the Roman Catholic Church in Upper Rissington. But they are devout.'

Gillard worked on a different, less celestial, system of accounting and knew there was a fair number of criminal convictions attached to the Ticketts' address. However it was not his job to share that information.

'So there is hostility?'

'No, suspicion maybe. The Ticketts' yard is on land leased from Willow Farm. Michael, who runs the farm, is quite reclusive and hostile to the Tickett family, but his sisters Crystal and Vicky and the rest of the Willow family are quite outgoing and mix with them well enough. There was some upset at the fact that while most of the village is up in arms about the negligence of the water company, the Tickett family are getting well paid working for them.'

'But isn't the work intended to put right the sewer problems?'

'That's what Chris Tickett keeps saying, and he does have a point. And a good proportion of what the Ticketts earn finds its way into the till at the Anvil Arms, so you could say the village as a whole does benefit.'

'Did you ever meet any of the other Aqua Western people? I know they spent a fair amount of time here.'

'Yes, a couple of times. Trevor Collier. A bit elusive when things got unpleasant. Oh, and some officious senior manager called Arrowsmith. Didn't like him at all.'

'So I heard.'

'You will also discover that I attended a demonstration outside their office in Windsor just a few weeks after I arrived, and another one in London. There's bound to be a record of my arrest. We were protesting against the pollution, and the lack of action by the company. That, of course, was before the remedial work was started last October.'

Gillard had read the statement. 'You were arrested with Sheila Ransome, as I recall.'

Cleaver chuckled. 'Yes indeed, she is a power to behold! Never underestimate the elderly. They can move mountains.'

Gillard heard the sound of a key in the front door, and a woman's voice called out to him, addressing him as Matt.

'I'm just in here with the detective, Mr Gillard. I'll be a few minutes.'

Gillard's ears pricked up at the sound of shoes being removed, cupboard doors clicking, and the light tread of feet on the staircase. He had recognised the voice, and his eyes switched back to those of the vicar with a question in them. The Rev Matt Cleaver clearly understood what the detective was asking of him. 'We're in a work bubble together, over the various finds that have been made in the churchyard. All the documentation is stored upstairs.'

'I see,' said Gillard, dubiously. The voice he had heard was Rowena Willow's, a girl of sixteen, who seemed very much at home in this house, apparently with her own key and the easy familiarity that comes with such a possession.

Cleaver smiled at Gillard, seeming to sense his suspicion. 'Rowena is also my cleaner, which is why she has a key.'

'Cleaning on a Sunday. That's a great service.' Gillard couldn't hear any banging or clattering upstairs. 'And very quiet, too.'

'Look, I only have one passion these days, detective chief inspector, and that is for the service of our Lord.'

The detective said nothing, but nodded. Cleaver seemed to believe his own words, and despite himself Gillard found he believed him. It was time to escape the aura of this convincing man. He stood to leave.

–

When Gillard emerged from the house, he could see Sheila Ransome in the street in conversation with two of the other elderly ladies. 'Mrs Ransome, could I perhaps have a word with you in private?'

She agreed with alacrity. 'I think it would be best if we sat in my garden, where we can keep a good distance.' She led the detective down to a cottage just three doors up from where the Rev Cleaver lived. She clicked open the latch on a small side door, which took them both through a low passageway in the terraced row and into a back garden. There were two apple trees, and between them a small wrought iron garden table and two matching chairs. She indicated that Gillard should sit down, and he picked up one of the chairs and set it back a few feet.

'I do hope you've come to ask me about the criminal acts committed by Aqua Western,' she said.

'Not directly, and neither am I interested in the criminal acts apparently committed by you when you glued yourself to the doors of the company's London headquarters.'

'Detective chief inspector, when I choose a task, I do tend to stick with it,' she said with a smile.

'So I hear. I want to ask you about Mr Blanchard, whom I believe you know.'

'He's dead, isn't he? Wasn't that his body that you discovered?'

'We're keeping an open mind until we have conclusive proof,' Gillard said, hoping that Mrs Ransome's comment was a leap from what had appeared in the newspapers rather than yet more inside information leaked by Clive Hancock.

'Oh, I thought you had proof. Well, I would be relieved if he is alive, naturally. Also because I have to say he was a rather sympathetic man compared to the others I've spoken to. When I described to him the pollution we suffered...'

'And when exactly was this?'

'I have it precisely in my notes on the computer, inside, just bear with me while I print them out.'

'No need for that at this stage, if you can tell me roughly.'

'Well I would say that I first met him three or four years ago. He rang me up, we walked around the village together, and he talked about what could be done to relieve the problems about the sewer overflows. He seemed quite knowledgeable. He came along to a village meeting just over two years ago, and I suppose he told us what we wanted to hear.'

'Are you saying that he misled you?'

'Yes. Or perhaps he promised something that he was later unable to deliver.' She eyed him shrewdly. 'I know how these corporate organisations work. If they meet fierce and determined opposition they promise you the earth, and then short-change you at the last minute. My campaign was just something for them to manage. I don't think they ever had the intention of spending the kind of money required to fix the problem. Ozzy rather gave the game away when he said the water company had a formula for dealing with floods. That is, the capital the company would spend was always directed to where the most number of households or consumers would benefit. And right here, there are only sixty people affected by the pollution of this land. The bottom edge of the village basically, Bourne Lane down to the river, and of course the bottom third of the Willow family farm. So what would happen is that every year some more urgent task would come up for the remedial money they had available to spend, and it would go elsewhere. We would always be left waiting.'

'So what exactly did they do?'

'Well, Ozzy kept talking about phase one, this all-singing all-dancing system. And they employed the Ticketts of all people to work on it. There were plenty of diggers and pipes and all those things, but they have only recently found out that it's only a small fraction of what they should have done. They laid some sections of new sewer but lots of it remains unfinished.'

'When did you discover this?'

'I think I got hints of it about November-time. Ozzy became very evasive, but I had done my research, and managed to phone him at home during the evening a couple of times. He basically blamed his boss for holding back the money.'

'His name?' Gillard knew, but wanted to see what Mrs Ransome knew.

'Kelvin Arrowsmith. Far too high and mighty to deal with us, apparently. Regional financial controller. Anyway, it was around Christmas when we stopped getting any visits from Ozzy. He had been seen about, apparently, but he wouldn't come to any of our meetings like before.'

'Do you think anyone had been threatening him?'

'You mean apart from me?' She smiled. 'I was on his case the whole time.'

'I mean physically threatened?'

'Well, that could be any number of people in the village. He let us down, you see. People want to sell their houses, but even those who weren't flooded last time are tainted by their proximity to an unresolved flooding issue. Lots of us can't get insurance, except at prohibitive cost. We're blighted, the whole village is blighted. I had hoped that when I die, my little cottage here would provide money so that Stewie can be looked after if he needs to go into residential care. But I doubt there'll be enough. This lovely charming little cottage is worth less than a half of what similar places go for in Haslemere. So I want compensation, as well as the work completed to get everything fixed.'

'But aren't they completing the work now?'

'My understanding is that most of what they're spending is on the water mains to supply the new houses outside Upper Rissington.'

'I do understand your predicament, but you have to understand I'm here about something else. We have a dead body, and we want to find out who killed him.'

At that moment Stewie emerged from the passageway into the garden. 'Mum, I'm going to play Cluedo with Callum and Rowena. Are you coming too?'

'Not this time, Stewie. Remember to take your mask and hand sanitiser.'

'All right,' he said, and almost skipped back down the passageway.

'He adores Rowena,' Mrs Ransome told Gillard. 'In fact I think he's got a bit of a crush on her. Such a lovely girl. She's always got time for him; she's so patient and sweet. And of course she is terribly pretty when she can bother to make the effort. If only she'd remove that nose ring.'

'I presume the Rev Cleaver has been a great asset to your campaign?'

'Oh yes. I don't know how we managed without him. I'm all right at the research, and ferreting out facts and details, but he can hold a crowd in the palm of his hand. When he came along to a demonstration outside the London HQ, he even got passers-by joining in. We passed out flyers to commuters and got dozens of email addresses, and hundreds of pounds in contributions for the campaign. Whatever he puts himself into he commits a hundred and ten per cent.'

Gillard nodded.

'Detective chief inspector, I've always believed in redemption through atonement. Matthew is the living embodiment of that. He's done wonders for our community, not just the church.'

Chapter Thirteen

It was Sunday evening, seven p.m., when Gillard's grey Vauxhall turned into his home street. His thoughts shifted from work worries to domestic worries. They were every bit as challenging. Trish had agreed to move into her bungalow tomorrow. She had her cats back, and Sam had given the place a thorough airing. It was about time, but he didn't expect it to go smoothly.

So as he reversed up the drive, he took a deep breath to prepare himself for the difficulties that the evening was bound to bring. But they didn't come from quite the expected direction. He was just getting out of the car when his mobile rang. He answered it expecting it to be the office, but it wasn't. It was Sheila Ransome.

'Mrs Ransome, I think I've told you not to call this number directly.'

'When you hear what I've got to say you'll be glad I did. You know my Stewie; he does some gardening for the Rev Cleaver. A bit of lawn mowing, usually. Well, this afternoon he was asked to dig out the old compost heap, and he found something quite interesting.'

Gillard tried to be patient, but this meandering introduction was the last thing he needed. 'And that was?'

'Fingers. What looked like two human fingers, underneath. All black and horrible.'

She had his full attention now. 'When exactly did he discover them?'

'Well, I'm not really sure. He was being a bit evasive…'

'Has anyone mentioned this to Rev Cleaver?'

'No. He says he hasn't, neither have I.'

'Good. Where are these two digits now?'

'In a plastic food box in my fridge.'

'Good. Do not tell anybody, understand? Keep it entirely to yourself, and keep Stewie at home and away from people until I get an officer to you. I'm off duty at the moment, but I'll come and interview you about it tomorrow.'

'Stewie told me that the Rev Cleaver was a murderer, but I just thought he was being silly.'

'Yes, he mentioned that to me too,' Gillard said. 'In relation to Cluedo.'

'On the stairs, with the dagger,' she said. 'That's what he kept saying.'

'Has Stewie found anything else, something that could be a murder weapon?'

'I don't think so.'

Gillard thanked her and hung up. The case had just got more complex. How did the two fingers missing from Rissington Man end up in the compost heap at the vicar's home? And was the vicar responsible?

–

Within an hour Surrey Police had a CSI team at the Bourne Lane home of the Rev Matthew Cleaver. Once team leader Kirsty Mockett had identified the two fingers in Mrs Ransome's fridge as human, the priest was asked to accompany officers to Reigate Police Station. PC Sarah

Noakes was left behind to interview Stewie Ransome at home about the circumstances of the discovery. Although it was nearly eleven p.m. before the interview began, his mother was present, and he was in familiar surroundings. The officer had only last week completed her course in interviewing vulnerable adults and was keen to put what she had learned into practice. Stewie was thirty-three, and apart from his Down's syndrome suffered from mild learning difficulties. Mrs Ransome said that he had been doing odd jobs like gardening for many years for people up and down the lane.

'Is Matt going to get into trouble?' Stewie asked.

'That depends, Stewie,' PC Noakes said. 'But it's important for you to tell us the truth.'

He looked to his mother, who nodded vigorously back at him.

'I swear by Almighty God—'

The officer smiled. 'You don't have to do that now, we're just asking some basic questions. So Stewie, when was it you began to work on Rev Cleaver's garden?'

'I start at two o'clock,' he replied, looking to his mother for guidance.

'No, I mean on which day?'

'I mow the lawn every other Monday after I come back from college, unless it's raining, then I do washing up.' Gradually, PC Noakes teased out that Stewie had been asked to dig over the compost heap the previous Friday, but had only begun to work on it on Sunday afternoon.

'So describe the compost heap to me, as it was before you started work?'

'It's a great big plastic box full of bits of grass and weeds that I've dug up before.'

'So this box was above the ground?'

'Yes, but the grass had gone all black and heavy at the bottom over the months, which makes it good for plants.'

'And did Matthew say why he wanted you to dig it all out?'

'For a community garden. He wanted the whole corner of his garden to grow vegetables. I was supposed to dig in the compost, and move the big box to another place.'

'So where exactly did you find the fingers?'

'Well, I'd shovelled all the compost to one side, and was digging the ground underneath. But it looked like it had been dug before, because it was all soft. Not so much clay. And it was in this soft earth that I found the fingers.'

'Did you find anything else of interest?'

Stewie looked to his mother, and then back at the officer.

'Did he tell you something?' PC Noakes asked her.

'He made some reference to Cluedo. He's obsessed with the game,' Mrs Ransome said.

'The Rev Green stabbed him on the stairs with the dagger,' Stewie said. 'He's a murderer.'

'Are you referring to Matthew Cleaver? Or is this just part of the game?'

'I don't like him,' Stewie said. 'He's not a nice man.'

'What makes you say that, Stewie? Has he done something horrible to you?'

He shook his head. 'Not to me.'

'To who?'

'Can't say.' He looked at his mother, and then down at the table.

'Did you witness something?' the PC asked.

There was no reply, and Stewie was looking straight down at the table in front of him, his face flushed.

'Do you know anything about this?' PC Noakes asked Mrs Ransome.

The elderly woman shook her head. 'I know he's taken against Matt for some reason, which is surprising because he's always been willing to play Cluedo with him. And Matt is ever so friendly with everybody.'

'All right. I think we'll leave it there for now.'

Monday

Gillard arrived with DC Carl Hoskins at Reigate Police Station at nine the next morning. The Rev Matthew Cleaver had been detained the previous evening, and was now sitting at an interview table in jeans and a rugby shirt, his hair pulled back in a ponytail, arms folded.

'I've been kept in all night because of something found in a compost heap in my garden,' he complained, as the two officers sat down. The duty solicitor had just arrived, and Gillard prepped the tape.

'Regardless of whether you were involved, we couldn't allow you to go back home because of the danger of contaminating any evidence that we might find,' Gillard said. 'As you know we are investigating the discovery of a body, and we have good reason to believe these two fingers may have been part of that body.'

'Well, I can tell you that I've had nothing whatever to do with it,' Cleaver said. 'The uniformed guys who cautioned me last night said whatever it was Stewie discovered was found in a compost heap.'

'That's right,' Hoskins said. 'In your garden.'

'But that compost heap was there long before I arrived. Stewie knows that. I don't have time to do the gardening, I'm an urban boy. I don't know a cucumber from a thistle.'

'So you say,' Hoskins said, looking down at an iPad where details of last night's interview were recorded.

'What explanation do you have for the discovery of these body parts?' Gillard asked.

'Why should I have an explanation? I've been renting this cottage for a year and it must presumably be something to do with the previous tenant.'

'Who is the landlord?'

'Well, I rent it from the Church of England, which took a lease from the Willow family.'

'So the Willows are the freeholders?' Gillard asked.

'As far as I know. When I had problems with the boiler, I used to ring Crystal.'

There was an 'ah' moment. 'Have you had cause to ring her recently?'

'No. I've not seen her for months. I pass on any messages through Rowena, when she comes to clean.'

'Rev Cleaver,' Hoskins asked. 'Have you fallen out with anyone in the village?'

'No, I haven't. Everyone has been absolutely charming to me, and I hope that I have been courteous and co-operative in turn.' Gillard couldn't help but find this man's answers convincing. He made eye contact and held it, and everything he said seemed utterly reasonable.

'You've got quite a criminal record,' Hoskins said. 'GBH, supply of class A drugs, affray, conspiracy to supply. It goes on and on.'

Cleaver closed his eyes briefly, and took a breath. 'That was all many years ago, officer, as you can see. Incarceration is intended to rehabilitate and, just occasionally, it works. Perhaps with just a spark from above.' He gestured to the heavens. 'I truly am a reformed character.'

'Time will tell,' Gillard said. CID had already taken a phone call from the office of the Bishop of Winchester, expressing concern and reinforcing the priest's standing. The detective wasn't keen to keep Cleaver under lock and key, but until CSI had finished excavating the bottom of the garden and a search of his home, he couldn't be allowed to return. Gillard explained that, and asked if Cleaver had anywhere else to go.

'Yes, I've had a couple of offers,' Cleaver said, brandishing the phone that had just been returned to him. Gillard didn't doubt the truth of that comment. Still, he would be interested to see what messages and texts showed up on that phone.

–

Driving from Reigate back to Rissington Common, Gillard found Bourne Lane clogged with police vehicles. He parked by the Tickett yard and walked the rest of the way, greeting the duty officer on the cottage gate, and going through the passageway that led to the rear of the terraced cottage. A white CSI tent occupied the bottom quarter of the garden, while beyond it a mini digger had been positioned on the other side of the garden wall where it could reach over to excavate. Kirsty Mockett, dressed in a white Tyvek suit, face mask and booties, emerged to greet Gillard.

'Have you found anything else?' he asked.

'Some scraps of clothing that appear to match what the corpse down by the river was wearing, and some more tatters of black bin bag. They'll have to be sent off for analysis, and it could take a few days.'

'Has anyone been through the house?'

'Yes. We've got a laptop, but nothing obviously incriminating so far.'

'It could well be that this predates his occupancy, couldn't it?'

She nodded. 'Somebody buried the body here, then moved it, somewhat clumsily, to the place we found it. I expect the fingers were cut off by a spade or something like that, and not noticed if it was done at night.'

'Timing is something we haven't had any clue about since we started this inquiry. But if the expected arrival of the reverend as a tenant prompted the killer to dig up and rebury the body, we can begin to build some timescales. Our victim may have been down amongst the willows for a year or so.'

'But we don't know how long he was here before that,' Kirsty said.

'No, we don't. And to my mind it makes it less likely that the body is Ozzy Blanchard. Some questions cannot be answered until we know who he is. I just wish those labs would hurry up with the results.'

'Covid is slowing everything up, that's what they tell me.'

–

By midday on Monday, Dr David Delahaye had rung Gillard to confirm that the fingers were indeed from the corpse found by the river, accounting for the two missing digits on the left hand. They fitted precisely, and exhibited the same waxy adipocere as the main corpse. The Home Office forensic pathologist had identified some of the scraps of material as coming from a sock. 'So it would appear to me that the body was moved, probably hurriedly, from one site to the other.'

'That's the conclusion that we came to,' Gillard responded. 'To me the most plausible idea is that the body was buried in the garden of the rental property while it was vacant, but as soon as the new tenant moved in, they realised it would eventually be discovered.'

'Hmm. It doesn't sound like a considered strategy to begin with,' the pathologist said. 'Ideally you want to bury a body somewhere that it will never be disturbed.'

Gillard chuckled. 'In my decades as an investigator, very few corpse disposals are carefully planned, even when the murder itself is premeditated. The fate of the body is almost always the critical forensic element of the crime, yet what I see most often is panic, hurried night-time disposal, and luckily for us, plenty of incriminating mistakes.'

'Well by that yardstick, the killer here has done quite a decent job,' Delahaye said. 'He's left us no clues as to who he is.'

'If it is Ozzy Blanchard, then the body must have been moved from the garden to the riverbank in the last six months, when Cleaver was already in occupation of the cottage. That puts him back in the frame. And there is a motive, because Cleaver was part of the group protesting about the pollution from Aqua Western sewers. There are a few complicating factors. One is that Ozzy was said to be having a relationship with Crystal Willow, a woman from the family of landowners whose land was polluted, and who is the owner of Dove Cottage where the fingers were found.'

'Ah, that does muddy the waters.'

'No one admits to knowing where she is, but neither has she been reported missing.'

'So if you find her, you solve the mystery,' Delahaye said.

'Well, it would be a good start. It's something I'll be looking at this afternoon.'

—

Following the first reopening of pubs on Saturday, Gillard returned to the Anvil Arms to find a new menu. Even though it was three o'clock on an overcast Monday, the outside tables were crowded. One central table was occupied by Aidan, Rory and Christopher Tickett, none of them masked, and decked with a dozen glasses, most of them empty. They saluted Gillard with their pints as he walked past and entered the bar. The hand sanitiser dispenser on the door was empty. Vicky Willow had agreed to be interviewed by Gillard anticipating it wouldn't be busy, but she was now pulling pints, while her niece Rowena was sitting playing with the baby and seven-year-old Callum in a corner of the lounge.

'I can see this is a bad time,' Gillard said.

'Don't worry, I'm chucking them out now. We've still got a few burgers if you'd like one.'

'No thanks, I've already eaten,' he lied.

She showed him to one the interior tables, flicking a tea towel to knock crumbs from the table and chairs. 'Sit yourself down, I'll be back in a mo.' In fact it took a good ten minutes for Vicky to persuade the Tickett family to depart, which they did with boisterous good humour. She took the baby from Rowena, as he had started to grizzle, and bounced him on her hip. She then she sat down opposite Gillard and lifted her mask into place.

'That'll be more wobbly water pipes laid this afternoon,' she said, indicating the Ticketts with an incline of
her head. 'They've each had at least three pints.'

'In a perfect world I'd go and intervene if there's a
danger of drink-driving, but now I have a bit of your time
I'd rather use that,' he said.

She smiled.

'I've got a simple question, Vicky. Where's Crystal? No
one has seen your sister for months, apparently. Not since
Ozzy Blanchard disappeared.'

'She's away in Devon, isn't she Rowena? Lockdown
wasn't kind to her business, so she just shut up shop.'

Rowena glanced up at the detective, and nodded her
assent.

'Where exactly is she staying? Caravan parks and campsites have only just reopened.'

'Dunno,' said Rowena, staring down at her phone.

'Would you pass me your phone? I want her mobile
number, so I can give her a ring,' Gillard said to the
youngster.

'It's just changed recently, hasn't it?' Vicky said to
Rowena, hurriedly pocketing her own phone.

Rowena called out a number beginning with zero
seven. 'That's Mum's new one.'

Gillard tapped it out on his own mobile. The call rang
for a few seconds then went to an anonymous voicemail.
As he'd suspected, Crystal wouldn't answer a call from an
unknown number. 'Your phone too please, Vicky, unless
you want me to get a warrant for it and search this place
top to bottom.'

Slightly flustered, Vicky pulled out her phone. 'I'll just
ring her now,' she said. As the call rang out, she rested her
eyes on Gillard's. 'Hi Crystal, no that wasn't me. It was

the police. They want to speak to you.' Vicky passed the phone across.

'Hello Crystal, my name is Detective Chief Inspector Craig Gillard. You've been rather elusive, haven't you?'

'I'm on holiday, that's all.'

'In your camper van, I understand. Where are you?'

'Errm. Not sure exactly. I'm parked in a layby in Devon at the moment.'

'Well, I need to speak to you in connection with the disappearance of your boyfriend, Ozzy Blanchard.'

'I don't know what you mean. He's not... he wasn't my boyfriend.' She sounded rattled, tripping over what tense to use to describe him.

'We'll track you down in a couple of days, so you might as well come back. You've some very serious questions to face.'

'I hear you've found his body,' she replied eventually.

'You tell me, Crystal. Did you kill him yourself?' Vicky and Rowena were staring at him. Whatever truth Crystal was hiding from him, they clearly knew part of it.

The line went dead, and Gillard looked at the two women, who seemed not to be breathing at all. 'With your permission, Vicky, I'd like to borrow your phone.'

'No, I need it. Lots of bookings for the pub get diverted onto it from the landline.'

'Look, if you give it to me now I can get it back to you within the day. If I have to get a warrant, you might be without it for a month.' He turned to Rowena and said: 'I'd like yours too, young lady.'

'You can't, it's personal!' she shouted, and taking her phone darted past him, out of the lounge into the pub garden. Gillard didn't attempt to go after her. He hoped Vicky at least would see sense, but she pocketed her phone, slid the baby into a plastic high chair, and ducked out of the room and into the kitchen, slamming the door behind her.

The boy twisted in the high chair, staring after her, his tiny stubby fingers flexing on the edge of the tray. He turned a perplexed expression to Gillard, searching the detective's face with his bright blue eyes. Gillard smiled at him. In what was a typical reaction in his experience, the child's face began to crumple, and he began an enormous inhalation. He was getting ready to cry.

'Come on, be a cheerful chappie for me,' Gillard said, gently offering his own index finger for the child to grasp. The crying had not yet begun, but with the unerring emotional radar of even the tiniest child, he knew something was not right.

The detective could only agree. The nature of the conspiracy between the three women was not yet clear to Gillard, only the certainty that one existed. Whether it reached to murder or was limited to something more mundane he was not yet sure. Vicky and Rowena could deny him their phones for now, but he only needed to get the numbers to order a warrant, and with that he would be able to unearth every text message and voicemail between them and others in the last six months.

He was still thinking about this when Vicky reappeared. At that moment his mobile rang. It was Kirsty Mockett from CSI. 'Sir, I think you should come and see what we've just found at Cleaver's house.'

'I'm on my way. Are you going to give me a hint?'

'Bloodstains. Lots of them.'

Chapter Fourteen

Given the congestion of police vehicles in Bourne Lane, Gillard decided to walk. He grabbed a fresh Tyvek suit, booties and gloves from the boot of his car. It was five minutes' brisk walk from the Anvil, across the war memorial to the bottom of the village green, and down Bourne Lane past the Tickett yard to Cleaver's home. He then made his way through the press of police patrol cars and CSI vans, under the crime tape, and signed in again with the PC in charge of the site. He noticed a couple of news reporters who had gathered beyond the tape but ignored their shouted questions.

Kirsty Mockett met him in the narrow hallway of the cramped house, and showed him a couple of close-up photographs of bloodstains while he climbed into his protective gear. She then led him up the narrow stairs to the landing. The upper floor was cluttered with books, clothing and clerical paraphernalia. She led him into the second bedroom, little more than a low-ceilinged box room. The light was on and the curtains drawn. It had three crammed bookcases, but had been turned into a makeshift gym. A rubber exercise mat occupied much of the floor. Beyond it, a weight training stand was full of dumbbells and free weights.

'This is what I spotted,' Kirsty said, kneeling in front of a wooden bookcase, bulging with hardbacks. There was what looked like a small paint run on the spine of one book, no bigger than a map pin and close to the skirting board. 'It looks like paint, but it's blood.'

Gillard crouched to look closely. 'I'm impressed you spotted that.'

Kirsty led him back to the doorway, and flipped off the light switch. Low down on one wall of the darkened room, just above a plug socket, was a spray of iridescent blue measles. The specks continued across a bookcase.

'BlueStar has done a good job here,' Gillard said.

'There's a directional sweep, as you can see,' Kirsty said. 'An arc from left to right, going towards the window, low across the bookcase. There are some runs down onto the skirting board too.'

'A cut artery, and a surge of blood. That fits with the injuries sustained by the victim. A knife wound to the neck, while he was prone.'

'It seems to me, sir, that we've found the site of the murder.'

Gillard nodded. 'And someone cleaned up, but not very well.'

'BlueStar is amazing. You can scrub and scrub with bleach and disinfectant, yet still get a reaction from the solvent. I sprayed this just forty-five minutes ago, and it tells us so much.'

'Rev Cleaver may have thought he cleaned up well enough. He probably replaced the original carpet, because there's not a single speck on this one,' Gillard said.

'It's not on most of the books either. What if the killing took place before his tenancy?'

'Maybe we can establish that,' Gillard said. He crouched down to look at the bottom row of books again. The blood run she had pointed out earlier stood out in kingfisher blue. 'If these are Cleaver's books, brought in with him, then this one drop of blood will prove the killing took place after his tenancy began.'

Looking over the bookcase, neither Gillard nor Kirsty could see any other drops of blood on other books, yet there were dozens of pinpricks of blue light from the edge of the shelves.

'It looks like most of the books were put here afterwards,' Kirsty said. 'You'd expect more contamination on them otherwise.'

Gillard carefully removed the blood-tainted book. In the gloom he couldn't see the title, so he retreated to the entrance to turn on the light. *A Pictorial History of the Bridges of London*, it was called. The paper dust jacket was ripped, but it wasn't too old. Published in 2012. Looking inside the frontispiece, Gillard could see a pencil mark giving the price. It looked to him like a charity shop buy.

'Pass me a large evidence bag,' Gillard said. 'I like to see if we can get any dabs off this. Perhaps you should take a selection of the other books as well.'

'That's good thinking. I'm going to dig out some samples of these stains for analysis. There's a process now called real-time reverse transcriptase PCR which can work out how old bloodstains are based on the degradation of the RNA in the blood. It came up in my forensic course. The crucial issue is the sample size. I'm not sure the single drop of blood on the spine of a book will be enough, and the bleach-treated droplets that BlueStar picked up may not work at all. But I'm going to try.'

'Hold on, Kirsty. Make sure you leave enough from that single drop to allow a test to see whether Ozzy was the victim here. That's the priority test.'

They both looked at the book. A single drop of blood, the kind you might get from a pinprick, and so much was riding on it.

'Okay.'

'And Kirsty, I'd like you to be in on the next interrogation of Rev Cleaver, tomorrow morning when we put the evidence to him. I'm having him re-arrested.'

—

Gillard didn't get back to the office until six. Research Intelligence Officer Rob Townsend was sitting at his desk, phone clamped under his chin as he liaised with the service provider to get a trace on the phones that had recently rung Vicky and Rowena Willow.

'How you getting on, Rob?' Gillard asked, after the call ended.

'Not too bad. I'm tracing Crystal's phone now. I've also got Vicky and Guy Naylor's mobile phone numbers from their own pub website. We'll get the metadata back, probably by ten tonight. To save you some time, I filled out the warrant form so we can see the contents of messages. The duty magistrate is in Oxford this evening.'

'That's good work.'

'We already have the metadata from Matthew Cleaver's phone, so I could identify Rowena Willow's phone number from that. She seems to ring him about twenty times a day.'

Gillard nodded. 'I think she's besotted with him. I just hope he hasn't done anything about it. She only had her sixteenth birthday six weeks ago.'

'Ah, I see,' Rob said, his pale ginger eyebrows flexing. 'We might find out once we get to see the texts and voicemails between them.'

'I don't want us to get distracted, Rob. We have to focus on our so-far unidentified corpse. Everything else is secondary.'

'Received and understood.'

'A lot now depends on how clever the Willow women have been about communicating with each other. We only need a few unguarded messages or texts and we'll know what's going on.'

Gillard felt his phone vibrate. Looking down he saw Dr Delahaye's number. 'I'd better get this,' Gillard said to Townsend before answering the call.

'Hello Craig,' Delahaye said. 'I've just had an email from Glasgow University giving the analysis of samples from the skeleton and teeth of the body. We have clear conclusions on the victim's age at time of death. He was between twenty and twenty-five.'

'Are they sure? Ozzy Blanchard was fifty-two.'

'It's quite robust, based on the known rate of decay of a particular acid in tooth dentine. And it's reinforced by what they call morphological characteristics of the skeleton, which basically means observable wear and tear on bones. They've separately managed to extract some DNA from the root pulp in those teeth, and it doesn't match Mr Blanchard's elimination sample, nor anyone on the national DNA database. Those are two independent tests, Craig. It's clearly not the body of the man you thought.'

Gillard thanked him and hung up.

'The body isn't Ozzy. We're going to have to rethink everything,' Gillard said.

'So Ozzy Blanchard isn't dead?' Townsend said.

'Probably not. He certainly isn't Rissington Man. But Rissington Man possesses Ozzy's comb. The question is, who planted it on him, and why?'

'Maybe we'll get the chance to ask Ozzy,' Townsend said.

'Right now, finding him is my top priority. And I think Crystal Willow will lead us to him.'

–

Gillard was on his way home at eight thirty when Townsend called him. Answering on the hands-free, he heard the research intelligence officer tell him that they had a trace for the location of Crystal Willow's phone at the time of Gillard's call to it that afternoon. 'It wasn't in Devon at all,' Townsend said. 'It was a caravan park a few miles west of Reading. I alerted Thames Valley Police who are on their way there now.'

'That's good news,' Gillard replied. 'If she's got any sense she'll have got herself a new phone and skedaddled. So for that reason I'd like you to check for any new numbers that turn up on either Vicky or Rowena Willow's phones this afternoon or evening. Chances are it will be Crystal's new burner phone.'

'Got to give you credit, sir, you're always one step ahead.'

'Not always, unfortunately.' Gillard thanked him before hanging up. The secrets of the Willow women would soon be uncovered. In the days of modern electronics, you need a very savvy technical mind to keep ahead of the police. Going on the run required cutting off communications entirely, something he didn't think Crystal would do. It was only five minutes later when Townsend patched through a call from the control room at Thames Valley Police.

'Two patrol units arrived at South View Caravan and Camping fifteen minutes ago, sir,' the female operative said. 'No sign of the target vehicle or the missing female.'

'Make sure they ask about Blanchard too, while they are searching,' Gillard said. He asked them to forward any ANPR details of the camper van from the region, thanked them and hung up.

The rest of the journey home was quiet. As he turned into his own street Gillard turned his thoughts to his aunt and wondered what Sam had been expected to deal with. The two days she had spent with them had been stressful. Gillard had on several occasions been stirred from his sleep by the tones of the BBC World Service coming from the next bedroom at two or three o'clock in the morning. It wasn't loud, but enough to disturb him. Trish, who had always had trouble sleeping, was in the habit of getting up at just after five a.m. The sound of her moving about the house, clattering about in the kitchen, always woke them both. They knew from previous experience that Trish had a tendency to poke her nose into every cupboard and drawer as if she owned the place. Sam, who was now working some weekend shifts, had never been happy about leaving Trish on her own in the house during the day, even though one of their retired neighbours popped in every couple of hours. The sheer presence of the woman chilled the atmosphere. Craig and Sam had few enough waking hours together as it was. Last night, for no apparent reason, they'd had a row about nothing in particular. Sam had stormed off, and when Gillard turned to see his aunt in the doorway, she had a look of grim satisfaction on her face.

'What are you so happy about?' he had shouted at her.

'Don't you worry, I'll be gone tomorrow. I know you don't want me around. You'll be happy when I'm dead.'

Gillard's attempts to deny this were as futile as they were half-hearted. They both knew the relationship had been broken for good by her abortive murder trial and the events surrounding it.

So when he was greeted by his wife at the door, he expected the worst. 'How's it going?' he asked, indicating the bungalow opposite.

Sam beckoned him in, then closed the door behind him. 'Fine to start with, but she's fallen out with Harry and Rosemary about the cats.'

Gillard's retired neighbours had kindly looked after Trish's three cats during the many months she was in a coma. They were a pleasant couple devoted to their gardening, and had always been a good but not intrusive set of eyes and ears for the neighbourhood.

'Is it about Lucretia's disappearance?' Gillard asked.

'And about how much weight Napoleon has put on,' Sam said. Napoleon was the neutered ginger tom which ruled the roost, and used all the gardens in the neighbourhood as a lavatory. 'Rosemary came round here in tears at the things that Trish had said to her.'

'She's got a nerve,' Gillard said. Harry and Rosemary had looked after the cats at their own expense, refusing offers of contributions. They had been mortified when Lucretia disappeared and posted notices all round the neighbourhood, even travelling up to the rescue centre on a couple of occasions. After changing and having a shower Gillard went round to visit his neighbours, who remained shocked and upset at Trish's accusations. After offering many apologies for the behaviour of his aunt, he was floored by Rosemary's final comment: 'Trish said that Sam reported to her that we had neglected Lucretia.'

'That is simply not true,' Gillard said. 'We both know that you looked after the cats extremely well. I must apologise for my aunt. She's had a difficult life, and doesn't have the sweetest temperament.'

'She's a murderer,' Harry said. 'I looked up the case online.'

'She was cleared,' Gillard corrected.

'Hung jury,' Harry said. 'After some of the things she said we're thinking of moving house.'

'I'm so sorry to hear that.'

'We just don't feel comfortable here anymore.'

Gillard shook his head. 'All I can do is apologise. Neither Sam nor I would want you to have been upset in this way.'

It was gone ten by the time Gillard sat down at home to some toasted cheese on crusty bread in front of the TV. Sam was upset to hear the tales that Trish had been making up about her, and once again raised the possibility of them too moving house to get away from her.

'Do you really think we should run away like Harry and Rosemary?' Gillard asked.

'I don't know, Craig. But she's only been back from hospital a few days and is already such a malign influence.'

He didn't have an answer for her, and after taking his dish back into the kitchen, checked the message that had just come up on his mobile. Thames Valley Police had a witness sighting of the camper van in Oxfordshire and a description that matched Crystal herself. But no sign of Ozzy.

Chapter Fifteen

Gillard wasn't the only one trying to find Ozzy Blanchard. Rain was lashing down driven by a chilly north-westerly wind as Ray Slater's Nissan coasted into Wantage Leisure Park at six on Monday evening. Carl Hoskins' last gift to him was to identify Crystal's camper van from the DVLA records. A white 2006 VW. Not the classic type, more like a boxy people-carrier with a concertina roof and just enough space for a good argument. And now he seemed to be scouring the world looking for it.

Since Hoskins had got cold feet, Slater had had to do more legwork himself. No ANPR to make life easier, no cell phone triangulation. Back to the old-fashioned stuff. At first he had telephoned likely caravan parks, but discovered that they were frantically busy, under-staffed and slow to answer the phone. When he did speak to anyone, they were reluctant to share any customer details. Each site was supposed to note vehicle registration numbers, but payment for casual guests was usually taken on arrival, and the rental forms they filled out themselves were often illegible. In the frenzy of reopening, Crystal Willow wouldn't have found it hard to cover her tracks, or to conceal her boyfriend. Slater had never bought the idea that Blanchard was dead. If he was, why would the Tickett family be racing all over the place? He'd watched their cars come and go, and sometimes followed them. He had inside information that showed they still had a score to settle with the missing water engineer. That much he was sure of.

Years of experience had demonstrated to Slater that to get the attention of potential witnesses you need photos. Ozzy's picture was taken from his LinkedIn account, while Crystal's was from her massage website. He hadn't so far met anybody in a campsite who recognised either of them, but quite a few had asked if there was a reward. That was when he would mention £50 in cash for a confirmed sighting, as long as it included an emailed picture. He'd handed out sheaves of business cards with his email address. He was open about being a private detective, and when asked what the couple had done said simply: 'Indecent pictures of kids.' If the cash wasn't enough to justify a holidaymaker touring his campsite to find them, this heinous (and false) accusation would often be. He knew that the word would get around very fast. Almost no one that he talked to amongst the holidaymakers questioned his right to be chasing such people rather than reporting them to the police.

Wantage Leisure Park was the eighth caravan park or campsite that he'd visited that day, and he'd decided it would be the last. Twenty miles south-west of Oxford, it was the farthest north he'd searched. The site was small, two or three big fields, mostly camper vans on hook-ups, but quite a few caravans, many of them with tented extensions. Holidaymakers were hurrying back and forth, anoraks over their heads, squelching through the mud. Children scampered behind their parents, chasing each other and splashing in puddles, clearly delighted that holiday venues had now reopened. Slater never ceased hto wonder at the typical Briton's optimistic summer dress code. Shorts, T-shirts, flip-flops. Perfect for the Costa del Sol, but rarely right for the UK. The reality was washed-out barbecues, muddy toys and sodden clothing. Disappointment was guaranteed, pretty much like this job. As he rumbled around the muddy fields of the site, sitting in damp clothes, looking at the pitches and the vehicles on them, he promised himself a hot bath and a cold beer when he was done.

Then he spotted the very vehicle he was looking for.

A white 2006 VW camper with the correct registration. It was surprisingly prominent, a pitch within a hundred yards of the main gate. Slater parked across the back of the van, blocking its exit. Rain was still tipping down, so he grabbed his still-damp raincoat and a baseball cap to protect him from the worst. In his pocket he had his mobile phone already set for camera mode. He could see the distinctive light of a TV from within the sleeping compartment. It seemed he was not expected.

He crossed over to the vehicle and rapped sharply on the door.

It took half a minute for the door to slide open. He saw a woman with pale dreadlocks wearing pyjamas with rabbits on them and behind her a shaven-headed man slouched watching sport on TV.

She was not Crystal Willow, and he was not Ozzy Blanchard.

–

After a few minutes of conversation the story emerged. The couple recognised the picture of Crystal, who had sold them the van for cash a week ago. The buyers had driven it around the field a couple of times, were happy enough at the steep discount to the market value, and agreed to the deal, no questions asked. There only query from the couple was a simple one: had it been stolen? Slater resisted the spiteful urge to say yes. Instead he got as much detail as he could from them about what Crystal had said during their brief meeting and if she'd mentioned what her plans were. 'Going back to Devon was all I remember,' the woman said. 'She's got family down there.'

There was no sighting of Ozzy, but that didn't necessarily mean anything. He might have been waiting somewhere for the deal to be done. Slater guessed that Crystal and Ozzy had traded down to a car and a tent. They had been smart enough not to directly swap the camper van for a car, but had broken the trail by taking their cash elsewhere. If they were being this smart, then he guessed they wouldn't be using cash machines or credit cards either. The last info he'd had from Carl Hoskins was many days' old now, but indicated they weren't. Everything now depended on how much ready money the couple could lay their hands on. Ultimately, it would need to be a lot to avoid laying a trail. Hence raising cash from the camper van.

Slater's client was expecting results. But he was back to square one. He'd have to think of something, or this was going to be embarrassing. The only plus point in the whole sorry saga was that the couple in the camper van had not yet been approached by the police. Thames Valley plods were doing an even worse job tracking this lot than he was.

That evening Ray Slater booked in at the Anvil Arms and took his hot bath there before coming down to the bar, where he sat chatting to Vicky Willow. Over the last couple of weeks the private detective had become a regular at the pub. He'd already stayed a couple of nights in their tired and dingy B&B rooms on the quiet, before it was allowed. The room was in need of redecoration but otherwise okay, and there was plenty of scaldingly hot water. The food was terrible, the service slow and at breakfast the lounge was a cross between a crèche and a war zone. Lego bricks and plastic soldiers were underfoot, there were discarded baby socks on the seats and numerous washed but still-stained baby bibs graced the radiators. Callum, the boisterous older child, would burst in, making the noise of explosions as he continued a tabletop siege that seemed a permanent fixture.

Slater reconsidered whether the intelligence gleaned was worth the risk of injury or food poisoning. He'd only tried the cooked breakfast once. The bacon shattered the moment he put his fork into it, and the fried eggs were solid enough to have been worn as medals. Still, he was there to get information, and information was what he would get. His cover was that he was a travelling salesman, but he hadn't gone into details. A few nights after the discovery of the body, he had tried to turn on the charm with Vicky Willow. She was a handsome girl, big boned and curvy, a good twenty years younger than him, and he couldn't help imagining her riding him energetically on the squeaky bed upstairs, naked and sweaty, her breasts flopping in his face. He fought the image away for the tenth time that evening. In typical barmaid style she responded neutrally to his chat-up lines. She had clearly heard it all, and flattery was getting him nowhere. She was, however, happy to drink at his expense. She downed only the first drink each evening. The rest he offered to buy her were just notched up on his bill.

'So are you an only child?' Slater asked, as Vicky prepared a round of lagers for the contractors laughing noisily in the other bar.

'No, I've got a sister, bit older than me.' While she was holding the beer tap down with one hand for one of the pints, she opened the dishwasher under the bar with another, feeding out hot glasses onto the shelf behind her.

'Does she live locally?'

'Crystal lives up in Haslemere, runs her own wellness centre from the back of her house.'

Slater knew all about it. He'd sat for many hours outside the place on and off over the last week to see who visited. Nobody, was the answer. 'So what exactly is wellness, then?'

Vicky smiled, and glanced at him for the first time. 'She does therapeutic massage, and ear candling, reflexology, and tattoos. She's a very good artist.'

Slater nodded. 'Massages, eh?'

'She doesn't do those kind,' Vicky said firmly.

'What kind?' Slater asked with as innocent a look as he could muster.

'I wasn't born yesterday,' Vicky said.

'Maybe the day before, from the way you look.' It came out all wrong, and she rolled her eyes. Slater knew that this was one aspect of private detective work he wasn't good at. He was shrewd enough to know that as a paunchy middle-aged bloke with a boozer's face, he was hardly going to charm the birds from the trees. But if he'd had the patter, at least he could lure them to the bird feeder.

'So what is it you sell, then?' she asked, clearly wanting to change the subject.

'Reconditioned smartphones.' He had a box of them up in his room. He'd waited days for her to ask. This was getting a bit more interesting. He watched as she took the beers out to the garden and waited for her to return.

'Who do you sell to?' she asked the moment she returned. She was more interested in this than anything he'd said about his timeshare in the Canaries, or his hot tub at home.

'The smaller high street retailers and repair shops, normally. Can't get into the big outlets like Carphone Warehouse, unfortunately. But I beat them on price every time.'

'Really? How much?' She bent down to change over a barrel of beer, and hauled the first few pints noisily into a bucket from the hand-pull. Slater noticed the strong arms and good muscle definition.

'Varying prices, obviously. From about forty quid. They're not the newest models. I can bring a couple down if you like.'

Vicky licked her lips, and stared out into the lounge. 'Okay,' she said quietly.

Slater went to his room and brought down a briefcase, which he opened to show a dozen different phones, mainly Samsung and LG models, still in their boxes.

'They look new,' she said, loading a tray of dirty glasses into the dishwasher. Slater opened a box and handed her a shiny maroon Samsung.

'They're in perfect condition,' he said. 'Latest software updates even though the handset isn't the newest model. You can do anything on them.' He listed the various features. 'And it's all pay-as-you-go, no contract. Already five quid credit on each. Just need to link it to your email.'

'No address?'

He shook his head. 'No, totally confidential. Data wiped. Guaranteed.'

Slater had used this gambit many times before when he'd had trouble tracking people down. He omitted to mention the smartphones had all been preloaded with an app, freely available from US websites, though illegal to use in the UK without the user's permission. The app had three features. The first was a tracker which connected with the phone's GPS, and forwarded the locations of the phone on Google Maps to his own phone. The second copied and forwarded all texts and voicemails, and the third stored voice recordings every time the phone was used. Slater couldn't listen in real time, but received a text each time a recording was finished, which he could then download onto his phone. He'd even shown some of his divorce clients how to load the tracking app onto their spouse's phone.

'How much is this one?' she said, picking up one of the older models.

'That's forty-five quid. But I tell you what. If you take the Samsung Galaxy, normally one-hundred-and-twenty, I can let you have the two for one-hundred-and-fifty. The cheap one would make a nice present for someone.'

Slater was really tempting fate here. But it was no good tracking Vicky, who was tied by her children and her various jobs to Rissington Common. He needed a device in the hands of Crystal Willow, so that he could be led right to her. It wasn't such an outlandish thought. Slater had done his homework. He knew Crystal's date of birth, and that she would celebrate her forty-fifth birthday on Friday. Like anyone on the run, she would always need an extra phone.

Vicky held up the two phones, and inspected them minutely. She was smart and she was cautious, two traits he definitely approved of. But he was devious and clever. As he watched her, he felt like he was visiting Snow White with a poisoned apple.

'Okay,' she said softly, and pulled a surprisingly large wad of cash from the back of her jeans.

Snared.

After another night in the cells Cleaver emerged on Tuesday morning looking haggard and angry, his blue eyes intense as Gillard and Kirsty Mockett sat opposite him. The detective ran through the formalities for the tape, while the duty solicitor settled himself down and shuffled through his papers. The duty sergeant had told Gillard that their prisoner had been praying, intermittently but loudly, throughout the night.

'Can you not release me while you continue your enquiries?' Cleaver asked.

'We can hold you for four days under the Police and Criminal Evidence Act 1984. We don't intend to infringe on your liberty more than we have to, but we have made significant forensic discoveries in your home.'

Cleaver's eyes widened.

At this point Kirsty Mockett showed Cleaver a clear plastic evidence bag with a thick paperback inside. 'Is this yours?'

Cleaver peered closer, then nodded.

'For the tape, the detainee acknowledged owning a copy of the *Collins Guide to Theology*,' she said. The next evidence bag she showed him contained a hardback about Christian evangelism.

'Why are you going through my bookshelves? What is the point of this?' Cleaver asked, his blue eyes focused on Kirsty. She avoided his gaze.

'Perhaps you'd just answer the question, reverend,' Gillard said.

'Yes, it's mine. I don't think I have the receipt any longer, if you think I stole it.' He leaned back, crossed his arms and rolled his eyes at the solicitor.

Kirsty went through three more books which had been drawn almost at random from bookshelves in the crime scene bedroom. One of them he said he didn't recognise. 'I own a lot of books,' he said.

The final book was the bridges of London hardback. 'That's not mine. It was already in the house when I moved in,' Cleaver said.

Damn. He's innocent, Gillard thought. If that was the one book that predated his occupation it indicated the killing predated it too. That would explain why it was the only bloodstained book in his collection. If Cleaver had been guilty, and had known about the stain, he would have disposed of the book. If he was guilty and *hadn't* known, there would be no reason to disclaim ownership of that particular book.

Despite Gillard's change of heart, they still hadn't put the main part of the evidence to Cleaver. Now was the time.

'We have found extensive bloodstains in the back bedroom of your home,' Gillard said. 'Can you explain that?'

Cleaver's mouth hung open. 'No,' he answered eventually. 'They must predate my arrival.'

For the next half an hour Gillard went over the details of Cleaver's possessions, from the weight gear through to the bookcases, and got a reasonably consistent picture. The furniture was in before he rented the place, as were a few books. Everything else was his. He hadn't redecorated, and there had been only a tatty piece of lino on the back bedroom floor when he took the tenancy. He'd replaced the lino with cheap carpet and turned the room into a gym.

'Do you know who the previous tenant was?' Gillard asked finally.

'Sorry,' Cleaver replied. 'You'd have to ask Crystal or Rowena.'

–

Gillard drove Kirsty Mockett back to Mount Browne to grab a late breakfast. They had discussed the forensics in detail, and were on the final approach to Guildford when she sighed heavily and stared out of the window. 'I hope Cleaver is innocent,' she said.

'Why is that?' Gillard responded.

She laughed. 'Because he is absolutely gorgeous. That wild rugged look. I like my criminals to be the usual ugly repulsive kind. I don't like to be conflicted.'

'Poldark with a dog collar, eh?'

'Well, not exactly.' She laughed.

'Remind me not to invite you to any more interviews. Devils can look like angels, and vice versa. We've got to go on facts.'

Kirsty's eyes slid sideways to Gillard. 'He was very convincing. I think he is telling the truth.'

'Charisma and self-confidence can carry us away,' he said. 'We have to stick to the evidence. There's plenty of blood on the wall of his spare room. Still, as it happens, the facts seem to favour your prejudice. Not owning the one book that was bloodstained. That to me was a crucial element.'

'I'm pleased about that.'

'I shan't mention any of this to Rob,' Gillard said, looking across at her. Research Intelligence Officer Rob Townsend and Kirsty Mockett had been an item for well over a year.

'Best if you don't,' she said, colouring slightly. 'Especially as we broke up a week ago.'

'Ah, sorry to hear that.' Gillard knew that now was not the time to ask searching questions, but Kirsty seemed to want to fill in the blanks anyway.

'It was mutual,' she said, closing off many of the other more speculative avenues. Even though the CSI officers work from a different building from CID, Kirsty was aware what a rumour mill Mount Browne was. 'We're still very good friends.'

In the final approach to the HQ car park she took a phone call. Her body language in his peripheral vision showed it was something important, and she turned to him. 'Yes, and that's confirmed is it?' she asked, before ending the call.

'That's the lab. The DNA in the blood on the book spine matches the stains from the wall, and the DNA from Rissington Man's teeth. Only one chance in ten million of an error.'

'So Rissington Man was killed in Cleaver's spare room.'

'And Ozzy Blanchard wasn't,' she said.

'The victim was murdered, buried in the garden and was later moved, minus a couple of fingers, to a new resting place by the river.' Gillard slipped his Vauxhall into a space in Mount Browne's car park. 'I was hoping forensics would simplify this, but it hasn't worked out that way.' He and the young CSI technician entered the building, headed to the canteen, and joined the breakfast queue.

'We still don't know if Cleaver was involved,' Kirsty said. She took her tray, loaded with melon, grapes and a grapefruit, and sat at a table. Gillard joined her, unloading his Danish pastry, croissant and bowl of fruit salad.

DC Carl Hoskins approached and dropped his jacket over a spare chair at the table, and stared at his boss's expression.

'Never mind, sir, it may never happen.'

'I'm afraid it has. Someone was murdered in a spare room at Rev Cleaver's home, and as I assume you've heard, it wasn't Ozzy Blanchard.'

'Yeah, someone planted that comb to try to put us off the scent.'

'Yes.' Gillard showed him the details of the email on his phone. 'It's not quite back to square one. Our dead guy, whoever he is, is not on the national DNA database either. But he is modern, that's quite clear.'

'So that means Ozzy Blanchard is still alive,' Hoskins said.

'Probably, but not guaranteed.'

Hoskins blew a sigh as he joined a queue at the counter to get his elevenses. Gillard spent the intervening three minutes emailing the members of his team to arrange a midday incident room meeting to consider the new evidence. When he looked up, he did a double-take. Hoskins had just sat down with a tray containing a portion of fruit salad and a grapefruit. The detective constable was known as the biggest salad-dodger in CID. To see him with fruit was like seeing a fish with a bicycle.

'Carl, this is amazing,' Kirsty said. 'Where's the bacon sandwich?'

'Start of a new era,' Hoskins said, nodding at his plate.

'It's certainly that. Are you on a diet?' Gillard asked.

Hoskins nodded, lifted a small spoonful of fruit salad to his mouth. 'I've been diagnosed with type two diabetes,' he said. 'Aiming to lose two stone in a month, almost ten per cent of my body weight. I've had dire warnings since I went to the quack with a sore on my ankle that wouldn't heal. For the first few weeks I just stuck my head in the sand. But my kids have been on to me over the weekend.'

'Better late than never, Carl. Well done for getting to grips with it,' Kirsty said.

'Yeah, well. It's cutting down on the beer that's going to hurt most,' he said wistfully. 'I've had problems with my eyesight too, which I thought was down to looking at screens too much. But it seems that it might be a diabetes-related issue with my retinas.'

'There you go, Carl,' Gillard said. 'The hidden cost of a chicken nugget. But seriously, I need you to look after yourself for the sake of our CID team. Who else would look at all the CCTV if you go blind?'

'Thanks a bunch, sir.'

'Now, eat up, it's nearly time for our incident room meeting.' Gillard got up, said goodbye to Kirsty and clapped Hoskins on the back as he left.

Chapter Sixteen

The Tuesday afternoon incident room meeting was short and to the point. Detective Constables Rainy Macintosh and Carl Hoskins were joined on Zoom by Shireen Corey Williams, self-isolating after her return from Greece two days ago.

'So now you're saying we don't even know who this wee dead fella is anymore?' Rainy asked.

'That's right. But I think it's fair to say that whoever reburied him also planted the comb because he wanted us to think he was Ozzy Blanchard.'

She looked up at him quizzically. 'Aye, someone with a strong stomach.'

'But what if the comb was just added at the moment of discovery?' Hoskins said. 'You wouldn't need to have such a strong stomach for that.'

'Och no, Carl, that disnae make sense. There would have had to be three of them in on it, with the comb to hand, and to delay reporting their find.'

'Yes, that would make a weird conspiracy,' Gillard said. 'One supervisor from the water company in league with the woman on her first week in the excavator, and Aidan Tickett nearby.'

'It wouldn't be the people that actually did want to kill Ozzy, would it?' Hoskins said. 'But it might be to try to fool them.'

'In which case the likeliest culprit for the forensic trick would be Ozzy Blanchard himself, trying to make his pursuers give up,' Gillard said.

'Aye, but you need a spare body, to hang the spurious evidence on, don't you?' Rainy said. 'Do we now think that Ozzy would kill someone else, bury him in a garden, then dig the wee fella up again to chuck him in a grave by the river hoping to fool his enemies?'

Gillard nodded, conceding that this would drastically change their understanding of the missing man.

'It wouldn't fool his enemies either,' Hoskins said. 'If I wanted to bump him off, it would be a bit of a coincidence to hear that somebody else had done the killing for me. And honestly, I'd never believe it without a heap of evidence.'

Rainy was stroking her chin. 'There is a circumstance in which Ozzy's enemies might want to mock up a body to look like his.'

Everyone turned to look at her.

'These enemies, whoever they are, are aware that we might still be looking for Ozzy, as we believe Hampshire Constabulary is too. So they offer us the dummy, which means they get to continue their search without much chance of running into us examining the same clues to his current whereabouts. Then, when they *do* get him, and dispose of the body, we don't think of Ozzy Blanchard because, hey, we've already got his body.'

'Rainy, your mind is as twisted as any killer's,' Hoskins said.

Gillard laughed. 'I prefer the simpler idea that Ozzy just wants us to think he's dead. Besides, the latest forensics open up a few new leads for us to follow. We already have a rough age for the victim and an imputed height, five foot nine or so. Rainy, would you compare that with the list of missing people in a hundred-mile radius?'

'Righto.'

Gillard peered at his screen, where his economic crime specialist had been sitting quietly. 'Shireen, glad to have you back. As you are aware, Hampshire Constabulary under DCS Stella Anderson seems to be investigating financial irregularities at Aqua Western, but not sharing intelligence with us. As you're self-isolating, you're in the perfect position to shadow that inquiry. I want you to dig into everything you can about the company if you can do so without getting under Anderson's feet.'

'I've already started my research,' she said. 'It seemed easier to start from the top down, where there is plenty of published material about the company's capital-light approach.'

Shireen combined fine Middle Eastern features and almond-shaped eyes with a nasal Birmingham twang she had picked up from her husband. She was a fully qualified accountant and had a work ethic second to none. He just hoped she didn't incur Anderson's wrath.

'None of this helps with the mystery of the Anglo-Saxon sword stuck in yon fella's neck, does it?' Rainy asked.

'That's true,' Gillard conceded. 'No sign of fragments of it in Cleaver's home, nor any other Anglo-Saxon items.'

'But what about the young Willow lassie, Rowena? She has access to Cleaver's house, as his cleaner and the landlady's daughter, and a keen interest in archaeology. Unlike any casual visitor she would have been able to clean up and change the bloodstained carpet without risk. So she has means and opportunity, but what about motive?'

Gillard struggled to picture Rowena as a murderer, but conceded that Rainy had raised an interesting idea. 'Those are good points, and I'll be following them up. But to get motive, the one thing missing from your hunch, we need to know who the victim is. We have to redouble our efforts on an ID. Once we get that, it may all click into place.'

–

Within an hour DC Rainy Macintosh had pulled together the ten most likely missing males in a broad age range between fifteen and forty with the right height to match the mystery corpse. When they had gone missing was a less significant variable, but varied between forty years ago and just two years. Well within the range of the type of dental fillings they had found, and within the guidelines for adipocere formation. Gillard sat at a terminal opposite hers as they examined the same documents.

'Stephen Hibbert is one of my favourites,' she said. 'Aged twenty-six, hitchhiking between London and South Wales in 1997, last seen at a motorway services station, with his thumb out.'

'What about this one?' Gillard asked. 'Mohammed Firoze, thirty, went missing from his home in Windlesham in 2008. His car last picked up on ANPR in Southampton. We have good and recent dental records we could check.'

'I think we can rule out Frank Machin, who disappeared in his car with his wife and bairn in 2001,' Rainy said. 'Even though they all lived in Haslemere. I would have expected those bodies to have been found together.'

The names listed included two Eastern European seasonal workers, one from Lithuania and one from

Romania who'd disappeared ten years apart after working on farms in Hampshire. 'What about these?' Gillard asked.

'There was a sighting of the more recent one, Tomas Valdovas, aged twenty-two, on CCTV getting on a National Express coach from Reading to Victoria,' Rainy said. 'He might well have gone home, although his family claim not to have seen him. But the older guy, Tadeus Romanescu, was last seen in September 2008. He was thirty-four.'

Gillard finished perusing the list and looked up. 'That's a good start, Rainy. See what dental records we have for any of them. I also need to know which of them we might be able to acquire a familial DNA sample for. That should cut down the list quite quickly.' He looked up at her. 'Now we think he's alive, I'd really like to find out where the hell Ozzy Blanchard is.'

–

It was late afternoon when Gillard left Mount Browne and drove back to Rissington Common to catch up with Rowena Willow. He found her at the dig by the river. She was working with a dozen others, crouching down close to a series of pits excavated around the area where the body had been found. She was wearing shorts, multi-coloured knee-socks and engineer's boots. When she saw a masked Gillard approach, she squinted up at him against the sun.

'Hello, Rowena. I left a couple of messages on your phone. Can I have a word?'

She stood up and shrugged. 'I only get one bar of phone signal down here.'

It was true, but Gillard thought it more likely that she simply didn't want to speak to him. 'I need to ask you about the tenants at Dove Cottage.'

'I've got all the details at home,' she said, ruffling her untidy brown hair.

'Trouble is, you're never there,' Gillard said. Rowena had given her address as Willow Cottage, four doors up from Dove Cottage where Cleaver lived. But every time Gillard or any of his team had rung her doorbell, or had rung the landline, there had been no reply.

'Well, we can go there now,' she said. She led Gillard across the meadow onto Bourne Lane and the hundred yards up to Willow Cottage. This attractive terraced house, with its small flower-filled front garden, showed what Dove Cottage could become with a little bit of care and attention.

'Are you the gardener?' Gillard asked, as Rowena unlocked the small rustic front door and let him in.

She laughed. 'No. Vicky used to do the garden, and she planted the flowers, but it's Stewie who maintains it. He's done a good job, hasn't he?'

The front door opened directly into a small and comfortable lounge painted in pastel colours, with new, pale carpets. Rowena took off her boots, and Gillard did likewise with his shoes. His eyes were drawn to a photograph of Crystal with Rowena, when the girl looked about twelve. On the mantelpiece there were a few oddments, beads and coins, that looked like they might have been archaeological finds.

'How long have you lived here?'

'All my life. I've pretty much had it to myself since Mum moved up into Haslemere a year ago.'

'Why the move?'

'Her business, really. She had a lot of evening bookings, and it just made more sense for her to be there most of the time. There was more space.'

'Easier for her when she had a boyfriend, right? Not having you around.'

She glanced shrewdly at him, trying to assess how much the detective already knew.

'Rowena, we already know Crystal was seeing Ozzy Blanchard.'

She nodded and turned away. 'I'll just go and get the tenancy book.' Without being asked, he followed her up the open-plan staircase to the upper floor. The upstairs was cramped, the landing crammed with shelves of history and archaeology hardbacks. As she went into the back box room, the one corresponding to the site of the murder had this been Dove Cottage, Gillard peeked into the girl's bedroom. A single bed, neatly made but with discarded clothes on it. There was a chest of drawers, a packet of contraceptive tablets on it and, hanging on a hook on the wall above, what looked like a fencing mask, with a black mesh face guard.

Hearing the sounds of Rowena emerging, he hurried out into the landing to see her appear with a big manila file. 'Have you just been in my room?' she asked indignantly.

'I peeked inside, but I could get a warrant if you'd prefer to have half a dozen uniformed officers turn the place over.'

She looked annoyed, but said nothing.

'I see from the mask that you're a fencer as well as an archaeologist,' Gillard continued.

'I did a term of it at school. I was rubbish, so gave it up.'

'Did they let you keep the sword?'

She looked at him as if he was stupid. 'It's not a sword, it's a foil. At least that's what I used. You can also use an épée or a sabre. And no, they didn't let me keep it. I only got the mask because it's too damaged to be used.'

'Have you ever used an Anglo-Saxon sword or dagger?'

'You mean did I kill the person found by the river? No, I haven't, and no, I didn't.'

Rowena led him downstairs. 'Right, this is a list of all the tenancies for the properties our family owns. There's quite a bit, actually, stuff Mum and Vicky inherited after my nan committed suicide.'

Gillard considered the tragedy of the Willows. Grandfather murdered in 1982, the grandmother committing suicide at Rissington Sluice a decade later. Michael inherited the farm, sisters Crystal and Vicky left to cope on their own. A steady stream of inherited income would be no substitute for the lack of an enfolding family.

Rowena pulled out a small file from within the folder. 'That's the formal tenancies for Dove Cottage going back to 1990,' she said. The documents were neatly laid out in what he presumed was Crystal's handwriting. He shuffled past the earlier residents, until he got to 2012. That was the year the bloodstained book was printed. It was impossible that the carnage in that bedroom could have occurred any earlier. The tenant at that time was the Rev Stephen Timpson, who stayed four years. From 2016, when he left, no tenants were noted until Cleaver's arrival last year.

'Is this it?' Gillard asked, holding up the sheaf of papers. 'Vacant for three years from Timpson's departure?'

'Well, it wasn't always empty. Rory stayed here for a couple of months—'

'Rory Tickett, the boxer?'

'Yes. Soon after he lost his big fight. He had a nervous breakdown, and fell out with his family. He came here for a few weeks to hide from the press.'

'That would be 2016. But there's no record of it,' Gillard said.

'No. I suppose he paid in… *cash*,' she whispered, holding her head in mock horror as if Gillard worked for the tax authorities.

'Any others?'

'There was a foreign guy who worked behind the bar at the Anvil for a while, he stayed for most of one summer, and there were occasional stays by contractors.'

'All these cash in hand?' Gillard said, looking in vain for any records. 'Who were the contractors? Were there any from the water company?'

Rowena stared at him. 'Possibly, there were loads of them down here for months. You'd have to ask Mum. I've only been looking after the paperwork for six months. I am only sixteen.'

'We've been trying to ask her, Rowena, but she seems determined to avoid me.'

The girl shrugged. 'We Willow women are very independent, you know.'

'So it seems. Including you, living on your own?'

'Yes. It's not hard. Vicky's up the road if I need anything.'

'Where exactly is your mother staying?'

'I don't know. She doesn't tell me. I think she's been moving about in her camper van.'

'She's been gone for six months, but caravan parks only reopened two weeks ago. So where was she staying in the interim?'

'No idea.'

'Is Ozzy Blanchard with her?'

Rowena shrugged, and gathered together the papers.

'Young lady, we are investigating a crime. As you know, a man is dead, buried down by the river, and perhaps killed in the house that your sister owns. Withholding evidence is a very serious offence. I'd like you to think very carefully. We will find your mother eventually, and you'll all be in much more trouble if you don't tell me what you know.'

Rowena narrowed her eyes. 'I'll tell you something I do know. Matt is *innocent*. He wouldn't harm a fly!'

'He's got a serious criminal record. In 2002 he beat a member of a rival drug gang with a crowbar badly enough to put him in a wheelchair for life.'

'He was different then! If you found something in that cottage, it isn't from him.' There were tears of anger in her eyes.

'Then from who?'

'Rory,' she whispered. 'It was probably him. He's a thug, and everyone is scared of him.'

'Do you have any direct evidence of this?'

'No. I just heard rumours.'

'Do know who the victim is?'

She shook her head.

'You're just making this up, aren't you?' Gillard asked softly. 'To protect Matthew Cleaver.'

'No I'm not!' she shouted, and began to sob.

'Have you been sleeping with him?'

'No.' Her reddening face said otherwise. 'Anyway, I'm sixteen!'

'Yes, but just a few weeks ago.'

There was no reply. Gillard had gone as far as he dared in an informal interview. He didn't discount the idea that

Rory Tickett could have been the murderer; the blood-stains he had seen looked lavish enough for the kind of power the ex-boxer possessed. Rowena was a tough girl, academically precocious but emotionally too; grown up before her time, cast into all the perils of an adult world. But anything she said had to be set against an abiding affection for Matthew Cleaver which she was incapable of hiding. That made her a poor liar, but a liar nonetheless. It would be hard to take anything she said at face value.

'I'll get someone to take your fingerprints and a DNA swab this afternoon,' Gillard said, as he stood to leave. 'It's just for elimination purposes.'

'Whatever,' she said, sniffing back tears.

'And as I mentioned, I need your phone. Just for a few hours.'

'No way. Arrest me if you want.' Her jaw was set, head high. A vision of martyrdom, ready to be nailed up on a cross next to the man she loved.

–

By nine p.m. Tuesday evening the CSI team were dismantling their tents at Dove Cottage. Gillard was standing with Kirsty Mockett in the garden, when he got emailed more forensic results. The fastest were, as usual, from the highly efficient fingerprint centre in Lewes, which Surrey Police shared with their Sussex counter-parts. The forensic list compiled by Kirsty Mockett now had fingerprints and elimination DNA samples from most of the village residents, many of whom had volunteered to be swabbed and printed to help speed up the inquiry. The DNA results would come in probably tomorrow morning, hopefully including a match for Crystal Willow.

Rowena had reluctantly surrendered the contents of her mother's wardrobe at Willow Cottage, and having looked over the clothing, Kirsty was confident of finding Crystal's DNA there.

'Have you seen these?' Gillard said, pointing to his iPad, as Kirsty was just rolling up her used Tyvek suit and fitting it into a large plastic evidence bag. She watched over his shoulder as he swiped through the attachments.

Cleaver's dabs were, as expected, found all over the house where he lived, and on some of the books. A single thumbprint of his was found on the bloodstained book that he claimed he didn't own. But that wasn't the only dab found there. Rowena's prints were on it too. There were plenty of hers in the house, particularly in the kitchen, but also on the metal frame of Cleaver's bed. Rowena was his cleaner, but it was still tempting to jump to other conclusions. This wasn't a direction Gillard wanted the inquiry to travel in. The girl was legal, just, and hadn't complained. As far as the law was concerned that was the end of it.

Stewie Ransome's prints were found downstairs, on a couple of door handles and in the shed, on the handles of various garden tools. On a few of those there were also prints from Vicky Willow and her partner Guy. Vicky's thumbprint also turned up on a bottle of bleach under the bathroom sink.

'There's no smoking gun,' Kirsty said. 'Cleaver could easily have innocently handled the bloodstained book after the crime took place. What about Vicky Willow? Dabs not only on the garden tools but on the bleach.'

'On its own it's not incriminating either,' Gillard said. 'Vicky could have been employed part-time as a cleaner between tenants for her sister, and we know she did some gardening along with her many other part-time jobs. She might've roped her husband in.'

'True. We've no prints from Rory Tickett,' Kirsty said. 'But maybe we'll find some DNA.'

While they were discussing this, they overheard a radio message broadcast to the various uniformed PCs in the vicinity.

'What was that?' Gillard asked the female officer nearby, having caught the words 'Aqua Western.'

She shrugged, and pressed the button to ask for a repeat from the control room.

Thames Valley Police just reported the abduction from home of Kelvin Arrowsmith, an employee of Aqua Western Ltd.

She acknowledged the message and glanced at Gillard. 'Does that mean anything to you, sir?'

'Yes, unfortunately it does. That man was Ozzy Blanchard's boss.'

Gillard swore silently to himself. If only Stella Anderson had shared details of her inquiry into Aqua Western, this news might make sense. As things stood, it merely made everything more urgent. Could it be that whoever Ozzie was in hiding from had turned their attention to his boss? Nothing else made sense. Gillard didn't doubt that Arrowsmith's life would be in danger.

Chapter Seventeen

Kelvin Arrowsmith resided in one of the best streets in Amersham. Finding the exact location in this secluded tree-lined avenue might have been tricky had Gillard not been guided towards the flashing blues of a half-dozen Thames Valley Police vehicles. The house was a new-build, accessed on a private drive squeezed between 1930s mock-Tudor detached homes. Gillard left his Vauxhall on the street, and after signing in with a uniformed officer at the perimeter of the crime scene tape, made his way up the laurel-lined driveway to the house. It was a typical executive-style home: a small wooden portico, a double garage, and detached – but only just. This second rank of new homes had all been built in the large gardens of the older houses, which had a street frontage. Apart from the police presence, there wasn't much here to indicate any kind of crime had been committed.

Detective Chief Inspector Eddie Nowak emerged from the front door to greet Gillard. He was youngish and prematurely bald, with metal rimmed glasses. After introductions, Nowak said: 'Two masked men abducted Arrowsmith at approximately eight twenty p.m. No one saw them arrive, and they left with Arrowsmith in his own Range Rover, which we've already found abandoned and burned out on farmland ten minutes away. Mrs Francesca Arrowsmith was tied up, but otherwise unharmed.'

'Was she able to give a statement?'

'Yes, a brief one. She says her husband had only been home from work for fifteen minutes, and was in the shower. She was watching TV when someone came into the room, and she assumed it was her husband. But it was some guy in overalls and a ski mask, who grabbed her, put a hand over her mouth, blindfolded her and tied her up.' Nowak looked down at his iPad, where the statement had been recorded. 'She then heard a disturbance, which indicated her husband was being beaten up.'

'Could she distinguish any voices?'

'No. All she heard was her husband begging for his life, and crying "No, no, no." Then the front door slammed, and she heard the car being driven away.'

'It sounds like whoever it was was lying in wait for him, having broken in earlier,' Gillard said.

'Yes. Seems fairly professional,' Nowak said. 'There is CCTV from next door which covers part of the drive, but because of the height of the hedges all it shows is the departing Range Rover. We've gone back two hours on the recording and there's nothing else to see. Mrs Arrowsmith was able to shuffle to a phone and raise the alarm within a few minutes.'

'Any contact with Arrowsmith's employer?'

'We rang them. They're in full panic mode.'

'I assume you've imposed a news blackout?'

'Yes. If there's a ransom demand we need to be able to deal with it without reporters breathing down our necks. Aqua Western are desperate to keep this quiet too.'

Gillard smiled to himself. 'I can see why. "To lose one water engineer may be regarded as a misfortune, but to lose two looks like carelessness".'

'Eh?'

'Lady Bracknell in *The Importance of Being Earnest*. Did it at school about a million years ago.' Gillard was always surprised at the useless things he remembered.

'She wrote about water engineers?' Nowak asked, incredulously. 'We didn't cover this book in my school in Warsaw.'

Gillard laughed. 'No. Never mind. Look, are we able to interview Francesca Arrowsmith yet?'

'No, she's in no state. Leave it an hour or two.'

'Okay, I'll take a look at the car then.' Gillard thanked Nowak and returned to his vehicle. It was a short drive to the edge of the built-up area, rural homes giving way to horse paddocks. A left turn led to a dead-end serving a couple of meadows. There in the gateway of one field was the smouldering wreck of the Range Rover, next to a fire tender and surrounded by half a dozen firemen. If a getaway vehicle had made tyre tracks, these had certainly now been expunged by the presence of a large fire appliance, and the thousands of gallons of water from a nearby hydrant that had been used to extinguish the fire.

The acrid stench of burned plastic in his nostrils, Gillard returned to his car, put on the aircon and rang Hoskins at Mount Browne. The nearest ANPR camera was a mile away, but would have been hard to avoid for anyone coming from the motorways. 'There are a couple of things I'd like you to do for me, Carl. I want to know if any of the Tickett's vehicles triggered a particular ANPR camera in Amersham yesterday.' He gave the location of the camera. 'See if you can get a triangulation of any of their phones since six this evening.'

He couldn't imagine the Willow women getting involved in an abduction, but the Tickett family was a different matter. Maybe they hadn't been paid for the work they did for Aqua Western. It might fit quite well with Ozzy Blanchard's fear.

–

Carl Hoskins had no sooner put down the phone to his boss when it rang again. It was Ray Slater, his former brother-in-law.

'I need another favour, Carl.'

'Jesus, Ray, give me a break.'

'I heard that someone at Aqua Western has been abducted.'

'How d'you hear that?'

'Never mind.'

'It's Thames Valley Police, you know that, don't you? Not us.'

'No problem, you can say you're digging for details on Gillard's behalf.'

'Sorry, Ray. I really can't, not this time.'

'All I need to know is who it is.'

'I can't tell you, Ray. News blackout. Can't even give you the location.'

'Is it Arrowsmith?'

'No comment.'

There was a pause on the other end of the phone. 'Carl. I can pay. A significant sum, honestly mate…'

Hoskins hung up. It was too tempting. He had debts, he needed a new car, the flat needed sprucing up. But he understood that once you started down that route there was no end to it. You were never coming back to the path of righteousness. Once a bent cop, always a bent cop.

Hoskins felt the familiar rumblings of hunger. All he could think of was the call of chips, preferably scaldingly hot, crispy and doused with vinegar, in the reassuring warmth of white crackly paper. What he had in front of him was a plastic box with the remains of a fruit salad, made for him by his daughter. Orange, grapes, and a banana now going black. He didn't fancy it, and in his head fought the temptation to slip out for chips. He took a deep breath, unclipped the lid of the box, and inhaled the sweet aroma of the fruit. With a plastic spoon he shovelled in the various pieces, then drained the syrup by holding the corner of the box above his mouth.

Feeling a little virtuous now, he started the process of making the traces that Gillard requested. But then he added an extra one. The registration number of his former brother-in-law's Nissan. It would be good to know how far and wide Ray Slater had been roaming. Hoskins had already made two fundamental decisions that night, both about choosing the right path: one for his health, and another on cutting links with his brother-in-law. And he felt good about both of them, as if he'd somehow started a new life.

–

The three a.m. incident room meeting was short and to the point. Gillard was joined by Detective Constables Rainy Macintosh and Carl Hoskins, and on Zoom by Shireen Corey Williams, still self-isolating. Hoskins, having worked the previous nightshift, was due to finish in an hour and presented the details of the ANPR searches he had done.

'There is one very important camera, on the back of an overhead gantry, which pretty much catches anyone coming off the M25,' he said. 'And it's done a good job.'

Two vehicles belonging to the Tickett family showed up. The first was an aged silver VW Golf belonging to Aidan and registered to his address in Upper Rissington. It had shown up as passing the camera on the way to Amersham at 5.13 p.m. and coming back at 8.26 p.m. A second vehicle, a midnight blue BMW X5 registered to Christopher Tickett, had passed once, coming back, at 8.26 p.m. 'There were no traces on any phones known to be registered to the family in that vicinity,' Hoskins said. 'Christopher Tickett's phone remained on and in place at the yard in Rissington Common throughout that day. So they must be using burner phones.' He made no mention of the final search, for Ray Slater's car. It had come back blank. If he had been anywhere near Amersham it was in a car they knew nothing about.

Gillard took over and gave Hoskins permission to go home. 'Our main focus now switches to the whereabouts of Kelvin Arrowsmith. Thames Valley Police remain in overall charge seeing as he was snatched on their patch, but now we know the Tickett family's cars were in the Amersham area, I think we bring the whole family in.'

He looked at his watch. 'We've got eight cars full of uniforms, a riot van full of our heftiest lads for the Tickett yard, and a single firearms unit just in case. We don't expect them to be tooled up, but you never know. That's forty-six officers in total, split between three locations: the builders' yard, Rory Tickett's new house near Haslemere, and Aidan's home in Upper Rissington. We're going in at five a.m. I'm going to brief them in half an hour.'

—

Christopher Tickett was detained after a siege of the yard in which two officers were bitten by guard dogs, and another fell over rusty machinery and gashed his cheek. Aidan Tickett and his girlfriend Jo were arrested without incident in the bedroom of his house in Upper Rissington. But the attempt to take Rory 'Typhoon' Tickett went pear-shaped right from the start. The first two patrol cars pulled up outside the wrong house, officers realising their mistake just before using the door ram. The correct address was 14 Rissington Lane, but they had missed the tiny turning and arrived at 14 Lower Rissington Road. By the time they had arrived at the correct address, Gillard was almost there himself. He was in a Ford Focus patrol car with PCs Michael Craven and Alan Dearing when a black SUV swept past them in the other direction.

'That's Rory Tickett's car,' Gillard said.

'Right, we'll get after it,' Craven said from the driver seat. He managed a rapid three-point turn, then set off to follow the Audi RS Q8. Tickett was going at a hell of a pace for a country lane. High hedges obscured visibility, so it was good fortune that there was no other traffic. Dearing called in the details of the escaping vehicle, and asked for assistance. Gillard, trying to keep tabs on the rest of the raid, was forced to look up from his iPad because the movement of the car was making him bilious.

Tickett led them to a T-junction on a major road, and went left. The patrol car followed but was clearly no match for the acceleration of the Audi, which pulled away even as Craven reached 90 mph. Dearing was told by the control room that another patrol car was heading towards them on the same road, and was one minute away. They could see its headlamps and flashing blues in the distance.

'Tickett might well try to surprise us here, there are a few small lanes on either—' Gillard began. Before he'd finished, the Audi had indeed made a screeching right-hand turn, and headed off down a narrow hedge-lined lane. The Ford followed, just in time to see the Audi's headlamps swing left into an ungated field parallel to the main road. Craven followed, and watched the car ahead squeeze down a narrow headland between a high hedge on the left and a crop of rape on the right. The rough and bumpy ground slowed their speed to less than twenty, and the Audi with its four-wheel-drive had a definite advantage. Dearing used his radio to try to contact the following patrol car directly to get it to go back and close off the far end of the field. The land descended gradually and became rougher.

Gillard, his teeth rattled by the bouncing of the suspension, felt that Tickett was drawing them into a trap, away from help. At a culvert, the lowest point of the field, the Audi crossed a muddy ditch and accelerated hard up the rising slope beyond. The Ford slewed right, then left, crashing through the crop, but finding some traction in a shallow part of the ditch. Craven's driving was impressive, but they had lost ground behind the SUV, which was a good hundred yards ahead.

The big car pulled a U-turn and stopped, its lights on full beam now facing them.

Craven accelerated up the slope and stopped five yards short of the Audi. Tickett himself was standing silhouetted in front of his own vehicle, hands on hips. He looked enormous, and totally confident. This was after all a man who had gone twelve rounds with some of the world's top middleweights.

The three cops extricated themselves from the vehicle, trying to shield their eyes from the dazzling lights. Gillard shouted for Tickett to turn the headlamps off and then lie on the ground. He guessed there was zero chance of this happening. 'Lie on the ground,' Dearing bellowed, while Craven was just fitting a new cartridge into his Taser.

Tickett picked his moment and crossed the few yards between them in two strides. The fist on Dearing's jaw seem to lift him right across the bonnet of the Ford, colliding with and unbalancing Craven, who dropped the Taser. Gillard leapt and grabbed Tickett's right arm, but the big man swung him around, trying to reach him with his left. Dearing seemed to be unconscious, Craven scrambling to pick up his weapon. Gillard dodged a left hook, but the following jab caught him straight in the ribs and knocked the breath out of him. At that moment Craven yelled 'Taser' and discharged the weapon. Gillard, still hanging on to Tickett's right arm, felt a searing jolt of electricity which seemed to jerk him away. Tickett fell too, but was already getting up when Craven fired a second time. Unconnected to the target now, Gillard was able to jump on the big man as he screamed from the second charge. But even with Craven's help, keeping Typhoon Tickett on the deck was no easy task. It was five minutes of undignified wrestling before the eventual arrival of Dearing, now properly conscious, which allowed them to handcuff him.

It was only when Tickett was finally installed in the back of the patrol car that Gillard had a moment to inspect himself and found drops of blood all over his shirt and jacket. For a few moments he looked for a stab wound that he hadn't felt, but then he saw Dearing's face. That was where the blood had come from. His nose was pouring.

At Winchester Police Station, the Ticketts were cautioned then kept in separate cells, as far away from each other as possible. It was gone eight a.m. by the time a duty solicitor was found so Gillard could interview them. In the intervening time he'd heard that Typhoon had been living up to his name, periodically throwing himself bodily at the door. The other two had been quieter. Christopher Tickett was brought up first. Gillard sat with Rainy Macintosh as the brief arrived. He wasn't one of the generic duty types, but a distinguished-looking fellow called Piers Tolliver from a top Winchester firm. Gillard knew he would be expensive, and realised that Tickett probably had more money than he imagined.

'So, Christopher. Bring back some happy memories does it?' Gillard gestured at the bleak surroundings.

'Fuck off,' he replied. 'And you can quote me on that,' he added, glancing at his brief.

'Whereabouts is Kelvin Arrowsmith, Christopher?'

'I don't know who you're talking about.'

'Really? We have photographic evidence showing your BMW was in the vicinity of his home at the time he was abducted.'

'Yeah, and I visited the World Trade Center in 2001. Don't mean I blew it up, does it?'

'Aidan's car was nearby too. Just too much for coincidence, don't you think?'

'Not really. We're thinking of buying some land up there.'

'Where?'

'Amersham way.' The moment he said it, Christopher Tickett blinked as if realising something.

'That's interesting,' Gillard said. 'How did you know it was Amersham that he lived in?'

The silence lasted half a minute. 'One of the cops told me while I was being arrested.'

'Och, that's a sad wee pack of lies, the kind you get free with petrol,' Rainy interjected.

'Excuse me, detective constable,' Tolliver said. 'It is my client's position that he was made aware of the location by an arresting officer. You're in no position to contradict it, are you?'

'I might well be,' Rainy retorted. 'As soon as we get inside his various computers and laptops recovered at the time of the arrest, we will be able to establish whether there have been any web searches for land in the area.'

'And I shall certainly be asking the arresting officers if they mentioned where Arrowsmith lived,' Gillard added. 'But I strongly suspect that the only reason for your client to have this knowledge is that he acquired it as part of planning the kidnap.'

'To what possible end?' Tolliver added. 'My client had no reason to be involved.'

'We have a few ideas,' Gillard said. 'So, Mr Tickett, you do not deny that at the time of the abduction you were in the vicinity of the victim's home?'

'I don't know exactly where he lived. The copper didn't give me the address, just the town.' Tickett folded his arms and leaned back with apparent satisfaction on the plastic chair, which creaked in agreement.

'So what is it that you have against Kelvin Arrow-smith?' Gillard asked.

'I told you, I don't know the guy.'

'Aye, but you know Ozzy Blanchard, don't you?'

'The name is vaguely familiar,' Tickett said.

Tolliver leaned forward. 'Detective Chief Inspector Gillard, I think it's very clear that my client is not in a position to answer any of your questions. It seems to me that you have no basis for holding him, so I'd ask that you release him on police bail while you continue your enquiries.'

'No, he's going nowhere,' Gillard said, pressing the tape recorder to end the interview. 'I've got ninety-six hours to hold him before charge, as you well know.'

Tickett was returned to the cells, but Tolliver remained. Aidan Tickett was then brought into the interview room. He looked tired and unhappy, and rubbed his hand through his short ginger hair.

'I'm missing work because of this,' he said.

'We're investigating a very serious offence,' Rainy said. 'Have you ever met Kelvin Arrowsmith?'

He rubbed his chin. 'A few months ago, maybe, when he came down to look at the work we were doing for Aqua Western. And when the body was discovered.'

'Do you know where he is now?' she asked.

'No idea.'

'Where were you yesterday evening at six o'clock?'

'At home with my girlfriend.'

'And the lassie would back up that story, would she?' Rainy continued.

'Yes.'

'So how come your car was spotted close to the home of Mr Arrowsmith at that time?'

'I lent my car to a friend.'

'Which friend?' Gillard said.

'Just a mate,' he said.

'Name?'

'John Smith.'

'Address?'

'Can't recall.'

'You're not even a good liar,' Gillard said. 'Isn't it the truth that you, your father and brother drove over to Mr Arrowsmith's house and abducted him?'

Aidan shook his head. 'That's complete bollocks. Why would I do that?'

At this point Tolliver intervened: 'That's a valid question, detective chief inspector, and I hope you're going to answer it.'

'Certainly. I suspect you're involved in some kind of fraud and were expecting him to pay up.'

–

After Aidan Tickett was taken back to the cells, Gillard got on the phone to his opposite number in Thames Valley Police. The DNA elimination samples taken from Kelvin Arrowsmith's home were in the process of being compared to samples his forensic teams had taken from the seized BMW and VW found at two Tickett premises. Results were due later in the day.

'We need those results quickly,' he told Rainy after he had hung up.

'Aye. We dinnae have a scrap of incriminating evidence,' Rainy said. 'The ANPR is a mile from Arrowsmith's home. We need much more than that.'

'Thames Valley Police are combing Arrowsmith's home for any other DNA, but I'm not holding my breath. This seems to have been well planned.'

'So is it time to tackle the Typhoon?' she asked.

'Yeah, let's bring him in. I think he might prove the weak link.' He told Rainy what he had in mind, and she agreed.

They had prepared for a difficult interview with Rory Tickett. Two extra uniformed officers were in the interview room, and two more stationed just outside. As it happened the interviewee was now more morose than furious. To repeated questions about the whereabouts of Arrowsmith he simply answered: 'No comment.' He fidgeted constantly, biting his nails, staring around the room or at the ceiling, and fidgeted his legs enough to disturb the tape. Gillard would have stopped him had anything been recorded they felt worth saving. After half an hour, he turned off the tape recorder, and announced the interview was over. Tolliver departed immediately, while the uniforms got ready to escort Rory back to his cell. Gillard indicated for them to wait.

'It's been a long night, Rory,' he said. 'Do you want a coffee?'

'I'd kill for one.'

Gillard asked one of the uniforms to get some coffee and biscuits. Rainy excused herself too, by prior arrangement, and left the room.

'I saw you fight against Lasorenko. You landed some great punches in the third round. That uppercut a few seconds before the bell would have floored any normal man.'

'I think his head is made of iron. I pounded it for so long.' He shook his head ruefully.

'His counterpunching was impressive too. Such a long reach.' Gillard had researched the bout on YouTube.

'He's just so tall,' Rory said, animatedly. 'A big reach comes with it. I was faster, but every time I got in close his right was smashing me on the left eye.'

'But even a loser's purse was enough to buy that very impressive house. Did that all come from the fight?'

'Yeah. Mostly, plus some of the earlier bouts.'

'How many bedrooms?' The coffee had arrived with a plate of chocolate digestives. Gillard offered them to Rory, who took one.

'Five. I need a good bit of space, and light. Full-length windows. Can't stand poky little places, does my head in. I've got my own gym at the back, there. I've got to keep exercising, or I run to fat.' He gave a slight smile, the first they had seen out of him. Gillard asked more: were the weigh-in confrontations stage-managed? Or were they a genuine enmity? Rory responded positively, as if he was being interviewed by the press.

'No, all that stuff is PR. I've often trained with some of these guys on the quiet.'

'You look very impressive to me; I just wondered why you gave it all up?'

There was a long drawn-out sigh. 'You have to pick your moment. I was going to retire after getting the title. But Denys Lasorenko got in the way. I had a broken jaw to contend with and it didn't heal well. Besides, Pa said he got a good bit of business for me that we would do well with.'

'Property development?'

Rory looked at his fingernails, and began to chew again. 'Yeah. Some.'

'Was that in Buckinghamshire?'

'No. Didn't have anything up there. It was more local—' He suddenly looked up at Gillard. 'No comment.'

'You didn't have a reason to be up there in Amersham, did you, Rory?'

'No comment.'

Gillard wanted to switch the tape back on, but couldn't do so without a solicitor present. Tolliver had departed, and getting a duty brief might take a while.

Rory drank from his coffee, his eyes shooting daggers at the detective.

'You're going down, Rory. I hope you understand that. A long stretch. In a tiny, dark, poky room, just like this one here.'

The man put down the coffee cup. His face was flecked with fear.

'Just tell me where, Rory. Where is Arrowsmith?'

There was no reply.

Chapter Eighteen

The searches of the various Tickett homes dragged on through Wednesday morning. The easiest was Rory's. For all its luxury, the newly built house had been sparsely furnished and apparently barely lived in. A brand-new and seemingly unused laptop computer was recovered, but little else for Rob Townsend to get his teeth into. There was no mobile phone there nor on Rory, and nothing was found in his car. Aidan Tickett's home in Upper Rissington yielded a couple of mobile phones and a laptop, which his girlfriend Jo insisted were hers. It was the Tickett yard and Christopher's static caravan that offered the real treasure trove. A dozen dumb phones, some still in their boxes, and a couple of grubby and ancient laptops.

Gillard called a hurried incident room meeting at Mount Browne at eleven a.m. Shireen Corey Williams was on Zoom, while Carl Hoskins, Rainy Macintosh and Michelle Tsu were there in person along with Rob Townsend.

'This is where things stand,' Gillard said, as he pointed to a whiteboard with adjacent circles around the names Blanchard, Arrowsmith and one around the label 'Rissington Man'. 'One murder, one disappearance, and one abduction. This definitely shifts the focus onto Aqua Western.'

'Have you got a definite ID for the body yet?' Shireen asked.

'No, we only know who it isn't. How have you been getting on with Aqua Western?'

'I initially focused on the idea that Ozzy Blanchard had been involved in some kind of fraud, but the documents I've been sent from their head office don't show anything untoward in the audit trail.'

'Can you be more specific?' Gillard asked.

'If there's a fraud it's probably of the plain vanilla kind. According to Arrowsmith, it looks like Blanchard and the contractors were simply inflating invoices beyond what the work actually cost and sharing the proceeds.'

'So just to be clear, you had been talking to Arrowsmith before his abduction?' Gillard asked.

'Yes, I spoke to him that afternoon. Aqua Western referred my queries to him because he was the regional financial controller. He told me he'd also been working with Stella Anderson from Hampshire Constabulary.'

'That would be very convenient for him if he was involved in the fraud too, wouldn't it?' Gillard asked. 'DCS Anderson might not have drawn the net wide enough.'

'Yes. If it was something elaborate involving Arrowsmith, it would be possible for the entire audit trail to have been falsified,' Shireen said. 'I have to emphasise there is no evidence of that, because I've only been able to scratch the surface so far. We would need a full-scale forensic accounting investigation that might take months. And maybe DCS Anderson is already doing that.'

'I might be dim,' Hoskins interjected. 'But the simple fact that Arrowsmith was abducted would indicate he was mixed up in something naughty.'

'What if he staged his own abduction, so that he can disappear with the money?' Rainy asked.

Gillard nodded. 'That had occurred to me. I'd already requested a financial order on Arrowsmith's accounts with Thames Valley Police. That should come through later today.'

'What about the Willow women?' Rainy asked. 'Crystal Willow left her home at the same time as Ozzy Blanchard disappeared. She is apparently still in contact with her sister and daughter. Aye, there is something not quite right about it.'

Townsend raised his arm. 'I've just started to go through the messages and emails on Crystal Willow's burner phone. Most of them don't tell us very much, as they were clearly being careful. One from Rowena warns her mother that the police have been asking about Oz, presumably Ozzy Blanchard. "Say 0" is the reply. One message sent by Crystal to her sister Vicky was, "I've got my hands dirty quite enough, thank you."'

Gillard sighed. 'Hmm. Suspicious without being incriminating. Keep digging, see what else you find.'

Townsend nodded. 'The triangulation on Crystal's new phone showed that she moved around a fair bit; we got her located on three different campsites in the last week. I've sent Thames Valley images of Ozzy Blanchard to take around to the sites in case anyone recalls him travelling with Crystal, even though he may not be now.'

'That's good work,' Gillard said. 'Now I've one final decision to make, whether to let Rev Cleaver back into his house.'

Townsend shook his head. 'I need more time on his devices. I've got three technicians and they're all snowed under with stuff from the Tickett homes, tracing messages on the Willow women and so on. I had thought we could leave Cleaver's stuff until last.'

'We can't do everything at once,' Gillard said. 'Finding Arrowsmith has to be our priority. As for Cleaver, he's been cautioned but not charged, and I've only got a day or so left to keep him in a cell. As CSI has finished with his house and garden I can't see a reason not to let him return. But let's keep an eye on him.'

–

The financial order requested by Gillard was broader than the one already in force from Hampshire Constabulary. It covered not only Kelvin Arrowsmith's own bank accounts but those of his wife for the past year. In Gillard's experience a man engaged in financial skulduggery would often use the accounts of his wife or even his kids to hide illicit funds. It just made sense to draw the net as widely as possible. The details that came back showed nothing to attract attention – at first. Gillard copied in Shireen Corey Williams, and agreed to split the work so that he looked through the most recent month in detail, while she gave a quick scan to the older transactions and the couple's savings accounts. There had been no cash card withdrawals and no significant credit card spending from either of them in the last couple of weeks. On the day of the abduction the only transactions were a few small contactless payments made by Francesca Arrowsmith.

Gillard rang Shireen to see what she had discovered. 'There's a couple of interesting things,' she said. 'There is a movement of one-point-two million pounds into their joint savings account nine months ago, which was transferred out again in euros two days later from her current account. Then another payment of one-hundred-thousand from the same source just a month ago, which was again transferred in euros.'

'Those are interestingly large sums of money,' Gillard said.

'Well, they could be buying a property abroad. It doesn't have to be illicit.'

'True. But that's one substantial property. Perhaps you can investigate the source of the funds and the payee abroad.'

'I've got the IBAN codes, so I can get the banks making the payment, but that might only be half the story.'

'Okay. If they are buying a Spanish villa or something it would probably show up on their web search history, so I'll get Rob Townsend to take a look when he finally gets a moment. I'm going to ring Francesca Arrowsmith and ask her.'

Gillard hung up, and rang the landline at the Arrowsmith home in Amersham. It was answered by Family Liaison Officer Soraya Shah from Thames Valley Police, who said they had been peppered with press calls since news of the abduction emerged. Gillard asked her if she was within hearing of Mrs Arrowsmith. She wasn't.

'Has Mrs Arrowsmith said who she thinks might have done this?'

'No, sir. She has no idea. She's absolutely distraught.'

'Understandable. Have you heard her talk about plans to move abroad?'

'Oh yes. She kept telling me, especially in the first few hours, that it was their dream to retire to southern Italy. They had travelled there for many years, and bought a place last year.'

'Did she show you any photographs of it?'

'Yes, it's an absolutely gorgeous villa in the hills of Apulia. In fact there is a printout of the estate agent particulars on a coffee table.'

'How much was the asking price?'

'Just a tick,' the officer said. Gillard heard the shuffling of papers. 'One-point-three million.'

'That was very indiscreet of her,' Gillard said.

'Was it? She said that it was a thirtieth anniversary present from her husband last October, who had been saving up for this moment for decades. She is absolutely devastated that all their dreams might be shattered.'

Gillard thanked her and hung up. The Amersham house might be worth a million at a push, but it wasn't up for sale. The balances from the other accounts he could see didn't quite add up to the kind of money required for that villa. Could Arrowsmith have got a loan? Perhaps. While waiting for Shireen, he examined the photographs taken at the Arrowsmiths' home and the list of electronic items taken away. While the search history on the various computers had not yet been examined, the passwords to Arrowsmith's personal email accounts had been noted. According to the log, Thames Valley Police had examined those going back a month, and found nothing relating to the abduction. Gillard decided to have a look further into the past. There were thousands of emails, and he only really had time to judge by the subject lines, which proved Kelvin Arrowsmith had been heavily involved in the purchase of the property. He spent an hour and found nothing incriminating. Frustrated, he decided to take a very quick scan through Francesca Arrowsmith's account.

Just as he was about to log off he struck gold, in a completely different direction.

There was an online receipt for an Apple smartwatch bought last October. It was a fancier version of the one that Gillard had bought for Sam for her birthday, and he knew it had a GPS tracker on it. It could well have been an anniversary present for Arrowsmith, and if he had been wearing it at the time of the abduction, they might be able to trace him. Gillard rang the liaison officer again, asked her to find out if the watch was indeed bought for Arrowsmith, and if so could she get hold of the unique product ID which should be with the paperwork.

Ten minutes later Gillard had all the information he needed to approach Apple.

—

Gillard was awoken at two a.m. on Thursday by a call from the Met Police liaison unit which specialised in dealing with California's tech giants. Apple had come good, and had forwarded a dynamic trace of Kelvin Arrowsmith's smartwatch. He got out of bed and dressed rapidly, with a rising sense of excitement. This was a quicker result than he had expected. On a couple of previous occasions, when seeking the contents of messages on encrypted platforms, he had discovered that a court order had to be filed in the relevant district in the US.

A phone wasn't the ideal way to examine a map, but it showed enough detail to make it clear that the smartwatch had travelled from Arrowsmith's home to the vicinity of Rissington Common in the first two hours after his abduction. Then the signal went dead. That could be good news. If Arrowsmith was being held inside a building, the chances were that GPS satellite signal would not get through. Likewise, it could be bad news. If they'd killed him and buried the body, you'd get no signal either. The other option was that the abductors had discovered the watch, realised its significance and destroyed it.

Michelle Tsu was covering the nightshift at Mount Browne, and he messaged to ask her to maximise the map and pinpoint the exact location where the last signal was received. He would be at Mount Browne in half an hour, and they would rope in a couple of patrol cars to head down to the village. He reminded her to copy in Thames Valley Police.

He was already in the car when Michelle rang him. Answering on the hands-free, he listened as she described the last location as being in a field close to the river. 'It's pretty much where the first body was discovered,' she said.

'I don't want you thinking about a second body, Michelle. Be optimistic. He might still be alive.' As he rang off, he heard her mutter: 'And pigs might fly.'

By the time he arrived at Mount Browne, Michelle was already in the car park talking to uniformed officers from the two patrol cars that were going to take them to the site. Gillard remembered to move his grab bag of wellingtons and torch from the boot of the Vauxhall before they set off.

–

The two patrol cars slid quietly through Rissington Common as the first predawn light was beginning to seep over the horizon. There was no traffic, and no one about. The vehicles eased their way down Bourne Lane past the Tickett yard on the left, and beyond Willow and Dove cottages on the right. The first fingers of rosy dawn silhouetted the spire of St Crispin's church. In the second car, Gillard was looking at his iPad, on which their GPS position was marked relative to the fixed point of the last known position of Arrowsmith's watch. The two dots were almost in eclipse. Next to him, DC Michelle Tsu had an iPad with the dynamic map on it. There was no change in position, no fresh signal.

A uniformed officer from the first car opened the gate into the meadow, and the two vehicles trundled across the uneven grassland until they reached the high embankment on which the excavator still stood. Gillard magnified the map as far as possible, which indicated that they still needed to go further east, deeper into the meadow. 'At the other end of this is Rissington Lock, but that's more than half a mile away. I think we need to go on foot from here.'

Five uniformed officers led by a sergeant joined the two detectives, leaving one PC with the cars. They began on the embankment, whose firm stony surface was easier underfoot than the overgrown and soggy meadow. After 200 yards, Gillard stopped them and cross-checked his map with that of DC Tsu. 'It looks to be about here,' he said.

'Well that's it,' said the sergeant, shining a powerful torch across the ground. 'He's dead and buried, somewhere here.' Michelle Tsu nodded her agreement.

There was already enough light to see their footing, and Gillard descended from the embankment. 'This looks like part of the earlier excavation,' he said. 'The vegetation hasn't fully regrown.'

'The dog handler should be here in half an hour,' the sergeant said from the top of the embankment. Gillard had requested a cadaver search dog, which was being driven over from Kent. In the meantime, he could do his own searching. The detective crouched down and shone his torch, moving along the compacted plant-free soil which marked a recently buried pipe. He spent five minutes edging along the scarred meadow, while his colleagues watched him.

'There's an inspection cover under here,' he said. He took some photographs on and around the metal plate, which showed that someone had carefully spread fresh earth around to hide it. Michelle and the uniformed cops joined him, and traced the 3' x 2' lid set in a concrete surround. Gillard knelt down on it and with the metallic shaft of his torch tapped against the metal plate. 'Anyone down there?' he called.

He pressed an ear against the cool manhole cover. There was no sound except an echoing drip.

'I still think this is the place. Let's get the lid off.' There were two recessed handles in the thick iron lid. He took one, and the larger of the uniformed officers took the other. There was a scraping sound as the heavy plate was heaved out and slid across its concrete surround. The stench of sewage was overpowering, but what they saw within shocked them even more.

Chapter Nineteen

A three-foot-wide shaft with access ladder descended twenty feet until it met a seemingly full sewer, noxious liquid drifting left to right. From the lower rungs an inert gagged figure dangled by his tied wrists, chest deep into the filth. Gillard called out to him, and saw slight movement in his head, and heard a muffled moan. Arrowsmith, still definitely alive.

Not getting any other volunteers, the detective began to descend the slippery and corroded ladder into the stench, until his feet were below the wrists and immediately above the hostage's head.

'We'll soon have you out, don't worry,' he said.

The hostage's body was trembling and he was groaning through his gag. Rats swam for cover in the side pipes as Gillard crouched down, just two feet above the sewage, then reached below his own feet to untie the gag. Arrowsmith was exhausted, fearful and desperate. 'Don't free my hands,' he croaked, 'My legs are dangling below the end of the ladder, and I'll fall in.'

The detective realised he wasn't in a position to effect a rescue single-handedly, and could not take Arrowsmith's weight. It took the arrival fifteen minutes later of fire service officers with a lifting harness to get the captive to the surface, where paramedics gave him oxygen. Conscious but shivering and terrified, he was taken by ambulance to hospital. He had said nothing about his abductors, but simply asked that his wife be informed that he had been found. It was three hours later when Gillard was given medical permission for a five-minute interview at his bedside. Arrowsmith didn't look too bad now he'd been cleaned up, only complaining about being cold, wet and filthy in the pipe.

'So who put you in there, Kelvin?'

Arrowsmith shut his eyes, and licked his lips. 'I can't say.'

'Was it the Tickett family? We've already got them in custody. Rory, Aidan and Christopher. You're quite safe. There's a PC on the door here, and Thames Valley Police have promised you the liaison officer can stay with your wife for another week at least.'

'I'm scared.'

'That's understandable, but we do need your co-operation to nail them.'

Arrowsmith shut his eyes again and nodded. 'I do get that.'

Gillard had saved the most important question for last. 'Did you double-cross them? Is that why they grabbed you?'

Arrowsmith looked at Gillard and shook his head slowly: 'I uncovered their little scam with Ozzy Blanchard. That's why they came for me. Ozzy must have realised. They rang me a few times at home, and warned me to keep my mouth shut.'

He wanted to ask how the scam was constructed, but it was at that point that a nurse came in and asked Gillard to leave. What Arrowsmith had told him was a tenable motive, but there were other ways of making sense of the abduction. He'd keep an open mind. The sooner he got to talk to Ozzy Blanchard, the happier he would be.

–

Back at Mount Browne for the ten a.m. incident room meeting, Gillard was exhausted after the all-nighter. It seemed to have been Thursday for days already. He got to work updating the whiteboard. As he did so, Carl Hoskins approached, coffee in hand. 'If Arrowsmith had died in there, I suppose he would have been interred.'

'Yes, Carl. But as it was, he was only going through the motions.'

'Aye, you're a rare double act of poor taste,' Rainy Macintosh said, as she pulled up a chair. 'I'm surprised the poor wee hen wasn't overcome by fumes in such a clarty place.'

'Well according to the man himself, the flow release had been set on a timer, to gradually pump out the storm tanks,' Gillard said. 'When he was first put in there, it was only up to his ankles.'

Rainy blew a sigh. 'Och, that's evil genius. They knew how to punish the man.'

'But for what?'

'Arrowsmith reckons he'd uncovered a fraud, and when he held back the money they expected to be paid, they came for him.'

'So it's obviously the Ticketts,' Rainy said. 'They're the contractors. They did the work.'

'So it would seem,' Gillard said. 'I'd much prefer if we had a confirmation from an independent source of the nature of the fraud. And I'd really like to talk to Ozzy Blanchard.'

'Aye, the Scarlet Pimpernel of the water industry,' Rainy said.

Carl Hoskins scratched his head. 'Pardon me if I'm being stupid, but how did the Ticketts know which person in Aqua Western signed the cheques, unless they'd already met?'

'Maybe Blanchard told them,' Rainy said. 'Or maybe they read the signature. They can read, can they not?'

'Or maybe they were all in it together,' Carl said.

'That's certainly a possibility I favour,' Gillard said. 'Maybe we'll find out later on. Arrowsmith is about to be released from hospital. Thames Valley Police are interviewing him at home later and I hope to be there.'

'Och, his poor wee wife must be relieved.'

'I'm sure.' Gillard broke off to answer a call. It was DCS Stella Anderson.

'Hello Craig, I'm delighted that you discovered Mr Arrowsmith. Now, just to keep you in the loop, as you had asked. I've just got off the phone with DCI Eddie Nowak at Thames Valley, and told him the news embargo is being retained until the Serious Fraud Office has gone in at the water company's London head office.'

'That's fine with me,' Gillard said. 'I understand there were local news reporters snooping around at Amersham, but I don't think anything significant has broken through to the national press. I'll make sure my team is on-message.'

'I knew I could rely on you, Craig. We had originally hoped for another couple of weeks, just to see how extensive the fraud is. However, events have overtaken us and we have to act quickly.'

'I'd guessed that this was what you were working on.'

'Not surprising, really, given my background. Look, I'm catching the Waterloo train for an emergency meeting at the SFO this evening. I could break the journey at Woking, if you're able to meet me for an early bite to eat. Say five p.m. at the sushi place by the station? I can finally fill you in on all the details.'

'Yes, that would be fine. I'd happily eat anywhere except the Anvil Arms at Rissington Common.'

She laughed. 'Yes, quite the worst food I've ever had.'

–

Slipping into the Mount Browne toilets with a fresh shirt from his locker, Gillard looked himself over. Stubble, as so often, was beginning to show on his chin, and his hair needed a good comb. The prospect of sharing a meal with Stella Anderson was a real opportunity to find out exactly how extensive the fraud was. But it was also making him nervous. Her superiority in rank, and the fact she had a personal score to settle with him, would have him on the defensive – and she'd know it. He texted Sam to say that he would be eating out that evening, just in case she was planning to prepare something. His thumbs hovered over the phone. Should he mention who he'd be dining with? He didn't think he'd ever mentioned Stella to Sam. Their one-night stand was ancient history. He had always promised to be honest with her, but couldn't see an upside to this disclosure. It would just lead to more questions.

So he said nothing.

He changed his shirt, had a quick shave with the battery-powered razor retrieved from his desk, and while combing his hair once again lamented its greying. Finally, with his tie looped over his shoulder, he brushed his teeth.

He was almost finished when the bathroom door crashed open, and Carl Hoskins wandered in.

'Thursday night date, sir?'

'Eh?' he said, toothbrush still protruding from his mouth.

'Brand-new shirt with creases from the packet, deodorant and razor laid out. Is it for Sam, or are you playing away with the gorgeous Rev Matt Cleaver?'

Gillard rinsed, then dried his mouth with a paper towel. He was used to DC Hoskins' good-natured insubordination, but had no intention of giving any extra information to the rumour mill.

'That's very funny, Carl. So how is the new diet going?'

He waggled his hand sceptically. 'It's fine for breakfast and grabbing a bite during the day. My daughter Diane has been making me fruit salads to bring in. Trouble is they don't fill you up, and by teatime I'm gagging for something with a bit of grease. Last night she cooked me some pasta with low-fat cream cheese.'

'Sounds like she's looking after you.'

'Yeah, but then after a couple of jars down the Three Feathers I couldn't resist a doner kebab.'

Gillard chuckled. 'Kebabs are the ultimate crime against the human gut.'

'Not to mention the stabbings and punch-ups at the shops at pub throwing-out time.'

'And the money laundering.'

'Y'know,' Hoskins said, 'I've forgotten the number of times I've woken up in the morning still in my suit, and wondering how just three or four pints of gave me such a cracking hangover. Finding the shredded cabbage in my trouser turn-ups and hot sauce on my lapels is the giveaway.'

'Well, Carl, you're still living a misspent middle age.' Gillard collected together his toiletries, quickly grimaced in the mirror, and left.

–

The restaurant Stella had chosen was small and intimate, hidden above a convenience store. He was five minutes early, and was shown to the secluded table she had booked. From the dark recesses of the booth it was possible to see the entrance without being seen. From that shrewd choice of table, it was clear she had been here before. There was a steady trickle of takeaway customers at the bar, but back here they certainly wouldn't be overheard.

The detective chief superintendent arrived exactly on time, in dark trouser suit, heels and a white embroidered blouse. Her big hazel eyes and fine cheekbones were subtly made up and she looked pretty damn good, almost too good just for a meeting at the Serious Fraud Office.

After briefly greeting him, she said, 'Let's order immediately. I've got to be in and out in an hour for the next train.' They chose the mixed sushi and sashimi set order, which came with a salad and miso soup, and fizzy water to drink.

As the menus were taken away, Gillard asked, 'So when is the raid?'

'Tomorrow morning. Fifty officers, full forensic accounting team.'

'I do wish you'd been able to keep us in the loop from the start.'

'Well, we had information that there was a mole in Surrey Police.'

Gillard was astounded. 'Not in my team.'

'We weren't sure, but we had to take precautions. It just seemed safer to keep it under wraps. That's why I'm rather annoyed with you that we keep stumbling across the work of one of your officers, DC Corey Williams.'

'Well, I take full responsibility for it. I needed someone to see what was fuelling the disappearances and abductions, and you weren't telling me. I don't want to get in your way, but my case can't make progress without those financial details.'

'The SFO are hopping mad. We've just one senior contact, a whistleblower in the holding company who has fed us details and documents about irregularities across the group. But now your officer has been in touch with the finance director and corporate treasurer. There's a danger she might have compromised the whole operation by asking too many questions. If documents end up being shredded before we get there, it will be on your head.'

'I asked her to be careful. But look, ma'am, from what you're describing, this goes way beyond Ozzy Blanchard just doing a little side-hustle.'

'Yes, he's a minor player, and his fraud is only one of several across Aqua Holdings companies.' She started to draw on a napkin, sketching out boxes connected by arrows. 'Basic construction fraud is very common. Contractors over-bill for hours worked, materials purchased, equipment hire, that kind of thing. If the on-site surveyor for the customer is complicit, they will just share the proceeds. It's the simplest fraud imaginable, because it doesn't leave much of a paper trail. However, this one is a bit more sophisticated.' She paused while the two elegant dark wood plates were laid down. Sushi roll with avocado and cucumber, beautifully cut pieces of salmon and tuna, and a delicately arranged flower of translucent pink pickled ginger, plus a little knob of fiery green wasabi paste.

Once the waiter was out of earshot, she continued: 'We spent a long time digging into the audit trail between CJT Contracting (Hants) Ltd, the Ticketts' main company, and Aqua Western, which look fine, and did not exceed the purchase order. However, we have discovered an additional stream of payments from a different Aqua Western account that do not show up in the bank accounts of the contractor.'

'Okay, I'm with you so far,' Gillard said as they both lifted their chopsticks and began to eat. The salmon was tender and delicious, the flavour balanced by the salty umami flavour of soy, and the fiery wasabi.

'There are regional contingency accounts, supposedly controlled and signed off at the head office level. The whistleblower noticed that several of these accounts across the group had been ransacked over the course of a year or two. Someone senior within Aqua Western had found a way to siphon off money while balancing the books.'

'So what was happening to this money?'

'By tracing the IBAN numbers, the unique code for the banks involved, we were able to discover that it went to CJT Contracting (Surrey) Ltd, a very similar sounding firm, which was bought out of receivership in 2017.'

'Another Tickett firm, just a different county?'

She shook her head. 'Originally, yes, it was owned by the Ticketts before it went belly-up in 2014. But the current ownership has been carefully concealed offshore, something I would say is too sophisticated for the Ticketts. It wasn't their company by the time payments began. That firm received over four million pounds in this financial back channel.'

'So who is your whistleblower?'

She smiled. 'My ex-husband, who works under the group financial controller. It's thanks to him that while I seem to be simply investigating a small-scale fraud involving Blanchard, I'm getting much more. I'm being passed documents from other group companies which show that the financial rot goes right to the core of Aqua Holdings. It was when I discovered the extent of it that I called the SFO in. It's simply too big for Hampshire Constabulary.'

'So who, in the end, was getting all this cash?'

She smiled. 'It took a lot of digging, but we have managed to get right up to the top of a chain of offshore companies. And the owner is one Kelvin J. Arrowsmith.'

'So Arrowsmith has been signing company cheques which siphon off money into his own company?'

'Exactly.'

'How long has it been going on?'

'That's more difficult to establish. In this project, the payments stopped in January after an audit from head office. But since 2017 this same cloned company was used in at least half a dozen multi-million pound infrastructure projects commissioned by Aqua Western and Aqua Southern to receive money from the company, including another one involving the Ticketts in 2018.'

'That fits in with when the family began to spend big money,' Gillard said.

'We've still got months' more work to untangle it all.'

'So if Aqua Holdings initiated an audit, were they aware what was going on?'

'In some ways that's the most interesting part of the whole case. We uncovered plenty of evidence that someone senior at Aqua Holdings was aware of significant accounting irregularities at several subsidiaries as long as nine months ago. Thanks to Thames Valley Police, we found on Arrowsmith's laptop communications between him and the group financial controller. It was clear that when Arrowsmith was challenged he peddled the idea to senior management that he had been working for years to try to pin down Ozzy Blanchard's fraudulent activity. In fact it's now clear to me that he and Blanchard, and several other employees, must have been in cahoots. Blanchard was simply one of the minor players who Arrowsmith needed on the ground. However, Arrowsmith and his boss weren't as much intent on uncovering the fraud as on covering it up. Arrowsmith was asked to untangle the source of the embezzlement, but to keep secret the fact he was doing so. The company authorised the use of a private detective, but again this was known only to a few senior executives.'

'Why on earth would they do that?' Gillard asked.

'Because the water regulator Ofwat was just finalising a two-year-long investigation of the company, and whether it breached its statutory duties. It's a bit like an Ofsted inspection of a school, with the final report having huge implications for investors, and how cheaply the parent company can continue to borrow money in the financial markets. The company couldn't afford to have any bad news emerge before the report was published.'

'And when was that?'

'The end of June. Just a few weeks ago. Pity me, Craig, because I've ploughed through the entire thing, all 216 pages. There is plenty of mention of the poor operational performance in terms of sewage spills and so forth, for which it will continue to be fined, and some recognition of the investment made to prevent future occurrences. But ironically it is for financial management of all things that the company gets its best marks.'

'So to boil it all down,' Gillard said. 'The water company was taking at face value what the regional financial controller Kelvin Arrowsmith told it about the source of the fraud?'

'Yes.'

'And then conspiring with him to prevent the regulator and the financial markets discovering what has been going on.'

'It's not unusual, Craig. I've dealt with fraud and embezzlement for decades, and every time the reaction of companies is the same. Batten down the hatches, pay off the miscreants in exchange for a gagging clause, and pray that no one ever knows. It's true of hacking, of cyber-attacks, basically anything that affects the reputation of a company.'

'So they would have hated the fact you were investigating them?'

She laughed. 'In the early days I was told in no uncertain terms that it would be investigated internally, but they didn't think any crimes had been committed.'

Gillard shook his head with incredulity. 'It's going to be a big wake-up call for them tomorrow.'

'Damn right,' Stella said. 'I'm looking forward to it. And from then on, I will share all our findings with you.'

'Thank you. That would be appreciated. It will be fascinating to hear what Arrowsmith has to say for himself. I had wanted to be there myself to hear the story at first hand.'

She looked at her watch. 'Yes. DI Eddie Nowak will be interviewing him about now. And I have to go.' She rose from the table, gathered up her bag and phone, and surprised Gillard by giving him a peck on the cheek before turning and walking out.

-

While Gillard and Anderson were sharing a meal, Thames Valley Police brought Kelvin Arrowsmith home from hospital in an unmarked people carrier. Family Liaison Officer PC Soraya Shah gave him and his wife some space, and stepped out onto the front doorstep to talk to the young PC, Oliver Woodward, whose job it was to sign everyone in and out.

'He's lucky to be alive, from what I heard,' Woodward said, squinting into the light. 'They found him half buried in shit in a sewer.'

'Unbelievable what some people will do,' Soraya responded. 'She was so relieved when she got the call to say he was safe. Cried for half an hour.'

'Yeah, not surprising.'

'Should find out more when he's interviewed this evening,' Soraya said.

'Good job Surrey has nabbed the three guys responsible.'

'That saves you having to fight them off single-handedly when they come for a second go,' Soraya said with a chuckle. 'Fancy a cuppa?'

'Aw, yeah, I could murder one,' Woodward said. 'It's so boring just standing here.'

Soraya stepped back inside. She could hear the radio on in the kitchen, but no conversation. She shrugged. Maybe they had gone upstairs for a cuddle, or more. She considered they were perhaps a little too conventional to do this when someone else was in the house. She filled the kettle and flicked on the switch, and having already found her way round the cupboards, grabbed two fresh mugs, a couple of teabags and milk from the fridge. While the water was boiling, she wandered through to the dining room, which looked out over the back garden. On a hunch, she went to the loo upstairs instead of the usual downstairs toilet. The door to the marital bedroom was open, and after listening and hearing nothing she peeked inside.

They weren't there. But there were a heap of clothes on the bed, and the double wardrobe doors were open.

She guessed immediately. They'd done a runner.

She entered the room, checked in the en suite bathroom, and then looked out of the window. There was absolutely no sign of either of them. There was no back gate, and the sturdy wood-panelled fence was six feet high. It was one of the things that she had checked on her first day, when they were worried about Francesca Arrowsmith being targeted. The officer who'd come to assess the security had been equally reassuring that there was only one way in and out, and that was out of the front drive.

So how had they got away?

Soraya checked the time, and realised that DI Nowak was due in fifteen minutes to interview Kelvin Arrowsmith. If Soraya had let them escape she would be as deep in the unmentionable as Arrowsmith himself had been. With a rising sense of panic, she went through the rooms upstairs, opening every door. Then downstairs: the lounge, the sun lounge, Arrowsmith's private office. She made an urgent call to the control room with the bad news, then went back to PC Woodward on the doorstep.

He turned round smiling, expecting tea. What he got was something different.

'They've disappeared, Ollie.'

'You're joking! How?'

'I don't know. You've got to come and help me find them. I've got the key to the garage, but let's look at the fence first.'

The two officers made their way around the garden, until they reached a shed. There was a gap of eighteen inches between the shed and the fence, and it was in this spot, invisible from the house, that they discovered a pair of aluminium stepladders. Woodward climbed the ladder, and looked over the fence. 'It goes into another garden, but it's shielded from that house by some big laurel bushes. There is a wooden gate into a street, and it's open.'

The sound of a vehicle approaching at the front of the house made them turn.

'Shit! It's Nowak,' said Soraya. 'He's early.'

'We are going to get fired for this,' Woodward said.

'It's my fault, you were only on the door. It was my job to keep them in view.'

–

Gillard was driving home after the meal when he took a call from Stella Anderson. 'I've got some bad news, Craig.'

'Bad enough that I should pull over to hear it?'

She laughed. 'Not that bad, but bad enough. Kelvin Arrowsmith and his wife have disappeared from under the noses of Thames Valley Police.'

'Abducted *again*?'

'No, I think not. According to the family liaison officer, Mrs Arrowsmith had propped up a stepladder against the back fence behind the shed where it couldn't be seen, and when her husband was released from hospital they climbed the fence and into an adjacent cul-de-sac. Thames Valley thinks they may have taken a taxi. She's of Italian extraction and they've got some bolthole in Italy, so wouldn't be surprised if that's where they are heading.'

'Do you need any help from me?'

'I don't think so. Nowak's team has notified all the nearest airports and the ferry ports. I don't think they've got false ID. There was a big series of cash withdrawals across Mrs Arrowsmith's various bank accounts yesterday, so it has clearly been planned. Every other part of the raid is going ahead as expected. It will be weeks if not months before we know the full extent of the fraud, but we can now be sure that Arrowsmith was a major part of it.'

She hung up. Some things were falling into place. The Ticketts were double-crossed by Arrowsmith and Blanchard. The two water company employees had different strategies to cope with the unravelling of the fraud. Blanchard had disappeared, while Arrowsmith cast himself as gamekeeper, not poacher. All this made sense as far as it went. But what about Rissington Man, killed by an Anglo-Saxon blade in a room in Rev Matt Cleaver's house? The mysterious young man, murdered, buried, then dug up, moved and reburied to be discovered again. How did that fit in?

Chapter Twenty

Ray Slater was sweating as he headed north towards the M4. He was in his Nissan, following in the satnav cradle a trace from one of the phones he'd sold to Vicky Willow. He'd already watched her leave the pub at half-three in the afternoon, get into her aged Citroën C3 and drive away. Leaving a few minutes later, dressed in a subtle wig, stained overalls and engineer's boots, he followed. The Google map of her position appeared on his own satnav, so he didn't have to keep her in sight. She was a smart and perceptive woman and might recognise his car.

Everything was going well, but the change in instructions gnawed at his mind. He'd got the go-ahead for something he'd offered half in jest, not expecting to be taken up on it. Using the weighty object in his overalls pocket, liberated from the Royal Marines quartermaster's stores in Portsmouth nearly forty years ago and carefully hidden at home all that time. Forget piffling divorce cases. This was serious money, the big boys' league. But it raised the stakes all round. He'd planned it in his head, going through every detail that could be prepared in advance. The trouble was, it didn't just depend on him, but the behaviour of the target. He'd have to think on his feet.

He tracked her on the ninety-minute journey to Chieveley Services at the intersection of the A34 and the M4. She had now been there for ten minutes, the trace not moving. And now he saw a second red dot pop up in the same place. The second phone. The meeting with her sister, arranged by Vicky the previous evening, was to take place in the car park of the Travelodge budget hotel at the service area. He knew that, because he had downloaded the voice file. Vicky had said little on the call that wasn't strictly necessary, but did mention she had a new phone for Crystal. No doubt the trackable one he'd sold her.

Perfect. It was going like clockwork. Wherever Crystal was, Ozzy Blanchard wouldn't be far away. Slater had never fallen for the ruse that Ozzy was dead. It was clever, he'd grant them that, but not good enough to fool him. Tracking him down had been hard, but once the deed was done Ray would be on for his performance bonus. More cash than he'd put away in a lifetime of being a Met Police dog handler.

He took the slip road from the A34 northbound, hit the roundabout under the M4, and took the exit into the services. He was looking for a distinctive red Citroën C3, 2006 model. With the child seat and a parcel shelf full of soft toys it wouldn't be hard to find.

Slater felt his pulse quicken as he turned into the Travelodge car park.

The car wasn't there.

He pulled out, and circled through the bigger car park for the services. It took three laps before he found it. The little Citroën was hidden away in the lorry park by the boundary fence. To avoid Vicky seeing his car, Slater chose a slot in the main car park about fifty yards away, where with binoculars he could keep the Citroën in view. Vicky was in the driving seat and Crystal in the passenger side, the silhouette of her big head of frizzy hair a giveaway. The two women were deep in conversation. There was no sign of Ozzy. Slater scanned the nearby vehicles, most of which were articulated lorries. He couldn't work out which vehicle Crystal had come from. Wherever it was, Ozzy would surely be inside. His view was suddenly blocked by a van which had pulled into the adjacent slot. Slater realised he had to get closer. He pulled on a baseball cap, big sunglasses and a face mask, then slipped on a grubby high-vis tabard, as worn by almost all truck drivers. Finally, he plucked out an empty plastic coffee container from the cupholder. He emerged from the Nissan and headed for the lorry nearest the Citroën.

The disguise was perfect. He'd used it many times before. Vicky and Crystal continued talking. Slater went in front of the truck, past a couple of picnic benches strewn with burger wrappers and coke bottles, and sat on the boundary fence pretending to drink from the coffee container. From this vantage point, with the Citroën just twenty yards away, he also could see the entire car park. He just didn't know where Crystal had parked. He didn't know her car, but the nearest non-commercial vehicle was a good sixty yards away. He risked looking at his watch.

Fifteen minutes later the women were still talking. Normally, he'd be as patient as a saint. Sitting and waiting is the default activity of all private investigators. But now, so close to the money, and so much money, he was getting itchy. Where the hell was Ozzy?

The women had been there half an hour. Slater, still pretending to sip coffee, felt he was becoming noticeable. He'd seen Vicky glance at him twice in the last ten minutes. He just prayed that she didn't recognise him. To forestall this he moved away, heading towards the trees which lined the boundary fence. Beyond it there was a litter-lined service road running in parallel to the lorry park. Then he spotted a car parked, apparently for concealment, in the shade of a tree. A compact white Honda Civic four-door. A bearded man with a ponytail, a heavily tattooed neck and sunglasses was sitting in the driving seat, and he seemed to be as interested in watching the red Citroën as Slater had been. He didn't look much like Ozzy Blanchard, but then that's the point of disappearing. Grow your hair, get some tattoos and you're halfway there. Slater was confident that Ozzy didn't know what *he* looked like, and approached the car. There was lots of luggage on the back seat, including some camping gear and a guitar case.

The man inside buzzed the window down. 'Can I help you?'

'I'm a bit lost, and my satnav is broken. Have you got a map of the area?'

'Yes.' He leaned towards the passenger door and pulled out an A3-sized AA atlas. 'Where are you trying to get to?'

'A place called Rissington Common. I'd never heard of it, to be honest.'

The man laughed. 'I know it very well.'

'I know you do, Ozzy.' Slater pulled the Browning 9mm from his pocket, and pointed it at Blanchard's head.

'Oh, Christ. Who are you?' the man said.

'Never mind that.' Slater opened the rear door, and squeezed in amongst all the gear on the seat immediately behind the driver. 'We're going for a little drive.'

Gun pressed to the back of Blanchard's neck, Slater directed him to restart the engine, and had him drive around the service road and take a side-turning off onto a country lane which headed away from the service station. After half a mile he got Blanchard to turn off onto a single-track hedge-lined lane between arable fields. Slater told him to park the car in the gateway of a field near a pile of fly-tipped tyres and refrigerators. He got out of the car, keeping a bead on his captive. With his left hand he brought out his phone, and took a picture of the terrified-looking Blanchard, telling him to keep both hands on the steering wheel.

'Are you going to kill me?'

'I'm afraid so.'

Blanchard began to whimper and lowered his head, which made it easier. The shot sounded deafening, quite unlike the crack of a rural shotgun or bird-scarer. The mess was less than he had expected, a small amount of spray over the passenger seat towards which Blanchard's body had slumped. Slater, his hands shaking, took another picture of the body. The money shot, worth a hundred thousand. Quickly he pulled out a lighter, and using a packet of tissues as tinder, set fire to the clothing and camping gear on the Honda's back seat. He made sure that the windows were slightly open to enable the fire to breathe, and do its job of eradicating forensic clues. Walking rapidly, he headed back to Chieveley Services. He got there in ten minutes, crossing the fence well away from where the Citroën was parked. Job done, dosh earned.

Chapter Twenty-one

Friday

Thames Valley Police had been good and copied Gillard in on every aspect of their search for Arrowsmith: witness reports, interviews, DNA and fingerprint results. Almost all of this voluminous daily briefing appeared to be there for a reason, but occasionally there was an apparently random contribution. One such was the report that popped up on his email on Friday morning. It was about a burned-out car containing a body behind Chieveley motorway services on the M4. He'd skimmed the details, but paid no attention until he was sent an urgent email by DCI Nowak. He was standing in the CID gents at a urinal with his phone in his left hand when he read it, a bad habit of the overworked who think they have to make every moment earn its keep.

When he read the contents he gasped, and stopped mid-flow.

A sample from the body in the car matched Ozzy Blanchard's DNA. And the body showed a bullet wound to the head. The elusive Ozzy was dead. And everything the victim knew might be lost for ever.

Gillard pocketed the phone and finished up, then washed his hands. He stared at himself in the mirror. In the harsh bathroom light he looked old, pale and defeated, outfoxed by events. He flicked the water off his fingers, then used a paper towel to grip the handle of the bathroom door as he exited, hurrying back into the fray with damp hands.

Returning to his desk, he went straight back to reread the first report about the body in the burned-out car. The 2002 Honda Civic was registered to a man in Reading, who claimed to have sold it for cash at a layby a week previously. The purchasers were described as a heavily tattooed and ponytailed man, and a large woman with frizzy hair. They looked to be in a hurry. The car was driven around the block to confirm it was a runner, money was exchanged, and the buyers drove away. Gillard knew of the location used. The layby was a well-known site for casual car trade. Many of the cars sold there had been stolen, but if the price was low enough, buyers often didn't care. The chance of anyone being caught was low. Although 100,000 uninsured vehicles were seized across the country by police every year, it was just the tip of the iceberg.

So Ozzy Blanchard was dead. Gillard would never have the chance to interrogate him and get to the bottom of what exactly was going on at Aqua Western. The big question now was what had happened to Crystal Willow. If she was still alive, it was more vital than ever that she was found. Then the next mystery: Ozzy couldn't have killed himself and somehow set fire to his own car. Somebody else had. And it couldn't be the Ticketts.

Because they were all in custody.

–

The photographs of Ozzy Blanchard's badly burned corpse were as horrifying as expected. Gillard had been forwarded the shots by Thames Valley Police, along with the DNA confirmation of identity. They had already broken the news to his wife Angela, and briefed the employer. The cause of death was not burns or smoke inhalation but the single gunshot wound to the head. An execution. This fact was being withheld from all except those closely involved in the inquiry.

Gillard sat back with his hands cupped behind his head. If none of the Tickett family had killed Ozzy, who did? The information he had received showed that Ozzy had been with Crystal Willow when they bought the car. Where on earth could she be now? The circumstances of the killing were curious too. A quiet rural farm lane, but so close to Chieveley Services. There were far more remote locations that the killer could have chosen. It made it seem like this was an arranged meeting.

Except for one thing.

There were absolutely no ANPR captures of the white Honda in its approach to Chieveley. It had not come down the M4 or A34, for which Chieveley was pretty much an intersection. It wasn't impossible to approach on more minor roads, but you would have to know your way around. Those routes tended not to come up on satnav. The data Gillard had been sent only covered the day of the killing, so he logged on to the database and extended the ANPR range back a further two weeks, a few days before the vehicle had been purchased for cash. That did show some captures of the Honda's number plate, but only two or three. Calling up the actual photographs, Gillard was able to see on one front-facing camera that there were two people in the vehicle. The one in the passenger seat had a large frizzy hairdo. Crystal Willow.

DC Rainy Macintosh made her way into the office for the start of her late shift. She waved a cheery greeting to her boss as she arrived at her workstation. She was walking a lot more easily now, and plonked herself down on her seat, rather than easing herself down carefully as she had done previously. He still hoped to persuade her to pursue charges against her ex. In the meantime he had something more urgent to talk to her about, and called her into the office.

'How did you get on chasing down Crystal Willow's relatives?' he asked.

'Those in the West Country were surprisingly co-operative. One farming family say they put Crystal and her boyfriend up for several months informally during lockdown. They parked the camper van behind one of the cow sheds and basically just stayed there, paying their way in cash. Oh, and Ozzy wasn't going by that name. They knew him as Charlie, but the description matches.'

'Have they any idea where she is now?'

Rainy shook her head. 'I dinnae think the rellies were kept in the loop. They complained that they can't even get through to the lassie on her mobile.'

'What about the burner phone?'

'Och, I think she must have a new one. We've nae trace. I also tried Rowena and Vicky Willow, and there are nae new numbers calling their phones. They're as canny as a bunch of drug pushers.'

Gillard nodded. 'We have some clues.' He turned to his screen and opened an online map of Chieveley services, pointing out where the burned-out car was found, and the lack of ANPR signals for the Honda. 'My thinking is that there was some kind of rendezvous at the services. I mean why else would you head for somewhere so busy, and with so many cameras, but avoid them all? The only answer I can think of is that Ozzy had gone there by arrangement.'

'So he picked the only unobservable approach route?' Rainy said.

'Yes. And presumably the other vehicle was parked in the main car park, or possibly at the hotel.'

'What about CCTV at the services itself?'

'Well, there's plenty of it, but it's mostly focused on the commercial side, the entrance to the Moto building, the petrol station and so on. I asked Thames Valley if they'd seen any sign of Ozzy or Crystal at Chieveley, but they haven't forwarded me anything of interest. Of course they are probably still looking through the footage from dozens of cameras.'

'Are ye thinking that Ozzy and Crystal were still travelling together?'

'I don't know. They were sharing that vehicle. But if Crystal was there, surely she would have raised the alarm. Not only if she witnessed the shooting, but also if they were separated, or he was abducted.'

Rainy shook her head. 'This case is doing my head in, sir. We've a body we can't identify, apparently killed in a house where no one was the tenant, by an Anglo–Saxon blade no one can find. We've three likely lads banged up for kidnapping an executive from the water company and leaving him marinating in a sewer, and we've got a second body, of another water company employee, killed near a motorway services, but not by the lads who abducted the first.'

'That's a good summary. Somehow, eventually, we've got to make sense of it. And I've got an idea how we can start.'

The search for the killer of Ozzy Blanchard had originally fallen to Thames Valley Police given the location of the body near Chieveley Services, but it was now handed back to Surrey Police following a conference call between the chief constables of each force. Gillard's team had a pre-existing interest in the victim, and his girlfriend Crystal Willow. But that didn't mean they had the resources to cope with this ever-enlarging inquiry. Radar Dobbs had provided just three extra bodies, recently qualified trainees, to help with the ever-mounting workload.

For DC Carl Hoskins, the three newly appointed female officers sitting opposite him were a distraction from a monstrous piece of work. A massive email file of 17,000 car number plate photographs from ANPR had fallen to him to check through. Every vehicle that had visited Chieveley in the two days leading up to the murder of Blanchard. What was he supposed to look for in that lot? He already knew that the white Honda that Blanchard's body had been found in did not register on any other cameras at the services that day. Nevertheless, Gillard was convinced Blanchard was there to meet somebody, he wanted to find out which vehicle they had arrived in. But he had nothing to go on. Starting from the other end, with needles not haystacks, he looked up the vehicle registrations for all the main players in the inquiry who lived at Rissington Common. He had already eliminated the vehicles owned by the Tickett family, the registration numbers of which were already on file, and that of Matthew Cleaver. Of course the three male Ticketts themselves were in custody, and had been at the time the vehicle was found, but that didn't mean that Blanchard hadn't already been dead for a day or two before the car was burned. Confirmation of an early time of death might put them back in the frame.

The next step was to look for vehicles owned by any member of the Willow family. A far less common name than Cleaver or even Blanchard, he found four, all of them registered to the Anvil Arms address. Cross-referencing one of them, a red Citroën C3, showed it had been at Chieveley Services just two hours before the body had been found. Rubbing his hands together with enthusiasm, Hoskins finished off with a final flourish. It was the standard ANPR search, now automated, which allowed all registration numbers of interest, i.e. anything amongst the current caseload, to be matched up against a particular subset of cameras and a date range.

He started the program running and stood to get a coffee from the machine. The three young female officers, currently looking through CCTV from Chieveley, glanced up at him. 'Coffee, ladies?' Hoskins said, enjoying what for him was the rarity of female attention. The complexity of the requests, one of which involved going down to the canteen to get some soy milk, quickly brought him back to reality. 'So one redbush tea without milk, one double espresso with Sweet and Low, a soy milk latte, and a bar of dark chocolate.'

Hoskins was back in ten minutes, and after distributing the drinks, sat down to see the results of the search. There was one there that astounded him.

Ray Slater, former brother-in-law and sometime private detective, had been parked at Chieveley for three hours, leaving at about the same time that the burning car was discovered.

That could not be a coincidence.

Gillard had a hunch, and decided to act on it. Why would there be no phone activity between Crystal Willow and the rest of her family after the death of her boyfriend Ozzy Blanchard? It could be because they each had a new phone, but that was not the only possible reason. He drove down to Rissington Common, getting into the car park of the Anvil at six p.m. The weather was fine, and the garden outside was already busy with drinkers enjoying their new-found freedom. He donned his face mask, pulled on a baseball cap and sunglasses and approached the door. He saw Vicky behind the bar, with her back to him. He slipped in and across the lounge towards the corridor leading to the toilets. Even if he was spotted she would assume that's where he was headed. The staircase to the upper floor was a right turn before the gents' toilet. He ascended as quietly as he could, and eased open the squeaky fire door at the top. The Anvil's office door was open, but no one was in there. There seemed to be three bedrooms. He listened at each door, but heard nothing. Then he spotted another small wooden staircase, ascending. As quietly as he could, he climbed the curving, cramped steps. They led to a short corridor, and a low door. He could hear the sound of a television. He knocked on the door, and the TV volume went down.

'Who's there?' called a woman's voice from within.

'It's about your dinner,' Gillard said quietly. He heard the sound of footsteps approaching, and the door opened to reveal a large woman with frizzy hair.

'Hello Crystal,' Gillard said. 'I've been looking forward to meeting you.'

Crystal Willow was taken to Winchester Police Station for questioning. Gillard had already cautioned her, and while waiting for the duty solicitor to arrive, he and DC Shireen Corey Williams stood in the corridor watching her through the one-way glass into the interview room. She had cried a little once she was left alone, and had since been staring into space.

'What was she like when you brought her in?' Shireen asked Gillard.

'Relieved, I think. Being on the run for six months is hard work. I asked her who she was meeting at Chieveley Services, and she replied that it was only her sister. She had left Ozzy in the car. When she returned he and the vehicle were gone.'

'Do you believe her?'

Gillard shrugged. 'Vicky Willow's red Citroën was at Chieveley. We haven't gone through all the CCTV yet, but we've nothing so far to contradict her.'

They were interrupted by the arrival of the young male duty solicitor. They all trooped into the interview room. Once the tape was running, Gillard asked Crystal to confirm her movements for the previous six months. She reeled off a list of caravan parks, but said that she had first stayed for over three months at a farm in Devon. That accorded with checks that had been made by Rainy Macintosh.

'And why did you and Ozzy run away together?'

She sighed, and looked at the solicitor. 'I suppose it doesn't matter to say, now. Given that he is dead.' Her eyes moistened, and she sniffed. Shireen passed her a tissue. 'Ozzy was entangled in a fraud at Aqua Western.'

'What kind of fraud?' Gillard asked. He wondered how much the woman would know.

'I don't know all the details. But it was more than a year ago when his boss came down for a meeting with the Tickett family in the back room of the pub.'

'His boss being Kelvin Arrowsmith?'

She nodded.

'For the tape, the interviewee agreed,' Shireen said.

'What exactly was the deal?' Gillard asked.

'Well, as far as I understand, the Ticketts would over-charge the work they did, Ozzy would sign it off as being done to spec, Arrowsmith would approve it for payment and all three of them would share the extra money.'

'So he was he being paid for doing this?' Gillard asked.

'Yes,' she whispered, her voice almost inaudible. Gillard had to ask her to repeat the answer more loudly.

'How much?' Shireen asked.

'Tens of thousands, I don't know exactly. He didn't like to tell me about it.'

'How was this money being paid?' Shireen asked. 'We've looked at all the accounts belonging to Ozzy Blanchard and his wife, and we can see no sign of it.'

'Arrowsmith told him exactly how to set up an offshore account. I was to be the signatory. His name wouldn't be on it.'

The solicitor was staring at her now. 'Mrs Willow, you need to be aware that as beneficiary to such an account you are implicated,' he said.

'No, not really, because the money was for him,' Crystal said to the brief. 'And hardly any has been withdrawn.'

The young lawyer sucked his teeth, and exchanged a meaningful glance with Gillard. He was right not to be convinced.

'So what went wrong with this little scheme?' Gillard said.

'What went wrong was that the audit team at Aqua Western got wind of it somehow, round about January time. Arrowsmith told him the company had frozen the accounts. The Ticketts hadn't yet been paid for all the work they really had done, so they were hopping mad. Because Ozzy was the one they knew, they came after him. Which means they also came after me, because they knew about us, as a couple.'

'And that was in January?'

'Yes. The night Ozzy had his accident. The Ticketts had been overheard saying they were going to kill him, so Ozzy brought forward all the plans that we had for running away together.'

'How did you hear?'

'Vicky overheard them at the pub. They were whispering, which isn't like them at all. So while clearing up the baby's toys she left a baby monitor on a chair under their table and listened to it in the back.'

'Clever.'

'She couldn't get hold of me, so rang Ozzy directly. What neither of them knew was that Rory and Aidan came round to my house and forced me to stay there with them, waiting for him. I couldn't leave or answer the phone to him, but they heard all the messages. Christopher Tickett was waiting in the lane in the car, and Ozzy only guessed at the last minute. They chased Ozzy's car all the way to the dual carriageway. Well, I think you know about the accident. Aidan kept my mobile and smashed up my answerphone before he left late in the evening. Ozzy had made his way along the river's edge to the churchyard, and then came round the back through the allotments. He heard the Ticketts depart, then climbed over the fence and knocked on the kitchen door. We got Vicky to give us a lift up to Haslemere, and that's when I took the camper van.'

'So you've been on the run for six months or so,' Gillard said.

Crystal nodded. 'It was only fun for the first week. Ozzy had managed to get quite a bit of cash from his own accounts, but I hadn't dared to transfer any in from the overseas account, because it would implicate us if you were looking at our bank activity.'

Shireen glanced at Gillard. He could tell she was impressed with their financial precautions.

'What did your sister and daughter know about this?' Gillard asked.

'They both knew about me and Ozzy. Rowena had even said "go for it" when I first said I'd fallen for him. But neither of them knew anything about the money.'

'Really?' Gillard said. 'But your sister worked for the Ticketts.'

'Only occasionally, back then. They're very close, that family. They wouldn't have said anything.'

'Let's move on to Chieveley Services. You told me that you had agreed to meet your sister, and that she was bringing in more cash for you, and some documents that you needed.'

'Yes, so we could access the overseas account to repay her. We thought Vicky might be followed, so we came into Chieveley on country roads and back lanes.'

'In the white Honda you bought with the cash raised from selling the camper van?' Shireen said, checking against details printed in front of her.

'Yes.'

'Did you hear gunfire at any point while at Chieveley?' Gillard asked.

'Well, I thought it was a car backfiring or a bird scarer, but yes. A single shot.'

'Did you make a note of the time you heard it?'

'No, but it would have been about three p.m. A few minutes later, when Vicky and I had finished talking, she pointed out a plume of smoke. I went back towards our car to tell Ozzy but it was gone. Even at that point I sort of knew, I started walking towards the smoke and this lorry driver was coming the other way on foot. I asked him what the fire was, and even though he said he didn't know, I thought he smelled of bonfires.'

'We'd certainly like a description of him,' Gillard said.

'It was hard to see beyond the hi-vis jacket, mask and sunglasses. But he was a stocky six-footer, with curly grey hair. I'm not sure I would recognise his face. I walked up to within fifty yards of the burning car fire, enough to see that there was someone inside. I was terrified, so I ran back and bumped into Vicky, who had come to see what was happening. I was in floods of tears, but she said we had to get out of there.' At this point Crystal broke down. Gillard nudged the box of tissues closer to her and waited while she used them.

'I never guessed it would turn out this badly,' Crystal sobbed. 'We were just following our dreams. But they turned into a total nightmare.'

–

The post-mortem of Ozzy Blanchard was going to be a grisly affair. Gillard wouldn't normally attend out-of-region autopsies, but he wanted to meet the forensic pathologist, Dr Maddie Robinson, before peppering her with questions. He arrived at the Royal Berkshire Hospital mortuary in Reading, which had recently been expanded to take many hundreds of Covid fatalities. Dr Robinson, a tall, pale woman in her early thirties, had just pulled the cadaver onto a stainless steel slab. Unzipping the body bag released a smell not unlike the Anvil's kitchen. Even with the overhead extractor on maximum, the smoky bacon aroma hung around.

Already masked, and fighting against the extractor noise, Gillard struggled to hear what Dr Robinson was saying. Their introduction was brief, punctuated by a touch of elbows. However, a glimpse of poor Ozzy Blanchard revealed the usual difficulties of car fires: not only the horrific flame and smoke injuries, but the inability to tell where the deceased ended and the vehicle began. He was extensively burned from the waist upwards, with large amounts of plasticised seat cover welded to his back and thighs, and fabric from the seatbelt incorporated into his chest and shoulder. Only the feet and ankles were unburned, still in pristine training shoes and socks, seemingly part of somebody else.

'I assume you're looking for time of death?' Dr Robinson said.

'A confirmation would be good. We have a witness hearing a gunshot at around three p.m. close to the site of the car fire. If your tests indicate anything much different from that I would be interested to know.'

She nodded. '*Prima facie* cause of death is clearly the single gunshot to the head, and we already have DNA confirmation of identity. What else are you looking for?'

'The bullet, if you can extract it, for ballistic tests.'

'If not, we'll get the best information from a CT scan,' she said.

Gillard watched as the burned body was gradually dismantled, the scalp slit and rolled forward ready for the cut into the skull. Poor Ozzy Blanchard had spent the last six months running away. Everybody had wanted to know where he was: not only the police, but Aqua Western, the Ticketts, Kelvin Arrowsmith and of course Ozzy's long-suffering wife Angela. Fate had caught up with him, and the tale he had to tell would not now be told.

Once the pathologist began revving up the electric saw, Gillard waved his goodbyes to Dr Robinson and turned away. The sound and smell of scorched bone accompanied him to the exit.

—

News that Ray Slater's car had been at Chieveley terrified Carl Hoskins. He'd overheard Gillard and Rainy discussing the mysterious man Crystal Willow had seen at the motorway services who smelled of bonfires, and called up the woman's statement. The description was imprecise, but the height and build would have matched Slater. Hoskins knew where his loyalties should lie. Slater might be his ex-brother-in-law, but he'd have to let Gillard know. The trouble was that Slater would undoubtedly pull Hoskins down with him. That was just the kind of guy he was. He wouldn't hesitate to mention who had been supplying him with ANPR matches. If that came out he'd be fired. No question. Gillard was not the kind of guy who would tolerate officers doing favours. It was well known within any police service that officers would be deluged with requests from mates who'd had some kind of road rage run-in to use the DVLA database to get addresses. Surrey Police had always made absolutely clear that abusing police resources like the vehicle licensing authority to allow personal scores to be settled was a dismissal offence.

Hoskins stroked his chin. His inclination was to simply supply his boss with the relevant information without comment but, knowing Gillard, he would either find out the family relationship or, more straightforwardly, Slater would tell him. Slater's mobile would be packed with calls to Hoskins' direct line. So the best course of action was one which included the truth; at least most of it. He waited until Gillard was in his glass box office, and had just finished a phone call. Hoskins approached, his armpits already sweaty. Gillard looked up and Hoskins felt his boss could read his mind.

'Sir, if you got a moment.'

Gillard nodded, then raised his eyes as he saw Hoskins carefully close the door behind him. 'Something confidential, Carl?' He gestured for the detective to sit. He did so.

'ANPR picked up Ray Slater's car at Chieveley services at the time Blanchard's car was set ablaze.'

'Yes, I've just seen the results. I was assuming he trailed Vicky Willow's car.'

'I want you to know that he'd been asking me for favours. I used to be his brother-in-law, he's the brother of my ex-wife.'

Gillard leaned forward, steepling his hands. 'Favours since when, Carl?'

'Shortly after the body was dug up. He's been looking for Ozzy Blanchard on behalf of the water company. He asked me for ANPR details and phone traces for him. I refused. He rang me a lot of times, badgering me based on our connection. For a long time I just thought it was an irritation, but now I'm thinking...'

'You should have told me immediately,' Gillard said. 'This has slowed up our inquiry. If Slater had been boasting to Aqua Western about having sources in this office, it must have got back to DCS Anderson's own whistleblower in the company. No wonder she wouldn't tell us anything. And in her shoes I'd have done the same.'

'I know. I didn't want to get in shit with the family, I just stonewalled him.'

Gillard inhaled deeply, leaned back, and cupped his hands behind his head. His eyes were studying the ceiling as if the answer to this conundrum was somehow written there.

'I need you to document every call and every request. I'm also going to download your search history on the case, to see if it tallies what with what you just told me. I can't afford to take your word for it, you do understand that? If I see anything, it goes up to Professional Standards.'

'Yes, sir.'

'Right. Carl, I'm really disappointed you didn't tell me straightaway, and now I'm doubly pissed off to have to lose you from this inquiry seeing as we're so short-staffed. But despite all that, you're off the case.'

Gillard dismissed him, and as Hoskins closed the door behind him he could see his boss, swearing quietly at the ceiling. He'd only gone five yards before Gillard called him back in.

'Right, Carl. We need Slater, and I imagine he's now gone to ground.'

'Yes.'

'Tell me everything you know about him: career, family, associates, interests, strengths, weaknesses. Everything.'

'So I'm not off the case?'

'You will be, Carl. But after I've wrung from you every piece of information about him I'm going to set a trap. And you will be the bait. I just have to get Radar Dobbs to sign off on it.'

–

'Craig, I'm very unhappy about this.' Chief Constable Alison Rigby was on a conference call with Gillard, his boss DCS Brian Dobbs and a senior lawyer for the Crown Prosecution Service, Pauline Wakefield.

'Detective Chief Inspector Gillard,' said Wakefield. 'Although entrapment is no defence in English law, you would give the defence counsel huge ammunition through this course of action.'

'It is not an offence for anyone to give in to blackmail,' Gillard said. 'The offender would not be committing an additional offence, but putting himself in a position where he could be rapidly arrested.'

Wakefield shook her head. 'Agreed, but one of your officers would be committing a crime. A serving officer extorting cash from a suspect…'

'Pretending to…' Dobbs interjected. 'Any monies supplied would be passed to the Crown.' Gillard was surprised to find his boss going into bat for him.

'We're sure Ray Slater has killed once and may kill again,' Gillard said. 'He is a former police officer and a private detective with, we must presume, significant forensic awareness. He won't be easy to track down, and could be a real danger to witnesses including Crystal Willow, and to our other fugitive Kelvin Arrowsmith. We may be able to protect some witnesses, but as Arrowsmith and his wife have gone into hiding, or have possibly fled, we are not able to do the same for them. We don't know quite how this all fits together, and if Arrowsmith is killed we may never find out.'

'That is the most persuasive aspect,' Rigby said. 'But is there not some way Slater could be enticed to meet DC Hoskins without creating a legal danger or ammunition for the defence?'

'The last thing Slater would want to do, even for his brother-in-law, is to meet in person,' Gillard said. 'We have his home and his business premises under surveillance. He's too smart to come back to be nabbed. The only way we can force him to a specific location is if something is being exchanged. Cash is the most obvious.'

'I'm against it,' Wakefield said. 'It would create huge difficulties for the prosecution.'

Gillard looked down at his paperwork. 'Naturally, I've looked up a few previous cases on this. May I draw your attention to the words of Lord Justice Nicholls in 2001 in R vs Loosely, in which he said the gravity of the case and the desire to prevent serious further offences as mitigating what he called "more unorthodox methods of detection". And we are trying to save at least one life.'

Pauline Wakefield arched an eyebrow. Gillard could see her bristling at the impertinence of a mere detective attempting to tell her how to do her job. It wasn't the first time he had waded into case discussions armed with quotes culled from previous legal judgements.

'Well, if your operational imperatives satisfy your chief constable, I will do my best at this end to secure a conviction,' Wakefield said. 'I can do no better than that.'

Gillard turned to Alison Rigby, who said: 'We'll go ahead, but please, Craig be very careful.'

Chapter Twenty-two

Ray Slater, oldest of three and the only boy, had grown up in a rough area of Bermondsey, south London. He was streetwise and wily rather than tough and more practical than academic. He joined the Royal Marines at eighteen, just before the Falklands War. He was in 3 Commando Brigade, expecting to head off to Norway for training when news came in of the Argentine invasion in April 1982. He used to brag to Hoskins about having 'killed Argies with my bare hands', but nobody quite believed him. His obvious skills were of the opportunistic fixer variety, securing scarce supplies, and driving or repairing Land Rovers. The family were surprised that he left the Marines within two years and joined the Metropolitan Police, where he became a dog handler. He always seemed to have a knack of turning up with various goods that he had secured through the police auction of stolen property. He always had a nose for an advantage.

Listening to this, Gillard wondered if Slater had already been bent when he was in the Met.

Precautions were essential. The fact that Ray Slater was being hunted at all was redacted from the official evidence file. Gillard felt there was a danger the private detective may have other contacts within the force able to tip him off. A surveillance unit had been dispatched to Slater's office, but so far there was no activity. Both of

Slater's cars were run through ANPR, but hadn't triggered any cameras since the day that Blanchard's body was found.

Once the plan was finalised, Gillard sat with Carl Hoskins while he rang Slater's mobile. He called from the same office number Slater had contacted him on. The message kicked in, so Hoskins said: 'Ray, give us a call. I've got some useful intelligence.'

There was no call back, and after half an hour Gillard went off to pursue other duties. Rob Townsend, already weighed down with work, was asked as a priority to put a cell-site trace on the mobile that Hoskins had called. If Slater turned on the phone to pick up the message, they would know where he was. A call back came after an hour, but from an unknown number, and it was to Hoskins' personal mobile, not the office direct line.

'It's me,' Slater said. 'What have you got?'

'I can't talk here,' Hoskins said. 'Let me meet you somewhere.'

'You must think I was born yesterday, son.'

'They're not on to you, yet, but I am. You've committed murder, but I can make it go away.'

'Bullshit.'

'Ray, I've got the ANPR records at Chieveley right in front of me, and your car's on the list, buried among 17,000 innocent vehicles. I can make it disappear.'

Slater blew a long nervous sigh. 'Can you?'

'I can delete the two images, entry and exit, for a fee. Your Nissan was never there. You'd be in the clear.'

There was a long pause. 'How much?'

'How much were you paid for the hit?'

There was a long pause. 'Hundred thou, roughly.'

'A hundred thousand pounds? I want half. In cash.'

'Fuck off. You've got a nerve.'

'Who paid you to do it? Was it Arrowsmith?'

'None of your business.'

'C'mon, it was bound to be him. Wasn't it?'

'I can't tell you.'

'You still got the shooter?'

'Yeah. Might still need it.'

'Pay me half and I can plant the shooter on the Tickett family.'

'How?'

'I've got the bona fides to visit Typhoon Tickett's house. Then pretend I found the shooter there. The Ticketts are already trussed up like turkeys for the Arrowsmith abduction. It's no great stretch to imagine they killed Blanchard too, several days before one of their associates planted the body in the car.'

There was a long silence before Slater spoke. 'You're a lifesaver, Carl, you really are.'

'Meet you at the Three Feathers?'

'No chance. I've got to take precautions. Take the Guildford to Waterloo train at 17.19 this evening, rear carriage, somewhere in the last couple of rows of seats. I'll meet you there.' He hung up.

–

Carl Hoskins was nervous as he waited on the Guildford platform. DS Vikram Singh, now recovered from Covid, was dressed as a commuter and stood with his nose in the *Times* a few yards away. There were two unmarked support vehicles which would head from station to station to match as far as possible the progress of the train, while Gillard co-ordinated back at Mount Browne. At short notice it was the best that could be done. Slater had been clever. This was a tricky meeting to put under surveillance. The train Hoskins was catching started in Portsmouth, heading to London Waterloo. It was impossible to check every one of the dozen stations that Slater might get on at. Likewise it was impossible to check all stations that he might require Hoskins to get off at if he rang the detective and asked him to meet away from the train.

The train arrived. The rear carriage was first class, and as expected less busy than the rest of the train. At this time of day most of the commuter traffic was coming in the other direction, leaving London to return to the suburbs. Hoskins got on and sat in a rear seat by the platform window. The only passenger nearby was an elderly woman in walking boots and carrying a small rucksack, who was reading a hardback about wildflowers.

Worplesdon, Woking, West Byfleet. The first three stations passed with no message from Slater. Hoskins checked his phone for the umpteenth time. Somewhere else a phone rang. Hoskins and the woman looked at each other. It wasn't clear where it was coming from. Hoskins leaned forward a couple of feet and peered into the bin that was between two rows of seats. It was definitely coming from there. He fished his hand in, and pulled out a McDonald's burger bag. He peered inside and saw a phone, an envelope and a Browning 9mm. Hoskins retrieved the phone and answered it. The elderly woman hid her laugh with a hand.

'Ray, is that you?'

'It is. Have you seen everything?'

'Yes. Three items.' Hoskins didn't dare bring out the gun, but retrieved the envelope, and opening the flap, could see it was stuffed with the giveaway pink of fifty pound notes. He turned away from the woman, who was now openly staring at him. 'Got it,' he whispered. 'You took a risk, Ray.'

'Not really. I put it in at Godalming, the stop before yours. There's not much chance of anyone going through the bins before Waterloo, when the cleaners come on. It's only a five grand down payment. I can't raise more that quick.'

Hoskins had to admit this was clever. There was going to be no face-to-face meeting. Gillard's high-risk ruse had failed. The inquiry's legal basis had been undermined, yet Slater had not bitten. It was with some trepidation that Hoskins rang his boss, knowing he would be angry.

–

Gillard somehow knew before he answered the call. Slater was proving more slippery than expected, and the detective had to admit a grudging respect for the intelligence and finesse revealed by planting a phone in a bin on the train.

'All right, Carl. Get back here as soon as you can,' Gillard said. 'I've changed my mind. I'm too short-staffed to keep you off the case.' Gillard stared across the office, dozens of work-stations, almost all unmanned. The only other detective sitting there was Rainy Macintosh, just returned from the abortive surveillance operation, and with a long Friday evening ahead of her tracking Slater's financial records. Rob Townsend wasn't there, nor Claire Mulholland. She was still on her way back from the surveillance op. The three trainees would be going in an hour, their normal office hours over. An incident room meeting would be useful to throw out some ideas, but it was pointless. He'd be talking to himself. Everyone was strung out between too many simultaneous inquiries, of which nailing Slater remained firmly top priority. They had some clues. Credit card records showed the private detective had rented a vehicle from Europcar in Croydon the day after the murder of Blanchard, and returned it to an outlet in Redhill just yesterday. Redhill was on the train line to Gatwick Airport. Maybe he was trying to leave the country? That would be hard. The Met Police had his passport and that of his wife.

The big unknown was exactly who Slater had been working for. When he had first run into him at the Aqua Western HQ in Windsor, Gillard had assumed that Slater was working for the water company, on a secretive mission to track down the source of an embezzlement. Stella Anderson had confirmed that. For them, using a private detective made sense if they were worried about publicity. Gillard had assumed that if they had succeeded in finding Blanchard they would have paid him off, and tied him up in a non-disclosure agreement. The crucial regulatory overview might then proceed smoothly, the existence of the fraud buried.

But since the killing, Gillard no longer took that view. Even the most ruthless corporation would baulk at killing an employee, at least in a country like the UK. Once Ozzy Blanchard had been murdered, the suspicion fell on either the Tickett family or Arrowsmith. If Arrowsmith was bent, which seemed likely, then there was clearly an incentive to rub out his partner in crime. From Arrowsmith's perspective, Ozzy Blanchard's death had the dual advantages of removing a key witness to the fraud and providing a conveniently dead suspect on whom to hang the entire crime, a man who was in no position to protest his innocence. And Slater had been the instrument to make it happen. Gillard admitted to himself that he had underestimated Slater's ruthlessness.

Even having given up the gun, the man was dangerous.

With no one else to do it, Gillard ended up manning the phones for the next half-hour, updating returning officers on the failed sting. The hardest calls were from his boss, Radar Dobbs, and Chief Constable Alison Rigby. He felt he was being blamed for Slater's ingenuity. Well, tough. You do your best, and let the chips land where they must. It was worth a try. Everyone needs a bit of luck.

Then he got some.

A call from security at Gatwick Airport.

They'd made arrests. Not Slater, but Arrowsmith and his wife. Just as they were trying to board a flight for Rome.

It seemed the pandemic had actually done the police some favours. In more normal times the Arrowsmiths might have got away with it. But with holiday travel only just allowed since 4 July, there were more questions, more manual passport checks, and several opportunities for offi- cials to spot that the Arrowsmiths were on the UK Border Force watchlist. As it was, they got as far as the boarding gate, when a sharp-eyed member of staff saw the names on the boarding passes and asked them to stand aside while others were boarding. They looked at each other for a moment, then circled round and tried to slip into the queue further down. They were spotted and detained by two security staff. Francesca Arrowsmith burst into tears; their escape to Italy ruined.

Chapter Twenty-three

It was early on Saturday morning when Gillard was able to get a glimpse of Kelvin Arrowsmith through the one-way glass at Staines Police Station. He had been transferred from Gatwick's detention unit to the cells during the night, while his wife had been allowed to go home. Arrowsmith looked exhausted, mask dangling by his neck, his arrogant, feline eyes roaming the walls of the interview room, as if somewhere there was a secret escape door if he could just find it. Gillard was joined by DC Shireen Corey Williams for the interview, and by Arrowsmith's own solicitor, a large woman with librarian-style spectacles on a chain.

The moment Gillard and Shireen entered the interview room, Arrowsmith unleashed a barrage of complaints. 'Why are you holding me here? I'm just recovering from a kidnap where, as I might remind you, I nearly drowned in sewage. I have had no access to my medication, and I'm getting anxiety attacks.'

Gillard had already been briefed by the Staines duty sergeant on the various demands Arrowsmith had made during the night. Francesca Arrowsmith was supposedly returning by midmorning with the required blood pressure medication, while the sergeant had contacted Gatwick to get the seized luggage released and sent over so that any medication within could be accessed.

'You've already been told that the medication is on its way. I would strongly suggest you calm down in the meantime so you're less likely to need it.'

'It's not clear to me on what charges my client is being detained,' the brief said.

'Those charges have not been finalised, but he has been cautioned,' Gillard replied. 'Charges are likely to relate to fraud at Aqua Western.'

'Oh, this is outrageous,' Arrowsmith said, eyes narrowed. 'It was *me* that reported the irregularities to the group financial controller. It was *me* that tracked down the overcharging by the subcontractor. It was *me* that the Ticketts abducted. I was hot on their trail, with the help of a private detective. I am the bloody victim here and I demand to be released.'

Gillard smiled. 'One of the reasons you are here is because of your relationship with Ray Slater.'

'My relationship?' He looked around the room as if someone was going to explain this to him. 'It's all above board. Slater was appointed by the group financial controller Shane Devlin. Yes, of course I worked with Slater. He did the legwork to try to find Blanchard while I combed through the books. We needed to find Blanchard to work out exactly how the fraud had been perpetrated.'

Shireen spoke for the first time. 'Mr Arrowsmith. I'm from the economic crime unit, and I deal with frauds all the time. For a fraud to work, someone has to sign the cheques. You as regional financial controller were in a position to do that.'

'Of course I signed the cheques. Blanchard had confirmed that the work had been completed. The costs were in line with the spec; that was my job to check. How was I to know that he failed to complete the job to spec?

260

The Ticketts had cut corners and inflated the wage bill. You have to remember that I'm not generally on site. I reconcile incoming and outgoing bills. Ozzy Blanchard was my eyes and ears on the ground. I was shocked to discover that he was corrupt.'

Gillard thought back to the famous scene in *Casablanca*, when Captain Renault declared himself shocked to discover that gambling was taking place at the club Rick managed, only for the croupier to whisper to him that his winnings were ready for collection. 'If you were so keen on catching your subordinate, why did you tip him off about the investigation?' Gillard asked.

'I didn't!'

'Somebody did. He left home in January with the fear of God in him, at least to judge by his driving. Blanchard's wife confirmed that you rang their home.'

'Yes, after he'd already gone! I'll tell you what that was. I withheld certain payments, and I can imagine that the Tickett family were not best pleased. That's what Ozzy was scared of. I'm sure he was furious with me, but I was simply doing my job. I couldn't allow any further payments to be made until we could get to the bottom of it.'

Gillard and Shireen exchanged frustrated glances. Arrowsmith's account was entirely plausible, and it would take much more work from the SFO's forensic accounting team to prove that it wasn't true. Gillard decided to return to firmer ground.

'Do you know where Ray Slater currently is?' Gillard asked.

'I have no idea, why should I? He reports to Shane Devlin.'

Gillard was careful with how he phrased the question 'We urgently need to speak to him in relation to the death of Ozzy Blanchard.'

Arrowsmith rearranged his face into an expression of utter perplexity: 'Detective chief inspector, are you seriously thinking that a professional private detective would be involved? Surely it's the Ticketts who did this?'

'The entire Tickett family were in custody at the time of the killing.' Gillard leaned forward and steepled his fingers. 'We have Slater, on tape, admitting he was paid a hundred grand for the hit. We think you paid him.'

'You're being absurd.'

Gillard opened a manila file in front of him, and slid forward a photograph culled from the Chieveley CCTV. 'Do you recognise this man?' The picture was of a thickset fellow wearing sunglasses, a face mask and a stained hi-vis jacket.

'No.' Arrowsmith pushed the photograph back across the desk.

'It's Ray Slater, incognito. This image was captured at Chieveley Services at around the time that Blanchard was killed. On your orders.'

'This is utter nonsense. I'm as shocked as everyone else that Ozzy was killed.'

'Sure you are. There is a phone call from your landline to Slater's phone just a couple of hours earlier.'

'What day are we talking about here?'

'The day you were released from hospital. You rang home, and a few minutes later someone from your home, almost certainly Francesca, rang Slater. Presumably to tell him to go ahead with the plan you had previously discussed.'

Arrowsmith shrugged. 'You have a lucid imagination, but not a shred of evidence.'

Shireen leaned forward. 'Mr Arrowsmith, we are taking apart your finances. You paid Ray Slater to kill Blanchard, and we will find out how. There's always an audit trail.'

'Look, I liked Ozzy Blanchard. He was reliable, hard-working and spent many hours more than he could have got away with on his work. That was how he fooled me for such a long time.'

Arrowsmith had clung tenaciously to his story. Gillard knew that the admission by Slater, made in a phone call with Hoskins, might be inadmissible in context of the entrapment. They really needed hard financial proof, and Arrowsmith rightly guessed they didn't have it. If they did, why press him so hard for an admission? Seeing as they could make no further progress, Gillard terminated the interview and the prisoner was returned, still bitterly complaining, to his cell.

'How long will it take to get every scrap of his financial records?' Gillard asked Shireen.

'It depends how complex they are and how clever he has been. I don't think Anderson's people have examined the link between Arrowsmith and Slater, they're looking higher up the food chain.'

'Look, all we need is proof he paid Slater outside normal channels,' Gillard said. 'Either a withdrawal of cash or a bank transfer.'

'It would be easier to find it at Slater's end,' Shireen said. 'He's probably less financially savvy than Arrowsmith, so we'll look for a big wodge of money coming in from an unusual account.'

'How long might that take?'

'Days to find it, but weeks or months to piece it all together enough to satisfy the CPS. It's never quick.'

Gillard nodded. 'All right. I have a plan. We release Arrowsmith on police bail, and keep him and Francesca under surveillance. Phone taps, the full works. Slater is bound to contact him, or vice versa.'

'Arrowsmith is pretty clever. First thing he'll do is get himself a new phone.'

'I'm sure, but it's the best we can do. In the meantime I'm going to dig around Slater's place of work.'

–

The search for Ray Slater was intensified. Now the Met had finished searching, Gillard made time to take a look at Slater's small office in West Croydon, and his modest home around the corner. Surveillance teams had reported no significant visitors to either location.

Slater's office was above a Turkish barber shop, which on a Saturday morning was packed with an ethnically diverse clientele. The office entrance was easy to miss, hidden between the barber's and a Chinese supermarket. The door was neat and tidy, with a small surveillance camera above and a buzzer, plus a brass plate inscribed RAS Business Services. It would have been as discreet and obscure as you could get, except for the hefty Met Police padlock securing the place after it had first been raided. Gillard fiddled for the key in the envelope given to him by the surveillance officer, tackled the padlock and opened the door. He was dearly hoping that he would spot something that the Met Police had missed. They'd raided the office, Slater's home, and interviewed nearby relatives in Croydon. There was no sign of Slater's whereabouts.

Nor of his wife, which made Gillard think they might be planning a runner.

Still, the Met claimed to have their passports. There was nowhere for them to go.

The stairs were uncarpeted, and the wallpaper a tired beige woodchip. As he climbed Gillard got a whiff of unemptied bins. A piece of lino ran from the stairs to the office door, which was cracked from top to bottom from what appeared to be an enthusiastic use of the police ram. The padlock here was superfluous. The frame was so splintered a toddler could have barged in.

Slater's workplace was shockingly basic. The desk, tooled with inlaid leather, was the only decent piece of furniture. The desk drawers had been forced and emptied, each one labelled with a cross-reference to an evidence bag. An unfashionably squat plastic dial handset, circa 1970, lay on the floor, still connected to the wall socket. The client side of the room had some coffee-stained soft chairs, a round glass coffee table, a well-stuffed magazine rack and some dirty mugs. A solitary bluebottle banged its head repeatedly against the window, trying to get out. Gillard could well understand its motivation. This place was a dump. Surprising that Slater had got the Aqua Western contract, when there were bigger, slicker guys in the business.

A hunch was beginning to form in his head.

He picked a handful of magazines from the rack, and spread them over the coffee table. Several editions of *Marie Claire* reflected the gender of Slater's usual divorce-job clients. *House & Garden*, a few copies of *Metro*, and some holiday brochures.

Italy. Plenty about Italy.

Interesting that Slater, like Arrowsmith, had on interest in Italy. Arrowsmith's wife was of Italian descent, but what about Slater? Gillard flicked through the dog-eared brochures, from which a few pages looked to have been torn out. Looking around the office, he saw some other Italian influences: a framed photo of Slater and his wife in front of the Colosseum, a hand-painted Rimini ashtray, a book about Pompei and Herculaneum.

Gillard scanned the office for anything else of interest. Nothing.

He scooped up a sheaf of Italy brochures to take with him to Slater's semi, a five-minute walk away. Gillard let himself in past a police padlock. The place was modern, modestly furnished, with mass-produced furniture and no signs of unexplained wealth. There was, however, more evidence of Italian holidays. The Met had made less mess here than at the office. Slater's home office had been stripped of its computers and phones, but otherwise the place looked reasonably intact. Not much surprised Gillard, except the metal detector in the garage. That might explain the night-time incursion at the crime scene. It fitted what Hoskins had told him about Slater: opportunistic, with an eye to a quick profit on anything he could find.

It was the kitchen, however, that yielded the break-through. A pile of opened post on top of the kitchen table had been neatly stacked. It included an empty envelope, postmarked from Italy. The apparent contents of that envelope, at least to judge by the matching paper, was held to the side of the fridge by an Italy-themed magnet, together with three or four photographs. They showed a whitewashed villa, either under construction or renova-tion. Slater did not appear in these pictures. Removing them from the fridge, Gillard looked on the back and saw an address in the Apulia region.

Something clicked in his memory. He took out his mobile and rang PC Soraya Shah, the Thames Valley Police family liaison officer who had looked after Francesca Arrowsmith while her husband had been abducted. After greeting her he said. 'Soraya, you recall the Italian holiday home of Kelvin Arrowsmith?'

'Yes, sir.'

'Can you dig up the address for me, and any photographs of the place?'

'I'll get right on it.'

It was less than ten minutes later when she rang back. 'I've emailed you the details, sir. There were dozens of photographs of the villa on Francesca's phone. She's back in the house now, and her phone has been returned to her, so I can't look at anything she may have added in the last couple of days.'

'That's no problem.' Gillard thanked her and hung up. He was beginning to get an idea as to how Arrowsmith had paid Slater – untraceably – for the hit on Blanchard.

–

Back at Mount Browne, Gillard did half an hour's useful web searching before the Saturday afternoon incident room meeting. Shireen Corey Williams and a stressed-looking Rob Townsend were the first to arrive, followed by Rainy Macintosh, looking distinctly upbeat.

'So how are we doing?' Gillard asked. 'Let's start with you, Shireen. Connections between Ray Slater and Kelvin Arrowsmith.'

'I've got all Ray Slater's bank accounts, business and personal, savings both in his name and in his wife's and, sad to say, it all looks totally legit. He was awarded the contract from Aqua Western in March, the agreed monthly retainer plus expenses have been made ever since. I've matched them up, and they were signed off not by Arrowsmith but by his boss Shane Devlin. It's all itemised, and not unreasonable amounts.'

Gillard nodded. 'Rob, how you getting on tracing Slater?'

'The burner phone he left on the train had not been used for anything else. To be honest I'm struggling to find the time to think outside the box on this one. He's obviously got lots of phones.'

Rainy Macintosh was looking rather smug at this moment, clearly dying to say her piece. Gillard let her.

'I think I've got an answer, sir, or part of one anyway. As you know, the Met Police have Slater's UK passport, seized from his home. But an Irish citizen named Raymond Slater flew out of Stansted to Naples two days ago. A woman named Anne Slater was on the next seat. She used a UK passport that had previously been reported lost. It's the replacement document that the Met seized.'

Two different ways to get second passports. Gillard wasn't surprised that a private detective would have this kind of precaution in place. 'I know exactly where they've gone,' he said. He described his discovery of Slater's interest in Italy, which matched the region where Arrowsmith had acquired a holiday home.

'Both families have homes in the town of Casamassima in Apulia, southern Italy,' Gillard said. 'With the help of Google Maps and some holiday listings I have established that those homes adjoin. I also found a couple of emails in Italian which were sent to Francesca Arrowsmith, and her replies in Italian. What effectively seems to have happened is that Arrowsmith has paid for the renovation of an existing cottage adjoining their large newly purchased villa. They added a swimming pool and various other mod cons to the tune of €115,000.'

'And he's given it to Slater!' Corey Williams said.

'That's it. The amount is roughly a hundred grand in sterling. All covered by the large payment in euros we previously discovered for his own holiday home. Virtually untraceable. If I hadn't put the emails through Google translate I wouldn't have realised.'

'So a free holiday home in exchange for a murder,' Rainy said.

'Yes. And I'm pretty sure that's where we'll find Slater. At his ill-gotten villa.'

'Nae problem. I'll get on to the international liaison team,' Rainy said. 'We can get the carabinieri to pick them up in a day or two.'

Sunday

Having been charged with abduction, Christopher Tickett had been remanded in custody. The kidnapping offence wasn't going to be difficult to prove now that some DNA matching Arrowsmith had been recovered from clothing found at Tickett's home. But it was getting to the bottom of the fraud that was proving more difficult. Arrowsmith claimed no part of it, but his abduction itself proved the Tickett family thought otherwise. Gillard took the journey to Belmarsh Prison in south-east London to find out for himself. He brought with him DC Shireen Corey Williams. The underground interview room where Tickett had been installed was for all its modernity as grim an enclosure as Gillard had ever seen. Flickering artificial light, dark walls, and no view of the outside world. He could feel Shireen shrinking by his side as they took their seats opposite the prisoner.

Being on remand in Belmarsh was considered to be one of the worst experiences in British prisons. The constant coming and going of prisoners ferried off to court appearances, and worst of all the unsettled power structure amongst inmates, made for a high level of conflict. Self-harming by remand prisoners was at epidemic levels.

Tickett, however, had seen it all. The twelve years he had already served for the murder of Henry Willow would have been in jails at least as bad as this. His body language, chin jutting, arms folded, legs apart, radiated unrepentance. The brief this time was not Tolliver, but one of the juniors from his office, a young man who seemed as intimidated by the surroundings as Shireen was.

'How are they looking after you, Christopher?' Gillard began.

'Like you give a fuck anyway,' he retorted.

'Okay, so much for the small talk. I want to know why you abducted Kelvin Arrowsmith.'

'No comment.'

'Do you deny abducting him?'

'No comment.'

A further half dozen questions were answered the same way. Gillard had prepared for this and looked to his right to Shireen, who asked the next question. 'Mr Tickett, your family company has been quite active over the years, hasn't it? Was it just work for water companies that you did?'

His gaze softened a little. 'No, lots of general contracting.'

'And what about Buckingham Pallets Ltd? It hasn't reported any accounts to Companies House since inception.'

'Well, paperwork was never my strong point. I'd have caught up with it by now if you hadn't locked me up.'

'If you were to tell us a little bit more about the fraud, we would put in a good word on the sentence for the abduction,' she said.

Tickett squeezed out a half smile. 'Butter wouldn't melt in that pretty mouth, would it? That kind of patter might sway someone who doesn't know the legal system. If I go down for the abduction, the fraud wouldn't be here nor there in terms of sentence.'

'A guilty plea is always something we can work with,' she said, giving her most winning smile.

Tickett rolled his eyes at Gillard. 'You must think I'm a complete eejit to fall for this. There was no fraud. You just can't prove something that doesn't exist.'

'Your son Aidan admitted it,' Shireen said. 'So why don't you?'

'Liar!' Christopher Tickett's explosion of anger was immediate. He lunged over the table and Shireen screamed. Gillard intercepted Tickett's open right hand just before it closed around her throat. Tickett was a big man, but straining across the table put him off balance. Gillard seized the wrist, and rounding the table, forced it behind Tickett's back. With the other hand on the scruff of Tickett's neck he rammed him face-first into the wall.

'Okay, okay,' Tickett said, as Gillard pulled back, readying him for a second charge. By the time two prison officers arrived, Tickett was back on his chair, arms hand-cuffed behind him. They took a look at Gillard, and the bloody smear on the wall from the prisoner's nose and mouth.

'Just look at the CCTV,' Gillard said, in response to their suspicious glances. 'I dealt with an attack on my colleague.'

The brief was cowering in the corner, speechless.

Tickett was quickly manhandled out, but not before bellowing: 'The Ticketts are not grasses; Aidan would not say a thing. You hear me?'

Gillard turned to Shireen and asked if she was okay. 'I am, thanks to you. That was a very quick reaction you had.'

He guided her out of the interview room and away from the solicitor. 'Shireen, I have to say, the moment you provoked him, I was ready. That's a hot button you pressed, by labelling Aidan a snitch.'

'I thought it was worth a try.'

'Next time give me a heads-up before you plan to do it. Right, now on to Aidan.'

—

Aidan Tickett was held on remand in HMP High Down near Banstead, just a handful of miles from Gillard's home. Relatively modern, the jail's interview rooms were light and airy, and Aidan was sitting in one of them by the time Gillard and Shireen arrived. Through the observation window he looked bored, chewing his nails absentmindedly. The paperwork showed his behaviour had been good since arrest. The two police officers went in, accompanied by a female lawyer from Tolliver's firm. Aidan's eyes followed Shireen as if he'd never seen a woman before.

Gillard prepped the tape, and began the interview.

'Now Aidan, you're being held on—'

'You accused me of grassing my pa up, didn't you?'

Gillard was gobsmacked that Aidan had in two hours got word of Shireen's accusation. He hadn't even decided how to deal with it before Aidan said. 'And you're the bitch that said it.'

Shireen hadn't managed to get a word out before Gillard decided to suspend the interview. They retreated to the corridor outside to regroup. 'How on earth did he hear?' she asked.

'There are phones in every prison, and if you're willing to pay enough, you can get contact with whoever you want. But that was very quick,' Gillard conceded.

'You don't think it was the lawyers talking to each other?'

'Have you ever known a solicitor move that fast? No, I'm pretty sure it wasn't that.'

They went back in and resumed the interview, but Aidan simply ignored them, saying nothing. After a half-hour, Gillard called proceedings to an end, and after the prisoner was taken away turned to Shireen. 'Not very informative, was he?'

'Should we bother with Rory Tickett?' she asked. 'Is it worth going all the way to Winchester?'

'Why not? He was the weak link last time.'

—

During the two-hour drive to HMP Winchester, Gillard heard about all the paperwork that Shireen had been sent by the SFO's forensic accounting specialists. They had found duplicate invoices at Aqua Western for much of the work supposedly done by the Tickett contracting firm. 'That in itself isn't proof of anything but inefficiency, because most of them were not paid twice. However, the nearest to a smoking gun for Arrowsmith's involvement is that DCS Anderson's team found a similar pattern in some of his other work, with different contractors,' Shireen said.

'So he'd been doing this before?'

'Yes, if we can establish what "this" actually is. The point is that Ozzy Blanchard could only have been involved with one fraud at a time. But the SFO is trying to find a pattern for all the regional contract work overseen by Kelvin Arrowsmith, to show that it was fraudulent. They want to put him at the centre of the case.'

They arrived at Winchester to discover some good news. Rory Tickett had been moved out of B wing and into the segregation unit because of bad behaviour. That meant single-cell occupancy, limited association with other prisoners and consequently a much lower chance of access to phones or drugs.

The big man seemed almost pleased to see them. 'It's doing my head in, being in here,' he said, as soon as they sat down with him.

'If you co-operate, we can see what might be possible,' Gillard said, after prepping the tape.

'I'll not grass my family up, anything but that.'

'Okay. But why were you looking for Ozzy Blanchard that day when I came to visit the yard?'

'He owed us some money, that's all.'

'Did you ever get it?'

'Did we, fuck. I couldn't find the little bastard, nor his woman.'

'But you found Arrowsmith.'

He nodded. 'Yeah, we did. Got a result there.'

Gillard couldn't believe how readily Rory was spilling the beans.

'Must've been horrible for him down that sewer,' Shireen volunteered. 'How could you do that to someone?'

Rory laughed. 'You should have heard him squealing, when we dragged him across from the car. He knew what we was going to do. That's when he gave us the passwords. He said the money wouldn't clear until the Friday, so Pa said. "When it has, we will come and fetch you out." Oh, but that place stank. Aidan knew how to set the valves, so the shite rose higher and higher.'

'How did you know that he wouldn't drown?'

Rory shrugged and then chuckled. 'We didn't.'

'So you got the money?' Gillard asked.

'I don't know. No one tells me anything. Now, I'm not grassing anyone up, understand? I don't want you using this from me.' He glanced at the tape. 'Can you get me bail?' His brown eyes searched their faces pleadingly.

'I can't offer you bail,' Gillard said, reaching out to turn off the tape. 'Not with a case of violent abduction, plus of course some vulnerable witnesses who would be terrified if you got out. Still, it should all contribute to a lower sentence, ultimately.'

Rory shook his head. 'I can't take it. Cooped up on my own.'

'I know, it must be hard,' Shireen said. 'But you've done the right thing.'

'Now, Dove Cottage,' Gillard said, prepping the tape for a restart. 'You lived there for a while, didn't you?'

Rory looked stricken. 'Not that, I'm not saying anything about that.'

'Who was he, Rory? Who did you kill?'

The big man wrapped his arms around his own head and began to whimper. 'No, no. I can't. I didn't do it. Stop blaming me.'

For the next ten minutes there was nothing intelligible. They tried waiting it out, but to no avail. Rory wouldn't look at them, so they finished up and left with a mystery still unsolved. Who was the killer in that blood-soaked bedroom at Dove Cottage? And who was the victim?

Chapter Twenty-four

Monday

The mortal remains of an unknown murder victim looked more like pieces of a broken statue than anything that had been once human. Rissington Man was closer to a darkened plaster saint from a Catholic Church than a man who had lived, loved, and presumably had some kind of a job. Why was nobody missing him? Where amongst the legions of the vanished did his true identity lie? Gillard stared down at the wreck of humanity before him on the mortuary's stainless steel slab, while the hospital technician pointed out the features that at least on paper he already knew: the fillings, composite and metal, which allowed them to be sure this was a modern man; the other removed teeth from whose root pulp DNA had been recovered, the missing fingers, since recovered from a separate grave; and the damaged neck, now separated to allow the removal of the weapon shard. The search for DNA within that rusted splinter remained the last untried forensic hope for identifying the culprit.

For Rainy Macintosh, no longer a junior doctor but still with boundless medical curiosity, the remains laid out on a mortuary slab were fascinating. In her few years in the police, this was only the second dead body she had seen, and she could barely restrain herself from prodding and poking. That morning's visit to the hospital to see the cadaver had been inspired by two extra DNA tests whose mixed results had been sent to them. A familial DNA check had found no connection between this man and anyone else on the national DNA database. The reason for this was probably explained by the second result. The mitochondrial DNA tests showed Scandinavian and Eastern European origins.

'I'll home in on the two missing Eastern Europeans from our list,' Rainy said, as she held up a small piece of the man's jaw in her nylon-gloved hand.

'I think perhaps we should expand the radius too,' Gillard said. 'All Scandinavian and EU foreign nationals registered as missing across the UK. We should start on the more recent ones, but still go back to 2012.'

'Why 2012?' Rainy asked.

'That was the year the bloodstained book in Cleaver's house was published.'

She snapped her fingers. 'Aye, that's a canny piece of evidence. Getting a match between the droplet on the book and on the walls of the room.'

'But I really want to find out about the barman who stayed in Dove Cottage. The one mentioned by Rowena.'

'So we need to get Vicky Willow in. She and Guy Naylor would have employed him.'

Gillard nodded. 'Here's another curious thing, Rainy. Rowena Willow showed me around St Crispin's church, and told me a prophecy. It was along the lines of "an innocent prince killing a foreign crown". Something like that.'

Rainy laughed. 'Aye, sir, we know the victim is foreign. But if a member of European royalty had gone missing we wouldnae miss that news. The wee kingly fella would not have been grubbing up veg or working behind a bar in a shithole like the Anvil either.'

'Fair point, Rainy. I'm still curious about it, all the same.'

–

The moment they'd finished at the mortuary, Gillard rang the Anvil Arms. Vicky answered, amid a lot of background noise, the clattering of glasses and a shouting child. Once the detective had persuaded her to step away somewhere quieter, he asked the name of the East European barman who had worked there a few years ago.

'Which one?' she responded, before re-emerging into the noise. 'Callum, for Christ's sake, put them away. I've told you! No, now.'

Gillard waited out the thirty seconds until he heard the click of a door, and then they were back in silence. 'We must have had half a dozen. I don't think I even remember all their names. It was all cash in hand. Some of them only stayed a week or two, filling in between farm jobs.'

'All right,' Gillard said. 'Pull together what documentation you have. I'll send an officer down to collect it, and perhaps get another statement from you.'

'Can if you like,' she said. 'There won't be much. They never worked enough hours even for national insurance contributions. We liked to keep it simple. I'll ask Guy to take a look once we close this afternoon.'

–

By late afternoon on Monday, Rainy Macintosh had returned from Rissington Common and walked into the office waving a thickish couple of folders.

'Some success then?' Gillard said.

'Nae breakthrough, that's for sure,' she replied. Gillard waved her into a conference room where they had the space to lay out the documents. But the thickest of the two folders turned out to be photographs, many of them dog-eared and faded, some sorted into slim piles with elastic bands. Overall there were hundreds of pictures of joyful and often drunken youngsters at Christmas, Halloween, various other pub parties over the years. 'There wasnae a single scrap of documentation you could rely on. But they had a wall in the bar with a collage of this lot, plus sheaves more in drawers. We spent most of the time looking through those, trying to identify casual staff from years ago.'

'So they co-operated?'

'Aye, pretty much. I have a few names.' She slid off an elastic band, and spread out the pictures which showed a tall smiling youth with a shock of dark hair. 'Yon fella was called Paul. He's Polish, and we think his real Christian name is Pavel. Neither Vicky nor Guy have a clue about his surname. He stayed all one summer, 2014 or 2015, they aren't sure.'

'That really puts the casual in casual labour, doesn't it?' Gillard said.

'Aye, that it does.' Rainy undid another stack. 'This one they called Tom, and he was from one of the Baltic republics. These photos were from 2018, they think.'

'No surname?'

'Nope. But they think it was the same Lithuanian guy who went missing in London that year. Tomas Valdovas, I mentioned him before.' She flicked backwards and forwards through a stack of printouts.

'Do you think Guy and Vicky are trying to hide the truth?'

She waggled her hand ambivalently. 'They're plausibly casual about almost everything. The two of them manage to keep the Anvil show on the road with string and sticky tape. And terrible cooking.'

'I meant to warn you about that.'

'Och, the gammon was like shoe leather. It was the day's special for five pounds, and came with radioactive green slop that might have been mushy peas.'

'Yuck. Did you get to speak to Rowena?'

'Yes, and Crystal. There was a bit more paperwork about Dove Cottage, which Crystal managed to dig out. There are two gaps in the tenancy record, 2013 and 2018. It seems that over the years several bar staff have stayed at Dove Cottage, including Tomas Valdovas in the early summer of 2018. Anyway, Valdovas later disappeared in London after taking a National Express coach from Winchester to Victoria. He worked as a fruit picker before doing bar work at the Anvil.'

'How do we know all that?' Gillard said.

'There was a misper inquiry on him at the time, documented by Hampshire Constabulary.' She logged on to the meeting room screen and keyed into the evidence file.

'Do we have witnesses?'

'Not directly, the log says it was video evidence from the coach itself that showed him getting aboard at Winchester on 16 October 2018 and leaving at Victoria. His onward ticket was never used.'

'I wonder if Hampshire still has the files? I'd also like to know who it was ID'd him.'

'The case is closed, according to this.'

Gillard rolled his eyes. 'Pound to a penny they haven't retained the footage.'

-

He was wrong. Hampshire Constabulary were able to forward several files to Rainy. The first was a series of video stills taken from within the National Express coach, from a position above the driver's seat. It showed a young man with a distinctive purple hooded top getting on the bus with a sports bag. He was wearing a dark baseball cap which hid his face, but it became clearer on stills from the camera further back.

'So that is Mr Valdovas,' Gillard said. 'Let's look at the bar pictures again.'

The two detectives soon spotted the same purple top in several of the photos taken inside the Anvil. The man had a distinctive mass of blond curly hair in the pub pictures that was not evident on the stills from the coach.

'Maybe he had a haircut,' Rainy said. 'Or stuffed it in his cap'.

Gillard use the screen magnifier to get the best of the stills to a reasonable size. 'Who identified this guy as Valdovas?'

'Guy Naylor,' Rainy said. 'He's certainly wearing the clothes. There are the same high-top trainers and the hoodie.'

Gillard stroked his chin. 'That's exactly what's making me suspicious. I recognise this face on the coach. It took me a moment to put two and two together. I don't think it's Valdovas at all. Look at the shape of the jaw. It's Aidan Tickett.'

Chapter Twenty-five

The two detectives went from one set of images to the other. From the flash–illuminated pub pictures with all the distortions of colour, to the grainy images from the coach. 'Aye, I can see why you might think it was Valdovas, because of the clothing.'

'If it is Aidan Tickett,' Gillard said, looking through the other attachments that Hampshire had forwarded, 'it's an attempt to make it seem like Valdovas wasn't missing until he got to London. Here, look. Hampshire tracked down the pre-booked coach ticket from Victoria to Warsaw, which was never used. And a matching phone trace which ends at Victoria. There is also a translation of a statement by his mother saying he never came home to Vilnius.'

'Aye, it's canny. Let's say Aidan or Rory Tickett killed him in Dove Cottage, then buried him in the garden. They, after all, are in the digging business.'

'Okay, I grant you they are main suspects. But it can't be that straightforward. Why move the body?'

'When they heard about the new vicar as a tenant of Dove Cottage, maybe.'

'But why rebury it somewhere it's likely to be dug up again? By your own digger, of all things. And why to try to make the corpse look like it's Ozzy Blanchard's by using the comb? Why would anyone but Ozzy do that?'

Rainy sucked her teeth. 'Ozzy must have been involved. To provide the comb, if nothing else.'

'I see there's no DNA sample for Valdovas. Can you contact the international police liaison officer in Vilnius; the Met will have the number. We need to get a DNA sample from any clothing she has. We can then match it up with the bloodstain DNA at Dove Cottage.'

'That's a canny plan. I'll get on to it.'

–

Finally, that week saw progress being made quickly. On Tuesday DC Corey Williams' team, now with full assistance from Hampshire Constabulary and the SFO, had been notified of a payment from Aqua Western to Buckingham Pallets Ltd, one of the companies owned by the Ticketts. Tracing it back, it turned out to have been sent from a contingency fund at Aqua Western which had been set up to pay the victims of sewage flooding. By Wednesday it was discovered that Kelvin Arrowsmith's signature covered more than two dozen different accounts at the water company. The payment reference was compensation allotted to Rissington Common households. Shireen had described it as a 'breathtaking act of nerve to divert cash away from victims'.

The fraud investigation had gradually tied together the Tickett family, Ozzy Blanchard and Kelvin Arrowsmith. Evidence was mounting, and the CPS was impressed. DCI Stella Anderson's name was mentioned in glowing terms.

But for Gillard, nothing was settled until everything was settled. At the top of that to-do list was trying to find the identity of the victim, something that had eluded them since the very beginning. They now knew it wasn't Ozzy

Blanchard, and strongly suspected it was Tomas Valdovas, but had no proof. He was aware that Rainy was spending hours on the phone to the liaison officer in Vilnius, trying to get hold of a DNA sample for Valdovas, and then get it couriered back to London for testing against the samples from Dove Cottage. On that side, things were just moving too slowly. It was late on Thursday afternoon, and Rainy was clearing her desk. She was due to knock off at four to pick up her son from school, and had her bag over her shoulder when her desk phone rang. Gillard looked up and watched from his office as she reached across and clamped the receiver under her chin. Almost immediately, her body language changed from casual to upright, and she turned around to him, beckoning him over.

'Yes, that's right. It is? Fantastic! Thank you.' She hung up.

'What have you got?' Gillard said as he approached.

'It's confirmed, sir. The two samples match.'

Finally, they could be sure. The man killed at Dove Cottage, buried in the garden, and then reburied amongst the willows by the River Wey was indeed Tomas Valdovas. The Lithuanian barman's DNA matched the bloodstains on the wall and on the spine of the book, and it also matched those recovered from the roots of the teeth.

'That gives us some more pointers,' Gillard said. 'First off, it underlines Aidan Tickett's involvement, and it gives us an approximate date of death, in the days running up to the date of the reservation.'

It was 16 October 2018, when Aidan Tickett had got on the coach from Winchester to London dressed in Valdovas's clothes, using his reservation and taking with him the phone on which it was made. Aidan Tickett had plenty of questions to answer, but Gillard first wanted to arm himself with more detail about the Lithuanian's movements in the days running up to his death. Hampshire Constabulary had taken witness statements at the time, but Gillard wanted to check these against what the witnesses to Valdovas's working life said now.

–

Vicky Willow used childcare issues as an excuse to decline a formal interview at Winchester Police Station, but instead agreed to be questioned in the rear bar at the Anvil on Friday morning. Gillard didn't need to press the matter, and provided a duty solicitor and a portable recorder to give the session its proper gravitas.

Vicky seemed to take everything in her stride, as usual. She was clearing the dishwasher when Gillard arrived, and wearily showed them through to a large musty-smelling back bar in which furniture was stacked at one end. She was wearing a stained T-shirt with the single word BOSS on the front, and evidence of fresh baby dribble on the shoulder. She actually locked the glass door with a key that she then pocketed.

'It's the only way I can be sure we won't be disturbed,' she said.

Gillard set up the tape, intoned the formalities of who he was interviewing and where, then asked her to detail everything she could remember about Tomas Valdovas.

'Who?' was her first question.

'A twenty-two-year-old Lithuanian barman with frizzy blond hair from 2018. You knew him as Tom.'

Vicky squinted into the distance, as if trying to recall the man. Gillard assisted by passing back to her copies of the photographs that had originally been on the wall of this very same bar.

'Oh, Tom. The police asked about him a couple of years ago. He worked here a few weeks at the beginning of the summer, and alternated between farm work and bar work depending on what crop was in season. This wasn't the only pub he worked at. I think he did a few shifts at the Sun in Upper Rissington.'

Gillard wrote down the details. 'What kind of a man was he?'

'He was friendly, funny, and good with the locals generally.'

'Generally?'

'Well, there was always someone taking the piss out of his accent.'

'And when did he leave?'

She licked her lips. 'I think the last time we saw him was in the October. You should look at the statement I gave at the time.'

'I've got it right here, but you tell me what you remember.'

'I do recall it was really sad that he went missing in London. I don't think we ever heard whether he turned up again, but since it all went quiet, I assumed he did.'

'Come on, that's a bit casual even for you. You knew Hampshire Constabulary had a missing persons inquiry on him, but appear to have shown no interest in its outcome.'

'I thought he must have turned up. People do, I mean that's what the officer said at the time. Most missing people do turn up unharmed.'

'And at no time were you worried enough to check up on this poor young man.'

'Look, this is a busy pub. Barmen and barmaids come and go. We welcome them and look after them, but we don't keep track of them after they leave.'

Gillard held up a witness statement. 'Two years ago, your husband identified Valdovas from CCTV on a National Express coach video. I can now tell you that the man in those pictures was not Valdovas, even though he was wearing his clothing.'

'Really?'

'Yes, really. We believe that Valdovas never left the village. He was murdered in a bedroom of Dove Cottage, and buried in the garden. Do you know anything about that?'

Vicky Willow said nothing, but stared at the table in front of her, her normal ruddy complexion now pallid. She looked exhausted and defeated.

'Do you know anything about that, Vicky?'

'No,' she whispered. Gillard got her to repeat it for the tape.

A crash against the glass door made them all jump. Vicky's son Callum was pressing against the pane, palms flat, face squashed so that his upturned nose revealed giant nostrils, fogging the glass. He began to pound on the door, calling for his mother. Furious, she rounded on him and bellowed for him to leave her alone. 'Can't I ever get a minute's peace from all your trouble?'

The boy vanished, and Vicky turned round to her interlocutors. 'If he is dead, that's horrible,' she said. 'But I know nothing about it.'

'How did Mr Valdovas get on with the Tickett family?'

She shot him a narrow-eyed look that spoke volumes.

'You don't have to protect them, you know,' Gillard said. 'They're all going down for a long time anyway. They've been charged with abduction and they are about to be charged with fraud. There's no need to be afraid. You can do the right thing.'

The woman buried her face in her hands. 'All my life I have tried to do the right thing,' she said thickly. 'But it's not always obvious what the right thing is.'

–

It was Friday afternoon when Gillard slid his Vauxhall into the car park at HMP High Down. It was humid, with towering cumulus clouds building, their undersides the colour of slate. He and Rainy Macintosh left the car just as the first fat raindrops were beginning to fall, and the first peal of thunder sounded like a warehouse shelf collapse. They hurried inside, escorted along brightly lit corridors which echoed to the sound of thunderclaps.

Aidan Tickett sat impassively in the interview room with the same solicitor as last time. 'I've got nothing more to tell you,' Aidan announced before they'd even sat down.

'You don't know what I'm going to ask you yet,' Gillard said, as he prepped the tape. When everything was set he steepled his hands and asked: 'You killed Tom, didn't you?'

Aidan, pale to begin with, went ashen before recovering his poise. 'I don't know what you mean.'

'Tomas Valdovas, a twenty-two-year-old Lithuanian barman who worked at the Anvil in the summer of 2018. He died in the bedroom of Dove Cottage, sometime that October, stabbed in the neck. His spine was severed.'

'I don't know what you're talking about.'

Gillard could see a certain confusion in his face.

'Did you not know the man? He worked behind the bar.'

'I might have known him by sight, but he wasn't a friend or anything. I know nothing about him.'

Gillard swiped through his iPad until he came across an image of a purple hooded jacket culled from an online retailer. 'Recognise this item of clothing?' He showed Aidan the image.

Aidan shook his head. 'Never seen it before.'

Gillard swiped to a video, part of the footage taken from the National Express coach. 'Yet here you are wearing the very same item of clothing thing, travelling to London on Tom's ticket.'

'Yeah, but that's not me. We look very similar.'

'I thought you said you didn't know him?'

Aidan blinked, looking confused. 'I said I might know him by sight.'

'You "might" know him by sight but seem to be very clear that he looked like you.'

'People said he looked like me.'

'What people?'

Aidan's eyes scurried from Rainy's face to the video and back up to the ceiling. 'Don't remember. Friends, probably.'

'Do yers have many blind pals?' Rainy asked. 'Yon fella's got blond hair, and lots of it. You're a wee ginger laddie to my eyes.'

'Yeah, well, it depends on the light.' Aidan folded his arms and set his jaw.

'Aye, and works best when there isn't any.'

'So why were you on the coach, wearing Tom's clothing?' Gillard asked.

'I wasn't.'

Gillard turned the iPad back to Aidan and flicked through one picture after another. 'You only got away with this because Guy Naylor identified you as Tom.'

Aidan said nothing.

'And the only reason he would lie like that is to help cover up the crime you committed.'

'I didn't fucking kill him, all right?'

'If you didn't, who did?'

No reply.

'Was it Rory?'

No reply.

'Who were you covering for?'

No reply. Gillard decided to press the nuclear button: 'Aidan Tickett, I am charging you with the murder of Tomas Valdovas. You do not have to say anything, but it may harm your defence if you do not mention when questioned something which you later rely on in court. Anything you do say may be given in evidence.'

'You bastards. You've got nothing on me.'

'I beg to differ,' Gillard said. 'Why on earth would you have impersonated him, used his coach ticket and his phone, if you didn't want to cover up the fact that he had died by your hand in Dove Cottage? Even if you didn't kill him yourself, you know who did, so do yourself a favour and tell us.'

Aidan merely examined his fingernails, and began to chew at the already bitten tips. Gillard tried a few more questions, but there was no reply. He wrapped up the interview formalities, and watched as Aidan was taken back to his cell by two prison officers.

In the car park outside, Rainy asked: 'We cannae put him at the Dove Cottage crime scene, can we?'

'Forensically, no. I've tightened the screws on all of the Ticketts. They're all on a murder charge now. We just have to wait to see which one cracks first.'

'I wouldnae reckon they'll ever crack, sir. That wee bunch are as hard as nails.'

Chapter Twenty-six

On Saturday, Dr Clive Hancock and his volunteers opened the dig to the public, to see how much progress had been made on the Anglo-Saxon site. Trestle tables were laid out with glass display cases showing some of the coins and shards of crockery that had been recovered, along with interpretation boards which explained the process of dating the various artefacts found. The weather was fine, and by ten o'clock there were about fifty people present. Hancock sat in a central tent, running something of an Antiques Roadshow for residents and visitors who brought in their own finds to be evaluated. So far that day he had identified a few Roman-era coins, some Victorian glassware and a rusted pin with a mount for a gem, which he was convinced was a genuine Anglo-Saxon item. Sadly, the mount no longer had the gem in it.

Next in line was Sheila Ransome and her son. Stewie was quite excited, because he had with him a late-Victorian metal biscuit tin given to him by his grandmother, and in which he kept his other precious oddments. Eventually called forward to sit opposite the archaeologist, he wasted no time opening the tin, which was jam-packed with rusty items.

Hancock peered into the box and immediately spotted the largest item, a purple plastic handle, into which a piece of rusty metal had been jammed. 'Aha, what's this?' Hancock asked.

'It's my lightsabre,' Stewie replies. 'It's broken.'

'May I?' Hancock said, lifting up the item. 'Is this how you found it?'

Stewie laughed. 'Yes.'

'Oh don't be so silly,' Sheila said. 'That plastic handle doesn't belong on that rusty old thing. Aren't you going to show him your collection of coins?' She prodded her finger into the box and picked up a greenish corroded disc.

Hancock ignored the coin, but hefted the corroded item, gradually easing off the plastic handle. It revealed an eight-inch-long rusty metal tool, narrowing from a shank where a handle would have fitted down to a jagged broken tip.

'I think we have something very exciting here,' he said. 'Where did you find it?'

Stewie suddenly looked extremely shifty. 'I swapped it for some soldiers.'

'Soldiers?'

'Plastic figures,' Sheila intervened. 'With Callum. It must've been a couple of years ago now,' she said.

'I'd just like to borrow this for a few hours, if I may. It could be quite valuable,'

'Ooh, isn't that exciting, Stewie? What you think it could be?' Sheila turned to the archaeologist. 'Is it a Victorian tool of some kind?'

'No, I'm pretty sure it's not Victorian. It's much older than that.'

Hancock called Rowena Willow over. 'Would you be kind enough to hold the fort for a while? I have to nip off to the college.'

'How long will you be?' she asked.

'A couple of hours, probably.'

'But what about all the people waiting to see you? They've all brought their finds.'

'I've something even more important to do, and I'm sure you'll do an excellent job here,' he said.

–

It was early on Saturday evening when Gillard was called at home by Dr Hancock.

'I've got some very exciting news for you. I've found the murder weapon used on the buried body.'

'Where?'

'Stewie Ransome brought it in. He had a biscuit tin full of old rusting junk. It turns out that he has been in possession of an Anglo-Saxon dagger, minus its pommel. He'd jammed the hilt into a modern plastic handle from a Star Wars toy, so it could be grasped. The blade is broken in exactly the same place as the jagged piece found in the neck of our murder victim. I've X-rayed the item, and it matches the Biorthelm style.'

'Have you been handling it?'

'In gloves, but yes.'

'We need to get it checked out for fingerprints and DNA,' Gillard said. 'Please bring it in to your nearest police station.'

'I'd like to hold on to it for a couple more days, as there are some additional tests I'd like to do.'

'The archaeology can wait, this is a murder inquiry.'

'I would be very surprised if there are any fingerprints apart from Stewie's.'

'Nevertheless, I need it tested.'

'All right then.' Dr Hancock sounded crestfallen.

–

By nine a.m. on Sunday morning, Gillard was once again back in Rissington Common, this time interviewing Stewie Ransome in the presence of his mother in their cottage. Also present was PC Sarah Noakes, who had interviewed the young man before.

'I want to emphasise, Stewie, that you are not in trouble, we just need to know where you got the rusty dagger,'

'The officer means your lightsabre,' Sheila said.

'I forget,' Stewie replied.

'Didn't you get it in a swap with Callum?' Sheila said. 'You gave him your plastic soldiers.'

'When was that?' Gillard asked.

Stewie looked at his mother for clarification.

'You had it in that old biscuit tin for at least two years,' she said.

'Two years,' Stewie said, triumphantly.

The next question Gillard had prepared in advance with help from Sarah Noakes, who had experience interviewing vulnerable adults. 'Now Stewie, have you ever pretended to stab someone with your lightsabre? Have you ever hit anyone with it by accident?'

He shook his head. 'I don't hit people. Hitting is wrong.' He began chewing his lips, and staring at his mother. 'I didn't do anything.'

'Stewie, we're just trying to find the truth,' PC Noakes said with a smile. 'You're not in trouble.'

Stewie blinked. 'Can I go and play, Mum?'

'No, dear.'

'In a little while,' Gillard said.

'It was the vicar, in the library, with the dagger,' Stewie said.

'What library?' PC Noakes asked.

'He's just referring to Cluedo. He's obsessed with it,' Sheila said.

Gillard stared into the young man's face. He had an open countenance, radiating innocence. His pale eyelashes quivered. 'I didn't kill him,' Stewie said.

'Who didn't you kill?' Gillard asked.

'Anyone.'

Gillard was far from convinced they were making any progress. He and PC Noakes thanked Mrs Ransome and left the cottage, heading up the road to the next interview, with Vicky Willow and her son Callum. 'Whatever you do,' he said to PC Noakes. 'Do not accept any food at the Anvil.'

'Don't worry, sir, I've heard about its reputation. So this Callum is just a seven-year-old lad?'

'That's right. I'm far from convinced that any of this will shed any light on who wielded the dagger. It's much more likely that the rusty dagger was found by Callum after it had been used in the murder. We just need to know where he found it.'

Gillard casually checked his phone, where a text had just come through. The two-word message from DC Rainy Macintosh almost floored him.

Rory's confessed

Chapter Twenty-seven

Rory 'Typhoon' Tickett had admitted killing Tomas Valdovas. The confession was made to a prison psychiatrist assessing his mental health at HMP Winchester. The email forwarded by Rainy described how the former boxer had got into an argument with Valdovas in the bar late one night just as the Anvil was closing.

'Is that admissible?' PC Noakes asked 'Aren't conversations between psychiatrists and their patients legally privileged?'

'Yes, they are,' Gillard replied. 'But the therapist persuaded him to make a statement, and it would be sensible of us to try to replicate that statement on tape, then we can wrap this up. I'll go up to Winchester straightaway. Perhaps you could speak to Callum Willow alone, and give my apologies to his mother.'

'Right,' said PC Noakes. 'You just want to know where he found the dagger?'

'Yes, and when. Callum can't have been involved. He would only have been five at the time Valdovas was killed.'

–

Gillard met up with DC Rainy Macintosh at HMP Winchester. Rory Tickett was in a terrible state. Dishevelled, wild-eyed and as pale as a ghost, he sat opposite Gillard and the duty solicitor, flanked by two hefty prison officers. Rory seemed to look past them all.

'There are spiders in my room,' he whispered. 'Huge invisible spiders, that are beaming their thoughts into my head.'

'We've come to ask you about something else,' Gillard said. 'Your argument with Mr Tomas Valdovas.'

'He sent the spiders from hell, as vengeance,' Rory whispered. He banged his temple with the heel of his hand. 'They're in here, they don't leave me alone.' He punched his own head twice, hard enough to make Gillard wince. He was far from sure that this interview was going to achieve any more than the one with Stewie Ransome had.

'Do you remember Tomas Valdovas? Tom, with the blond hair.' Rainy passed across a photograph from Vicky Willow's collection. 'That's him.'

'I hurt Tom, but I didn't mean to. But the spiders don't care.'

'Why did you hurt him?' she asked.

'We had a barney, in the bar.'

'About what?' Gillard asked.

'A spilled pint, nothing really. I was tanked up, and waited for him in the car park.'

'This was after closing time?' Rainy asked.

'Yes.'

'Do you remember an exact day or date?' Gillard asked.

'It was a Sunday night in October, a couple of years ago. The pub had emptied out. I only punched him the once. Aidan pulled me away.'

'And this was in the car park? You didn't fight anywhere else?' Gillard was thinking of the bloodstains in Dove Cottage.

'No. I punched him in the temple, a right hook, and he went down and banged his head.'

'Why didn't you call an ambulance?' Rainy asked.

'Because he got up again, after a few minutes. He was all right, and I apologised and we shook hands. But then he died in the night.'

'How did you know?' she asked.

'Vicky told me. She went round to see him next day when he was due on shift at the bar. She couldn't rouse him. I couldn't believe it, but she took me to Dove Cottage and showed him lying dead on the bed. I felt terrible. I hadn't meant to kill him.'

'Did you notice any injuries on the body?' Gillard asked. 'On the neck, for example.'

'He had a massive great swelling on his forehead and a black eye. I didn't notice anything else. I'm so so sorry for what I did.'

Gillard exchanged a glance with the solicitor. This was a confession that didn't match the evidence. Blood from Valdovas had been sprayed across the room. That could only have come from an injury which matched the dagger wound. It didn't make sense.

'When you were fighting Tom, were there any other witnesses apart from Aidan?'

'I don't think so.'

Gillard asked a few more questions, but Rory Tickett's answers now focused on invisible spiders, that were talking to him *at this very moment*.

'What are they telling you to do?'

'To bite you,' Rory whispered. 'They're evil.'

Getting no more sense out of the interviewee, Gillard cut the tape, thanked the solicitor and stepped out of the room. Checking his phone, he saw he'd got a new

and shocking message from PC Sarah Noakes back in
Rissington Common.

Got a confession

Chapter Twenty-eight

Another confession? Gillard rang Noakes immediately. 'Are you telling me Vicky Willow killed Tomas Valdovas?'

'Not exactly. At first she wouldn't let me talk to Callum. Instead she gave me a story about how she helped Tomas home on the Sunday night after a fight at the pub.'

'I heard about that, Rory Tickett hit him.'

'Ah, yes, that was in the version I heard. She didn't see the fight. She'd just finished locking up when she walked out into the garden and saw the two Tickett brothers standing over Valdovas, who was sitting on the ground. The moment she saw the bruises on him, she threw the Ticketts off the premises and walked Valdovas back to Dove Cottage. He was pretty woozy, but seemed okay. She went round at breakfast time on the Monday, and apart from the bruises Valdovas seemed fully recovered. She asked him to look after Callum, who was then five, while she dealt with the usual Monday morning delivery from the brewer. Apparently Tomas was great with the kid, and used to cart him about in a wheelbarrow, give him piggybacks, and go running about with him on his shoulders.'

'Go on.'

'Now the story I was told is this.' At this point Sarah's voice changed to convey a certain scepticism. 'Half an hour later, which would be around 10.15 a.m., Callum came running up the road to the pub in hysterical tears, with bloody hands and bloodstains on his shirt and trousers. She said she was well used to this because he's a boisterous child and always getting into scrapes. But this time there was a lot of blood. The child didn't seem hurt, and she couldn't understand where the blood came from. Callum was inconsolable, and kept talking about Tom. She dropped everything and ran back with the boy to Dove Cottage. There, in the back room, she found Tomas Valdovas dead and covered in blood. "I stabbed him by mistake," the boy said. "We were playing cavalry." That's all he said. Having established that Valdovas was dead, Vicky stopped herself from ringing 999. Callum eventually explained that he was riding on Tomas's shoulders when they were playing, with his lightsabre in his hand. Tomas tripped and toppled backwards and onto the child, whose weapon pierced his neck.'

'A likely story,' Gillard said.

'Vicky Willow said she panicked. Callum was convinced he'd killed the man, but she persuaded him that Tomas wasn't dead, but knocked unconscious. She didn't want the child to have all that guilt. So she rang Guy, to bring fresh clothes for Callum, and then to take the boy back while she cleaned up. She washed the walls, pulled out the carpet and cut the bloody clothes off the body before washing him. She even put a dressing over the wound on the back of the victim's neck. Guy came back and together they dragged Tomas back to his bedroom, dressed him in clean clothes, jeans and a shirt with a collar that hid the dressing. They put him on the bed and then called Aidan Tickett with the news that Thomas had died last night. "That punch in the head from Rory was the death of him," she said.'

'Very clever,' Gillard said.

'An hour later Aidan and Rory Tickett came to Dove Cottage and were shown the body, now cleaned up and dressed. They had no reason to believe that Vicky and Guy had been lying. Vicky offered to keep quiet so long as the Ticketts disposed of the body somewhere sensible. They went through his belongings, phone and laptop and found the coach reservation. It was Vicky's suggestion that Aidan should impersonate Tomas, because they were a similar build. The Ticketts, needless to say, were incredibly grateful for Vicky's promise of silence on this. They came back in the evening, and though they never told her, buried him in the garden. When Vicky asked later where they had disposed of the body, Aidan said, "Miles away from here, no need to worry." Now mightily relieved, Vicky gave the house a much more thorough cleaning. She also told a white lie to Callum, along the lines of Tomas leaving to go back to Lithuania. She even got Aidan to write a postcard from London and send it to Callum as if it was from Tomas.'

'The whole thing is beginning to make some sense now,' Gillard said. 'Did you get to talk to the child?'

'No, she wouldn't let me.'

'Well, that has got to change. He's just about old enough to give a coherent account.' He thanked her and cut the call. He told Rainy what he had just heard.

'Aye, sir. This is beginning to make sense. Do you remember the prophecy from the church? "In ages hence when England flees the Frankish arm, an innocent wielding a lost scramsax will here fell a Viking lord".'

'Well remembered,' Gillard said.

'Och, I didnae remember it, I wrote it down. And yesterday I did a wee bit of research. Well, I suppose

Callum could be the innocent, wielding the scramsax, that nasty little weapon he found in the mud.'

'What is the Frankish arm in this context?'

'I'm tempted to say Brexit. But it could equally be the Battle of Hastings and all that.'

Gillard laughed. 'And the Viking lord?'

'Aye, that's where I had a breakthrough. We already have the Viking angle, from the victim's mitochondrial DNA, which shows a Scandinavian origin for him. The rest is about the name. In Lithuanian, lord, ruler, or sovereign are the same word: Valdovas.'

Gillard was by nature a sceptic, but he had to admit that those who wanted to believe in the prophecy had all the evidence they needed. But how could some seventh-century Anglo-Saxon scribe know that a young Lithuanian was to die here, a millennium and a half later, at the hands of a child?

–

Vicky Willow sat outside the rape suite at Winchester Police Station, while Gillard and PC Sarah Noakes sat inside with Callum and a social worker. Callum had a box of plastic soldiers, which he was playing with on the coffee table. The social worker, whose name was Charlotte, introduced the child to the two police officers, who were casually dressed in jumpers and trousers to help the child relax.

'Now Callum, we just want to play a little quiz with you,' Sarah said. 'We ask you things, and you give us the answer. Then we all have cake at the end. Okay?'

Callum nodded, but continued to play with the soldiers, making shooting noises as one plastic figure chased another amongst the coffee cups.

'Do you remember your friend, Tomas?' she asked 'The man who let you ride on his shoulders.'

Callum looked up at her, his mouth wetly open, his pink tongue resting on his bottom lip. 'I played cavalry with him.'

'Do you remember playing with Tom at his house, at Dove Cottage?'

The boy nodded, and continued to play. 'Tom went home, so I don't get to play cavalry anymore. Mum doesn't like me to play rough.'

'Why is that?'

'It's dangerous. I can have plastic guns, but not metal. No swords, knives or scissors.'

'Did you hurt Tom once?' Sarah asked.

Callum's concentration on one particular soldier seemed intense. He blinked several times, and then nodded. 'I was messing around. Being silly.'

'What happened?'

'Tom was my horse, and I was on his shoulders, and he was galloping. He tripped and fell over.' The boy's face coloured at the recollection. 'I won't play cavalry again.'

'It's all right, you're not in trouble. It's just part of the quiz.'

He nodded.

'So did he fall backwards?'

'Yes.'

'Did you have your lightsabre in your hand?'

'Yes.'

'What happened to it?'

'He fell backwards onto me, and the sharp bit went right in his neck. There was blood, and it made him go to sleep. Mummy made me give the lightsabre away afterwards.'

'She said she threw it away,' Sarah said.

'Yeah, but I got it out of the bin, and swapped it with Stewie.'

Gillard smiled to himself. Maybe Vicky had been telling the truth after all.

'That's great, thank you Callum,' Sarah said.

'Can I have cake now?'

'Yes.'

'Can Tom come and have cake too?' he blurted out.

The three adults looked at each other, before Gillard said: 'He lives far away now, but he sends you his love.'

–

Gillard was almost back at Mount Browne when the final piece of the double-murder inquiry fell into place. He was driving into Guildford when a call from the control room passed on the message that the Italian authorities had finally arrested Ray Slater at his holiday home, and he was now on a plane back to Gatwick. Gillard was keen to get his hands on Slater at the earliest opportunity and decided to join the airport police for the handover. That left him just half an hour to grab a bite at the canteen before heading off to the airport. He rubbed his hands in anticipation.

He joined a jovial queue of uniformed coppers anticipating the day's special of cottage pie. Doubting that any would be left by the time he got there, he glanced at the Surrey Police noticeboard. The long-vacant post of assistant chief constable had finally been filled. He looked at the picture of the new appointee and gasped. It was Stella Anderson. Reading down the glowing tributes that had been paid to her, one was: 'Detective Chief Superintendent Anderson played a key role in discovering a major water company fraud and an associated murder and abduction. Almost all the defendants are all in custody and the case is now awaiting trial.'

Gillard had plenty of experience of senior officers taking credit for the hard work of those further down the hierarchy, but this was a severe case of overreach, particularly jumping the gun on Slater, who wasn't yet on British soil. The fraud, yes, she had played the key role in that. But catching the murderer of Ozzy Blanchard had been nothing to do with her. If he was to share the credit with anyone, it would be Thames Valley Police, not Hampshire.

DI Claire Mulholland came up to him as he was reading. 'I didn't think you'd be impressed by that. She's got a nerve, hasn't she?'

'Radar Dobbs won't be happy about reporting to her,' Gillard said. 'She's got ambitions to sweep out the old guard.'

'Who knows, that might include you,' Claire said.

He turned to stare at her. 'I'm not that long in the tooth.'

'Yes, but didn't you sleep with her once, back in the dim and distant?'

Gillard stared at her open mouthed. 'I never told you that.'

'I heard it on the sisterly grapevine. I've no idea who the original source was, except it must've been someone who was at the same conference and saw you two disappearing together. I hadn't thought it was true until just now. Your reaction confirmed it.'

'Yes, I'm afraid it is true.' Gillard realised that he shouldn't be surprised a conference room full of detectives would notice two people slipping away together.

'Well, it's truly come back to haunt you now, Craig, hasn't it?'

—

Gillard was still fuming about Anderson when he arrived at Gatwick Airport. He drove to the secure police compound, having to show his credentials numerous times at various checkpoints. Leaving the car by a collection of anonymous Portakabins, normally used for abusive drunkards plucked from holiday flights, he went into the reception area, where the desk sergeant led him through to the correct interview room and unlocked the door. Ray Slater, arms folded, looked every bit the disappointed holidaymaker. He wore a short-sleeved flowered shirt, blue shorts, and below his hairy legs, a pair of canvas shoes without socks. The female duty solicitor sitting with him looked dressed for a funeral, in a black trouser suit. As far as Gillard was concerned she had the mood right.

'Did you enjoy your brief holiday?' Gillard said as he arranged his papers, and prepped the tape.

Slater gave a sarcastic smile through his two-day growth of beard.

Gillard cautioned him, then said: 'Mr Slater, we have in our possession the handgun which ballistic tests show was used to kill Ozzy Blanchard. We have CCTV evidence of you near the scene of the crime at Chieveley Services at the time of the killing, and we have witness statements too. We also have records of telephone conversations of you admitting to an undercover officer...'

'Undercover, my arse. Carl Hoskins set me up. It was entrapment. For weeks he had been feeding me information so that I could do my job, and then he stabs me in the back. My own brother-in-law.'

'DC Hoskins came to me and volunteered his relation-ship to you and the fact that you had been asking him for information. He was also instrumental in tracing your vehicle to Chieveley Services, and without him we would have struggled to catch you.'

Gillard knew Slater would try to implicate Hoskins, which offered the best chance of undermining the prosec-ution. However, he himself had checked Hoskins' access to records on the various police databases, and there was no evidence of rule breaking. Hoskins hadn't looked at anything that would not have been part of the inquiry he was working on. Gillard suspected that Hoskins had in fact fed Slater some information, but was secretly relieved to discover he couldn't prove it.

'You're fitting me up,' Slater said.

'Really? The serial number shows the Browning auto-matic used to kill Blanchard went missing from a Royal Marines quartermaster's depot in Portsmouth in 1984, when coincidentally you happened to be serving in that unit.'

'That's bollocks.'

'On the contrary, Mr Slater, I suspect a jury will find it quite convincing. Moreover, we are able to show that Kelvin Arrowsmith bought you a £100,000 holiday prop-erty in Italy, and we contend that was in exchange for the hit on Ozzy Blanchard. Not an easy transaction to trace, but we now have all the details we need, including the Italian title deeds. Arrowsmith will be going down for a series of frauds which he unsuccessfully tried to pin solely on his partner in crime, Ozzy Blanchard.'

'That holiday home is totally legit,' Slater said. 'I paid for it myself.' He turned to his brief as if attempting to convince her. 'You know, I was standing in the shell of my new swimming pool, talking to contractors, when the Italian cops came. They didn't even give me five minutes to change.'

Gillard then formally charged Slater with murder and theft of a firearm. 'There may be more charges coming if we think you were in on the Aqua Western fraud. You certainly benefitted from it,' he said.

The detective was smiling to himself as he left the building and headed for his car. The sun was warm on his back, and he took off his jacket and slung it over his shoulder as he unlocked the vehicle. Both killings were solved, one a conspiracy following an accident, the other a deliberate slaying to cover-up a fraud. The perpetrators were now ready to be remanded into custody, job done, bar weeks of paperwork. He squinted into the sky, where a jet was just heading off to some warmer clime. He wondered whether he might even be able to leave work on time today. It would make a nice change.

Chapter Twenty-nine

Gillard was relaxing at home that evening, having got in at seven o'clock, not quite on time but reasonable enough. Sam was able to report that everything was quiet across the way, where Aunt Trish had now settled in. Over a glass of wine, he told her about the competing confessions that came to explain the death of the Lithuanian barman Tomas Valdovas.

'So it was all an accident?' she asked.

'In a way, it was. No doubt being punched in the head by a former middleweight boxer did nothing for Valdovas's sense of balance. So if an energetic five-year-old was bouncing up and down on his shoulders while he ran around, it's quite possible to believe he lost his balance and toppled backwards onto the weapon. Stranger things have happened.'

'Vicky Willow and her husband presumably convinced the Tickett brothers that his death was their fault, to rope them in on a cover-up?'

'Yes. They didn't want their child to be traumatised by the knowledge of having caused a death, so they tried to pretend to Callum that Tom was still alive.'

'So how did they discover where he'd been buried?'

'Vicky had been creating a vegetable garden at the back of Dove Cottage a few months after the death and guessed, from the freshly dug earth, that the Tickett brothers had in fact buried the body there, rather than shifting it far away as they had promised. Vicky told Crystal, who owned the cottage, and they realised that it would only be a matter of time before the Church of England sent a new vicar, and it would then be impossible to do anything about it. They dithered about it for months, worried about the state of the corpse and whether it would have rotted too much to be moved. It's not an easy thing to contemplate. Then it was too late. Rev Matthew Cleaver arrived a week early to take up his post. Fortunately, he showed no interest in the garden, and for a while the Willow women forgot about it. Crystal was seeing more and more of Ozzy Blanchard; their affair had really taken off. She tried to persuade him to leave his wife, but like so many men in that position he wanted to have his cake and eat it.'

'Typical man,' Sam said.

'Ozzy boasted to her that he had some big money coming to him, and eventually asked her to receive it in an account in her name. Crystal admitted she liked the idea of stealing money from the company that had caused them so much trouble. It was in January when Ozzy was finally forced to choose. Arrowsmith had warned him that Aqua Western were suspicious about some of the transactions and put many of the payments on hold, including all of those going to Buckingham Pallets Ltd, the Ticketts' second company. Arrowsmith could see his plans for getting rich were going to be blocked, so diverted all the legitimate money for phase one of the new sewer scheme from the Ticketts' main company CJT Contracting (Hants) Ltd, making the payee the similar-sounding CJT Contracting (Surrey) Ltd, which he'd bought out of receivership.'

'So instead of paying the Ticketts he was paying himself?'

'Yes. And the Ticketts were not only failing to get the fraudulent cash but had only received a fraction of what they were entitled to for the real work they had done. So we come to January, and Vicky overhearing the Ticketts' plot to kill Ozzy. She told Crystal the Ticketts had mentioned Ozzy's home address. She rang Ozzy, who decided to go for it, leave his wife, pick up Crystal and skedaddle with the money they had already accumulated.'

'But at this point the dead barman was still in the original grave?'

'Yes. Ozzy drove like a bat out of hell to Rissington Common, not knowing that the Ticketts were waiting at Crystal's house, with her held captive. The chase ensued, and when Christopher Tickett saw the overturned water company car in the river, guessed that the man they'd been pursuing was either dead or seriously injured and decided to back away. It was only an hour after Aidan and Rory left Crystal's home, having warned her to keep her mouth shut, that Ozzy climbed over the back fence. He and Crystal returned the back way through allotments to the Anvil Arms, where Guy and Vicky gave them shelter overnight. Next morning Vicky gave them a lift to Crystal's home in Haslemere, from where they took the camper van.'

'What I still don't get, Craig, is how this poor Lithuanian got dug up again and moved.'

'That was in April this year. According to Crystal, Rowena had let slip that the Rev Matthew was going away for a long weekend back to Liverpool and she was going to miss him. Crystal was worried about her daughter. She had previously had a crush on Tomas, and had been told that he went away unexpectedly back to Lithuania, which upset her. She was only fourteen at the time. Crystal was terrified that Rowena would one day find out what had happened. Anyway, with Matthew Cleaver away, Vicky did an experimental dig in the garden, and when she reached the plastic bag containing the corpse slit it open enough to realise it hadn't rotted, but turned to adipocere. She rang Crystal and said "It's now or never." Vicky had just started doing some work for the Ticketts in a mini-digger, which was still on site. On the Friday she dug an extra practice trench with the mini digger down amongst the riverside willows. Late that same night, Vicky, Crystal and Guy dug up the body, still wrapped in bin bags, and using the Willow Farm quad bike, Vicky took it across to the construction site. They dumped the body in the trench and filled it in. The whole operation only took an hour.'

'But what about the comb, that initially identified the body as Blanchard's?'

'That was, according to Crystal, a last-minute idea from Ozzy himself. He had offered his comb to Crystal, suggesting that she plant it on the body. Crystal and Vicky had already looked up adipocere and having realised it destroyed DNA, agreed there was a chance to disguise the body as Ozzy's. So Vicky slipped the comb into the back pocket of Tomas' jeans. Ozzy knew it was unlikely to fool the Ticketts. They probably guessed who the body was, although they weren't told about the reburial. Ozzy hoped it might stop Arrowsmith and Aqua Western management trying to find him. He probably recognised that it was doomed to fail ultimately, but might give him some time to escape abroad.'

'What about the discovery? Why on earth did Vicky dig up the body with the excavator after having reburied it there?'

'She didn't have any choice. Trevor Collier, the replacement surveyor at Aqua Western, instructed them to lay a pipe where it should have been on the plan, not the cheaper shortcut version the Ticketts and Ozzy had built. Vicky thought they had a fighting chance of getting away with the deception, even after digging up Tomas Valdovas, so long as the body was badly damaged in the process. And I think that's just about right. It was only the more specialist forensic techniques that showed that the body was of a young man, not of a fifty-two-year-old.'

'So what did the Ticketts think?'

'I think at first they genuinely thought the body was a new discovery. It wasn't recognisable as the man they buried. But then various bits of information, leaked principally by the archaeologist, made them realise it was the same person. They just kept quiet about it, but it made them more determined to get the money they felt they were owed from Aqua Western. If not from Ozzy, who they couldn't find, then from Arrowsmith.'

'Did they get the cash? The water company had blocked the payments, hadn't they?'

'After they kidnapped Arrowsmith, and he saw where they planned to put him, he gave the Ticketts the banking details and passwords for his own company, where he'd channelled the funds. The transfers were just taking place at the time they were arrested.'

'So the new vicar was completely innocent?'

'Yes.' Gillard took a sip of wine. 'But it took co-ordinating all the statements of the various Willows and Ticketts to be sure of it. Two families torn apart years ago by the murder of Henry Willow were later bound together by a shared secret over a second death, that of Tomas Valdovas.'

Sam was smiling at him. 'Speaking of secrets, I'm going to share one with you.' She leaned forward and kissed him. 'Craig, I'm pregnant.'

Gillard's face broke out into a huge grin. He held his wife closely, and kissed her forehead. 'I'm thrilled, Sam. This is just the news I've been hoping for.'

'It turns out I'm already two months gone. Our child should be born next April.'

Epilogue

Kelvin Arrowsmith was charged with murder for commissioning the killing of Ozzy Blanchard. He maintained his innocence, but was found guilty. The sentence was life with a minimum of twenty years and five years to run concurrently for the fraud. Ray Slater, who admitted murder, got life with a minimum of fifteen years. Aidan and Rory Tickett pleaded guilty on the kidnapping charge and were each sentenced to nine years, with a three-year charge for the fraud to run concurrently. Christopher Tickett went down for another ten years on the same charges. Vicky Willow and Guy Naylor were given two-year suspended sentences for preventing a lawful burial, and ordered to do a hundred hours of community service. Crystal Willow, too, was given a suspended sentence. She returned to her massage and tattooing business in Haslemere.

Sheila and Stewie Ransome stayed living in their cottage on Bourne Lane. Stewie's friendship with Callum Willow developed further, now that the child was old enough to play Cluedo. Callum was never told what had happened to Tomas Valdovas, and in the excitement of childhood gradually forgot about the incident involving the Lithuanian barman. Only in his nightmares, which have worsened over the years, does that scene of horror ever come back to him.

Rowena Willow is still living in the same cottage, but goes to college full-time now. The Rev Matthew Cleaver moved away shortly after the case was closed, and now runs a thriving urban church in Wolverhampton. Rowena got over her attachment to him, which despite all appearances to the contrary was – and at the vicar's insistence – never consummated. Her ambition is to become a fully-fledged archaeologist, and she is still to be seen on sunny evenings with a metal detector, going over the grounds of her family farm on the banks of the River Wey looking for Anglo-Saxon coins. She was closely involved in the restoration of Biorthelm's dagger, which is now to be seen on display in the British Museum, along with the prophecy found in St Crispin's church.

ᛁᚾ×ᚠᚷᛗᚻ×ᚻᛗᛏᛚᛗ×ᛈᚻᛗᛏ×ᛗᛉᚠᛏᚦᛗ×ᚹᛈᛗᛗᚻ×ᚦᛗ×ᚹᚱᚠᛏᛚᛁᚻᚻ×ᚠᚱᛉ×ᚻᛗᚱᛗ×
ᚠᛏ×ᛁᛏᛏᚠᛚᛗᛏᛏ×ᛈᛁᛗᛁᛇᛁᚷ×ᚠ×ᛁᚠᚻᛏ×ᚻᛚᚱᚠᛉᚻᚠᛚᚻ×ᛈᛁᛁᛁ×ᚹᛗᛁᛁ×ᚠ×ᚹᛁᛚᛁᚷ×ᛚᚱᚠᛈᚻ×

Afterword

The boundaries between familiar truth and fiction need to be carefully drawn. So although readers may find the account of water company misdeeds familiar, I would like to stress that all the companies mentioned in the story, and their actions, are fictitious and unconnected to any of similar name to be found anywhere in the world. I have taken a few liberties with the geography around Chieveley Services. The village of Rissington Common is likewise an invention, although set within known territory south of Haslemere.

Archaeologist David Start was a great help on the intricacies of dating Anglo-Saxon iron weapons, Home Office forensic pathologist Dr Stuart Hamilton was as always of great assistance, particularly on the body's transition to adipocere. I would also like to thank Hester Russell, Kim Booth and John Campbell. The latter gave me some pointers on corporate fraud. The runes and (made up) Anglo-Saxon prophecy were translated with the help of a neat little text converter at Valhyr.com. Any mistakes are my own.

I am grateful to Michael Bhaskar and the rest of the team at Canelo, and copyeditor Miranda Ward. Last but not least, my wife Louise, for her boundless patience and support during the gestation of each and every book.

⊙ **CANELO**CRIME

Do you love crime fiction and are always on the lookout for brilliant authors?

Canelo Crime is home to some of the most exciting novels around. Thousands of readers are already enjoying our compulsive stories. Are you ready to find your new favourite writer?

Find out more and sign up to our newsletter at canelocrime.com